# LOVE
*on the*
## MISTY ISLES

Tom

Hope you enjoy this journey to the Misty Isles (Haida Gwaii)

Rosemary 11-3-2020

(aka your Solivita neighbor

Shirley Greves)

4PM GATOR ROOM

First Place in the Romance
Category of the first annual MCP
Author Awards Contest.
2017

# LOVE
*on the*
# MISTY ISLES

ROSEMARY VAUGHN

MCP MAITLAND, FL

Mill City Press, Inc.
2301 Lucien Way #415
Maitland, FL 32751
407·339·4217
www.millcitypress.net

ISBN-13: 978-1-63505-448-4
LCCN: 2016918983

Photo credit to: Jack Litrell Photography

Haida Gwaii Map - Davenport Maps Ltd.,
Victoria, BC maps@davenportmaps.com

*Printed in the United States of America*

Dedicated to my husband,
the grand romance of my life.

# To the Reader

*Love on the Misty Isles* is set on the former Queen Charlotte Islands, now officially known as Haida Gwaii, meaning "islands of the people." I lived on the Charlottes for two years in the mid-1970s. An author takes a risk when using a real geographic place for a setting, as some readers will invariably say, "She hasn't got that right!" As I have not returned to the archipelago since my time there, I admit my setting won't be completely accurate according to the Misty Isles of today. There have been many changes on the islands since the mid-1970s, and some specific details have also faded in my memory. Haida Gwaii is such a unique corner of the world with its rugged, pristine beauty and the culture and art of the Haida First Nation, that I was unable to resist such a fruitful setting for my first novel. I have, therefore, taken creative liberties with the setting.

The novel is in three parts, each with its own plot and main characters, but it comes together as a whole through the intertwining lives of the characters. Their stories cross cultures, generations, and sometimes borders. The time frame covers approximately ten years, beginning in the mid-1990s, with flashbacks to the early 1970s and 80s. For the purpose of plot, any references to real events outside this ten-year time frame have been meshed together within it and fictionalized. All the characters are creations of my imagination, and resemble no one in real life. Names of characters similar to real people is purely coincidental. References may be made to real people, but they do not appear as characters in the stories.

For further clarification of details and for the reader's interest, please read the "Author's Postscript for the Reader" at the end of the novel, or check my website. A bibliography of suggested readings, and lists of websites and search engine terms are also provided for the reader's own exploration of this unique setting.

The following map was developed by Davenport Maps in Victoria, British Columbia. It is a simplified map of Haida Gwaii. The archipelago consists of approximately 150 islands. The two largest islands are Graham in the north and Moresby in the south. For the most part, the events of the novel take place on Graham Island. This streamlined map of the islands focuses mainly on the places and points of reference mentioned within the novel. A corner of mainland British Columbia is also included, with Prince Rupert labeled to give the reader a reference for the location of the islands off the northwest coast of the province. For further clarification of their position, please refer to a map of Canada.

The cover photo of Agate Beach and Tow Hill, provided by Jack Litrell Photography of Masset, British Columbia, represents the rugged and pristine beauty of the Misty Isles. Both Agate Beach and Tow Hill are featured in the setting of the novel and are places visited by the characters.

Please come with me now to the Misty Isles, where I hope you will enjoy the twists and turns in each love story of the novel.

*Rosemary Vaughn*
*2016*
www.rosemaryvaughn.com

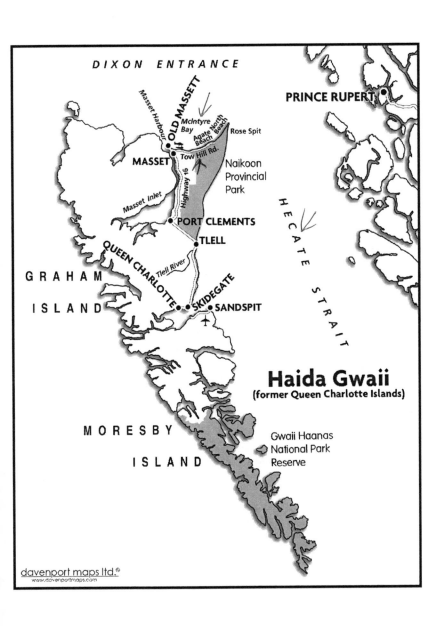

# PART I

# RUNNING TO FOREVER

# CHAPTER ONE

"*A*re you running away from something, Libby? Why would you go so far away when those who love you are right here?" her father asked, looking at her with sad eyes. "Your mother and I are worried about you."

Libby tried to reassure him. "No, Dad. I'm not running from something. I'm running to something." She paused, forming her argument. "Well, not running exactly, but embarking on a new adventure in a different place and culture. I'm excited about taking on this professional challenge."

In trying to rationalize her decision to her father and herself, Libby realized she sounded like she was in a job interview. Softening her tone, she casually tossed out, "Gotta see what kind of stuff I'm made of, Dad."

Replaying this conversation in her head as she waited for takeoff, Libby recognized that they had really been skirting the issue. *For months now, we've been dancing around the topic of my losing Ben. I know Mum and Dad wanted to talk about it, but I just couldn't. The pain is still too raw. And they're wrong. Not everyone who loved me is right there anymore. They think I'm just running away from it all. And maybe I am. Away from a life without Ben.*

She'd learned of the open teaching position from a friend who'd moved to British Columbia. All she knew about the Queen Charlotte Islands off the northwest coast of British Columbia was from her bit of research. Wanting to understand who her potential students would be, she discovered that the main residents were commercial fishermen, loggers, the Haida First Nation, and personnel from the Canadian Forces Station in Masset. Even though she didn't know much about her destination, she thought it at least couldn't be further from her prairie roots and the memories she hoped to forget. It seemed to be the perfect solution.

After a three-day car trip across the Canadian prairies, through the Rocky Mountains, and up the interior of British Columbia, Libby found herself pondering her situation and feeling slightly claustrophobic in this strange little eight-seater plane as it plunged into the water to prepare for takeoff. *Maybe I should have tried to work through things at home.* Her doubts didn't diminish when the body of the plane sank lower, bringing the water much too close to the bottom of the small windows. Eventually, the plane revved its motor, and, leaving a wake behind as it sped up, finally rose from the water, banked, and headed west across the Hecate Strait.

The Grumman Goose, a small amphibious plane, had an underbelly shaped like the hull of a boat rather than fitted with pontoons like most floatplanes. This design allowed it to take off and land on its belly in the water. The plane made the approximately fifty-minute trip once or twice a day between Prince Rupert on the mainland and Masset on Graham Island, the largest and most northern of the islands in the archipelago of the Queen Charlotte Islands. Libby would soon learn that the locals called the little plane "the Goose."

Once in the air, Libby looked for a distraction from second-guessing her decision, her memories of Ben, and whatever might lie ahead. She finally struck up a conversation with the young woman across the aisle, who was cradling what appeared to be a newborn baby.

Smiling at the young woman, she commented, "Looks like we have a very young, and I might add, very sweet, passenger on board."

The young woman returned the smile. "Yes, he's only five days old. I had him in the hospital at Prince Rupert, and I'm just praying he stays asleep for the entire trip home! Don't want to have to breastfeed in front of those two back there," she commented, nodding her head toward the two young men sitting in the back of the plane.

Libby nodded her head in agreement. The two servicemen, obviously still slightly hungover, were rehashing their exploits from a weekend leave on the mainland. Bumping along the aisle to the back seats as they boarded, one had blatantly ogled Libby, eyebrows shifting up and down like Groucho Marx. There was only one other passenger on this trip, an older gentleman in one of the front seats, who was engrossed with paperwork. There were no assigned seats on this plane, and definitely no attendants.

Returning to her conversation with the young mother, Libby wondered aloud, "I thought they had a hospital in Masset."

"Oh, they do, but Noah here decided to be breach, so Dr. Parker thought I should go to the mainland for his delivery in case there were complications."

Libby frowned. *Maybe this place is more isolated than I thought.*

"So, what brings you to the Charlottes? My name is Karen, by the way." She might have offered her hand, but her arms gently rocking the baby were obviously full.

"Nice to meet you, Karen—and baby Noah. I'm Libby, and I've come to teach English at the high school in Masset. Have you lived on the islands your whole life?"

"Oh, no. My husband was posted to the base here. We're on the last year of a three-year tour. He was on duty today, so he couldn't come over to help me bring Noah home."

5

"What can you tell me about living here? Anything a new-comer needs to know?" Libby asked, hoping to waylay some of her misgivings.

"Well, the islands are semi-isolated. We only get one radio station from Ketchikan, Alaska, and a very fuzzy CBC television channel. When we get fogged in with only the Goose to get off Graham Island, sometimes it feels just plain isolated. The weather is temperate though, and as well as fog, we get a lot of mist and rain. Guess that's why they call them the Misty Isles."

"I like that name. It has a pleasant, rather peaceful, sound to it," Libby responded, purposely avoiding the feeling of isolation the rest of the description had given her.

Realizing she may be painting a depressing picture, Karen brightened. "The good news is you can get a direct flight to Vancouver periodically from Sandspit on Moresby Island." Being realistic, she added, "That's a bit of a challenge, too. It's a seventy-mile drive on the only road down our island. Then you have to take a short trip on a small ferry to get to the Sandspit airport."

Wondering once again if she'd been too hasty in her escape, Libby related what she'd learned about the residents on the island from her research.

Karen started to laugh. "You probably didn't learn about the most interesting group here. Hippie squatters came in the seventies to collect magic mushrooms, and ended up staying. In fact, I was told by a woman who had come to the base back then that when they first arrived, she and her husband couldn't get into their PMQ—oh, sorry—base talk for Private Married Quarters. Anyway, they stayed at the Seegay Inn. She couldn't even do laundry 'cause the hippies had ruined the dryers at the laundromat. They apparently had used them to dry the mushrooms for sale off the island. At least that's what she told me. Don't know if it's true, but it made a good story, anyway."

"Whoa! Guess a prairie girl like me is in for a culture shock! Does that still go on? That can't be legal now, is it?"

At that moment, the aircraft suddenly dropped. Libby grabbed her armrests and sucked in her breath. Karen clutched her wee babe a little tighter, but seemed to take the drop in stride. "Not to worry, Libby. That wasn't a bad one. It happens all the time with the sudden air drafts over the Strait, but it can be scary at times. That's why we jokingly refer to TPA as Toilet Paper Airlines."

"It sure scared the crap out of me!" Libby quipped, gulping.

The pilot glanced back at his charges. "Sorry about that, folks. We'll be landing soon."

All Libby had seen of the pilot so far was a glimpse of a broad shoulder and a muscular arm through the doorless opening to the cockpit. She checked her seatbelt and grabbed the armrests again. Looking out the tiny window, she watched sea lions playing in the shallow water on a sandbar.

Descending into a small harbor, the plane's wingtips barely missed a rusty, run-down cannery. Libby could see fishermen on the wharf, presumably unloading salmon and halibut from their boats. Suddenly, the belly of the plane hit the water. Once again, Libby sucked in her breath as the water splashed over the windows, obscuring the view. Inside the cockpit, she could see a strong, masculine arm vigorously pumping a lever.

"Good grief! Does the pilot have to pump to keep the plane afloat? What kind of operation is this?"

Laughing, Karen responded, "No, Libby. He's releasing the wheels so that when we reach the shore, the plane can roll onto land." Moments later, that's exactly what happened. The Goose puttered across the bay to the shoreline, where the wheels rolled up the cement ramp and onto the gravel landing.

Wishing good luck to Karen and to Noah, who had mercifully slept throughout the trip, Libby followed them down the short staircase to the landing. She watched the handful of passengers be greeted by friends or family outside the plane. A uniformed serviceman swooped his wife and newborn son into his arms. The older gentleman walked toward his wife, who waved at him from outside the terminal door. A couple of boyish servicemen greeted their buddies, slapping them on their backs, anxious to hear about their weekend adventures in Prince Rupert.

Libby realized how truly alone she was. *Guess I'm just a stranger in a strange land.*

# CHAPTER TWO

With no one to meet her, Libby walked across the landing to the small airport building, which hardly qualified as a terminal. Just ahead of her, the pilot of the Goose sauntered toward the entrance. He was taller than she'd first thought, with dark hair curling over his collar. Bronzed skin indicated an outdoor lifestyle, maybe? Perhaps a Mediterranean heritage? Italian? The casual khaki shirt, with its sleeves rolled to the elbows, revealed taut, sinewy forearms. And those faded blue jeans hugged a butt rivaling that of Michelangelo's *David. Now what made my mind go there? Not a uniform one would expect of a professional pilot.*

As if reading her mind, the pilot turned, then saluted her with two fingers touching those cool wraparound sunglasses, and continued toward the building bearing a sign labelled "Trans Provincial Airlines,"—in other words, TPA.

By the time Libby entered the building, he was leaning against the counter, talking with the lone agent. "Took her kind of close to the cannery, didn't you, Connor?"

"Just had to give a nod to Chuck. He usually saves me a nice salmon or halibut that's too small for the cannery." The pilot turned toward Libby, who was approaching the counter. He took off his sunglasses, revealing the most strikingly blue eyes she had ever seen. He smiled, appreciating what those blue eyes drank in.

"Excuse me," she addressed the agent, "could you call a taxi for me?"

The agent chuckled, and a slow, slightly mocking smile spread across the pilot's face. "Yeah, you get right on that, Gus," he commented, and added, "Where are you from anyway, sweetheart?"

Pulling herself to her full five feet five inches, Libby retorted, "I'm not your sweetheart, and I'm from Manitoba—ever heard of it?"

"Oh, a prairie rose!" he replied, nonplussed, and offered his hand. "I'm Connor Ferguson, and this reprobate is Gus Davis. And who might this wild flower be?"

"Elizabeth Campbell," she responded. "Libby. Did you say your name is Ferguson?" Her brows knit together while taking in his dark hair and swarthy complexion. *Hmmm. With those bright blue eyes and that name, he's not Italian. But my, that bronze skin and those eyes are certainly an attractive combination.*

"Aye, a good Scottish name, not unlike your own," he noted with a phony burr. "Not what you'd expect for a black heart like myself, eh?" Not bothering to explain further, he added, "Now you, my bonnie lass, are the picture of your heritage, with your peaches-and-cream skin and strawberry-blond hair."

"You're going to scare the poor girl off, Connor," Gus interrupted. "Pay no mind to him, Ms. Campbell. Now, what brings you from the Canadian prairies to the islands?"

Ignoring Connor's amused smile, Libby replied, "I've taken the open English teaching position at the high school for the year. I'm renting Ed and Isabel Jordan's cottage for the term. Could you please tell me how I can get there? And *you* may call me Libby." She directed this last comment to Gus, pointedly ignoring Connor.

"I'm afraid not by taxi, Libby. We're without service right now. The area isn't that big, and most folks can get a ride or walk anywhere they might want to go. Perhaps the school could send someone for you."

"I can give her a lift," Connor broke in. "I'm going that way anyway. Let's get your bags."

Libby looked doubtful. Chuckling, Gus assured her, "Not to worry, Libby. He's harmless." Seeming to have no other choice, she reluctantly followed him to retrieve her bags, which had been dumped inside the door.

"Not much luggage for a whole year," Connor assessed.

"The rest of my things and my car will be coming by barge next week."

"Make sure you hose down the car so the salt water doesn't rust it," Connor advised.

They rode in silence around the harbor while Libby took in the rugged beauty of the water, rock, coniferous trees, and blue sky. Finally, Connor asked, "So why teach English here? No schools on the prairies?"

"Just wanted a change. A new challenge."

"Oh, running away from something," he stated matter-of-factly.

"No! I'm not running away from anything!" Libby retorted a little too vehemently.

"Here we are," said Connor, pulling up to a small cedar cottage surrounded by towering spruce and cedar trees. Welcoming window boxes bloomed with bright red geraniums. Libby climbed the few steps onto the porch and searched under the mat for the key the Jordans had said they would leave for her.

Taking her bags from his Jeep Cherokee, Connor followed her into the cottage. Libby was charmed by the open space, which consisted of a small kitchenette in one corner to the left of the cottage door, a large round wooden table in the center, and a worn leather couch and recliner facing a stone fireplace on the opposite wall.

Rosemary Vaughn

Alongside the fireplace was a desk where Libby could picture herself grading papers and designing lesson plans.

Libby moved to the far side of the fireplace, where a door led to the bedroom. She was pleased to see it furnished with a bed, dresser, and rocking chair of rough-hewn logs. An intricately woven blanket thrown casually over the back of the rocking chair caught her eye. She studied the geometric pattern, which had some birdlike features. Perhaps this was a raven or eagle motif designed in the traditional Haida style she'd read about. She'd have to become more familiar with Haida art.

Following her to the bedroom, Connor attempted to carry her bags inside. Sensing his presence, Libby suddenly whirled on him and commanded, "Put those down out there in the living room."

"OK, OK," Connor conceded. "I was just trying to be helpful, Prairie Rose."

"I am quite capable of handling my own bags, thank you very much. I'm no fragile flower."

"Sorry, again," Connor replied. Things weren't starting off very well.

Libby brushed past him as he set down her bags. He followed her tentatively as she crossed the room and walked to the entryway of a large back porch facing the harbor. Here, two inviting willow rocking chairs were placed side by side, beckoning onlookers to "sit a spell" and reflect. A worn path led to the dock, where a small rowboat was moored. "It's so peaceful," Libby sighed.

"Yes, it is," Connor agreed. "The Jordans did a great job in planning their retirement retreat. They loved the islands, and when Ed retired from being a Canadian Forces captain, they decided to spend their summers here. They spend the rest of the year on the mainland, enjoying their grandchildren. They made a lot of the furniture themselves, adding some of the local and aboriginal art."

"Their retreat certainly fits well with my needs and teaching schedule." Gazing on the tranquil water, Libby mused, "A person could lose herself here."

"That she could," responded Connor, cocking an eyebrow. "Why don't I take you to get some provisions?"

"No, but thanks anyway. The Jordans said they would leave canned goods and other nonperishables to hold me over while I settle in. I noticed it's a short walk to downtown, so I can go later to get staples like milk and bread." She smiled then and offered her hand. "Sorry we got off to a bad start. Thanks for the ride."

"Not a problem, Prairie Rose." He was gone, leaving Libby to fume over his parting comment. *Exasperating man! And I don't know why I found his butt so attractive.*

*Now, what would bring such a ravishing redhead to this isolated part of the country?* Connor's curiosity—and yes, his interest—were definitely piqued. Frowning, he climbed into the Jeep, still contemplating Libby. *She sure got prickly when I suggested she was running away from something. But then she mentioned being able to lose herself here, and how peaceful it is. Hmmm. I wonder why? Shouldn't have teased her about being a Prairie Rose, I guess. Must be a feminist.* Concluding that Ms. Campbell was a puzzle, Connor vowed to try to put the pieces together, because they would make a mighty pretty picture.

*Connor the Pilot.*

# CHAPTER THREE

*L*ibby had just finished unpacking the few things she'd brought on the plane, and was searching for a coffee pot when someone rapped on the door. A bubbly voice called, "Hello, anyone home?"

Through the screen door, Libby saw a petite young woman who was slightly older than she, with a mop of chestnut curls framing her pixie face and dancing brown eyes. The pixie was struggling to balance two coffee containers and a white bakery bag. Libby opened the door for her, and she bounced in. "Hi! You must be Libby. Connor said you'd arrived, so I thought I'd come to welcome you, and what better way to do it than with fresh coffee and pastries from Dr. Shirlee's Books 'n' Brew. Where can I set them? How was your flight? Are you unpacked?" She gushed this monologue in a chipper voice.

Somewhat overwhelmed by this whirlwind, Libby inquired, "And you would be…?"

A delightful giggle spilled from the waif, and she responded, "Oh, *pardonnez-moi!* Stephen always says I tend to overpower a room before I enter it." Setting the paper cups and pastries on the table, she reached out her hand and said, "Hi! I'm Aimée Parker, and I teach French at the high school. I'm officially here to welcome you to Masset and the islands." Aimée giggled again, "Well, I'm officially *self-appointed* to welcome you."

"Oh, hi!" Libby took her hand. "I'm Libby Campbell, but I guess you know that."

"Yes, we knew at the school, of course, that a new English teacher would be here to begin the school year, and Connor confirmed that a 'bonnie lass' had indeed arrived."

"He's rather arrogant, isn't he?" Libby scowled.

"Connor?" Aimée raised her eyebrows in surprise. "Why, no. He's a sweetheart!"

"Interesting. That's what he called me. I wasn't impressed." Aimée tipped her head, frowning, but Libby went on. "Enough about him. Do come in. That coffee smells wonderful! Let's sit on the back porch, and you can fill me in on the school and everything."

The women settled into the willow chairs, sipped their coffee, and looked out over the serenity of the bay. "Where did you say you got this coffee?" asked Libby.

"Dr. Shirlee's Books 'n' Brew. It's a delightful coffee shop and secondhand bookstore downtown. It's a nice place to go for a break, grade papers, or visit with Shirlee. She's a doll—the voice of common sense and intellect all rolled into one. You'll love her."

"Sounds nice. How long have you been here?"

"Stephen and I have been here two years. In fact, next summer, our three-year stint will be up and we'll be posted elsewhere. Oh, I should explain; Stephen is one of the medical officers at the base here. We met when he was posted in Montreal—maybe you noticed my slight Francophone accent."

"Yes, I did," replied Libby. "It's charming. Are you lonesome so far from home?"

"Sometimes. I come from a large family, and I miss *mes petits choux*. Oh, sorry. My little cabbages—my brothers and sisters. But I'm madly in love with my husband, and we hope to begin our own family very soon," Aimée responded with a giggle and a wink.

"Do you like it here?" Libby wondered, slight apprehension creeping into her voice. "It seems kind of isolated."

"*Oui*, that it is, but everyone is friendly. The base is a little community within the community, but that is changing, too. The base is being phased out. A station will be maintained here, but in a few years, 90 percent of the personnel will be eliminated, leaving behind a lot of empty houses and a huge impact on the local economy. There are plans, though, to rejuvenate the area by making it more of a vacation destination, and perhaps by selling some of the PMQs—oh, I mean Private Married Quarters—for retirement or vacation retreats. Much like how the Jordans use this cottage. There are plans to boost the tourist trade with fishing and hunting, and especially the cultural aspect with the sale of Haida art in boutiques. Shirlee's place, of course, lends itself well to that kind of trade. And the commercial fishing families will still be here, too."

"Sounds like a time of transition," mused Libby. Deciding she could be like Scarlett O'Hara and think about it tomorrow, she asked, "Now, what about the school? Tell me about the students and the other teachers."

"The building itself is typical, and we have finally become wired to the outside world. That should eventually open up a lot more learning opportunities for the students. It's dial-up, so it's not always reliable."

Aimée reached for her coffee cup, took a sip, and continued. "Some of the kids are from the base and have lived in a variety of places, coming from diverse backgrounds. The local ones have lived here all of their lives. For many, their parents came here from other areas for the commercial fishing and logging, or to squat on the land and pursue their own interests, such as crafts, writing, organic farming, or whatever. Then you have the Haida children, who come from a long heritage of their First Nation ancestors. Quite a variety, eh?"

"Yes," replied Libby. "I bet it's quite a challenge to teach such a blend. How do the teachers manage?"

"Most really are interested and try hard, but they come from varied backgrounds, too. A lot are here temporarily, like myself, because we've come in with spouses posted to the base. So there's a lot of turnover and not a lot of consistency. Most are dedicated, but some, knowing they are short-timers, are just putting in their time until they can go back to civilization."

"Good thing it's Labor Day weekend. Looks like I'd better get busy with my plans before it all begins next week."

"Me, too," replied Aimée. "But right now, I'd better get home to work on dinner. I'll see you at the staff meeting on Tuesday, but call if you need anything in the meantime. We'll have you over for dinner soon, or take you to a movie at the Officers' Mess. I'm so glad you're here!" she said, reaching out for a quick hug, and then the whirlwind was gone.

"I wanted a new challenge," sighed Libby, closing the door behind her. "Guess I got one." To her dismay, at the word "challenge," a certain hunky pilot came to mind.

\* \* \*

Connor sat with his feet propped on Stephen Parker's desk. He'd just run into Aimée, Stephen's wife, and had told her he had delivered the new English teacher to the Jordans' cottage. He was still puzzling about this newest resident of Masset when Stephen walked in. "Hey, Ferguson, feet off the polished walnut!"

"Oh, sorry. Kind of forgot myself for a moment. Are you done for the day?"

"You did look kind of far away. I was checking out a new baby just born in Prince Rupert. Cute little guy. Yeah, except for the mountain of endless charting, I'm done. What's up?"

"I don't know. The new English schoolteacher just came over on the Goose today, and I drove her to the Jordans', where she's staying for the term. She's nothing short of gorgeous. It seems odd, though, that she would come here to teach. She got a little defensive when I suggested she was running away from something. I was joshing, but I think I touched a nerve. She also got a little prickly when I called her a prairie rose."

"Sounds like you got a little prickly yourself. Pun intended."

"Knock it off, buddy. There's just something about her. Sure, she made my loins groan, but even though she puts up this independent front, she makes me want to protect her somehow."

"Geez. You just met the bird, and already you're making a nice little nest."

"Oh, I know, Steph, but I guess I really do want to get to know her."

"Well, I'm sure Aimée will be welcoming her by inviting her to dinner or a movie or something. If you behave yourself, I'll see that she includes you."

Connor brightened for the first time since Stephen had walked through the door. "I'm counting on it!"

# CHAPTER
# FOUR

O n a Sunday evening after school had started, Aimée came through with an invitation for Libby to join them for movie night at the Officers' Mess, and Stephen made sure Connor, who had a standing invitation to the Mess anyway, knew Libby was going to be there. He was already at the bar when the Parkers walked in with Libby. He strode quickly toward the group of three, two drinks in hand. Heads together, the women were chatting about the events of the first days in school, so Libby didn't notice Connor's approach.

"What's your pleasure, Prairie Rose? A Black Russian or a Shirley Temple?"

Startled by the familiar voice, Libby raised her own eyes to gaze into the two vivid blue ones appraising her appreciatively. She stammered, "Wha...what? I didn't know *you* were going to be here." Recovering her manners, she asked, "Uh, what's a Black Russian?"

Appearing to take no offense, Connor explained it was a favorite of the gals on movie night, a nice blend of vodka and Kahlúa. Suddenly, she felt flushed in all kinds of places. What was it about this man that got to her? Thinking she'd better keep her wits about her in such a state, she opted for the Shirley Temple. Aimée happily took the Black Russian.

"I've got a couple of two-seaters pushed together over here. Should be a good spot for viewing the film."

"Moving a little fast, aren't you, bud?" Stephen nudged Connor, moving toward the couches. Connor just shrugged.

"What's going on? Did he know I was coming?" Libby quizzed Aimée, who also shrugged but added lamely, "He's here almost every Sunday night."

The Parkers cuddled up on one small couch, while Libby sat down carefully and primly in the corner of the other. After grabbing a couple of beers for Stephen and himself, Connor joined her on the couch. "So, how's the Prairie Rose adjusting to the islands?"

"Certainly a lot of interesting characters," she responded, a little more tartly than she'd intended. He just grinned, blue eyes twinkling at her discomfort. She continued on to safer ground. "Now, how do they show a film? I see an old reel-to-reel projector, but no screen."

"It's a pretty makeshift deal. Movies are sent in for Wednesday and Sunday nights. Someone is always trained to run the projector, and the film is shown on the wall at the end of the room. Don't expect the most recent releases, either. I think tonight's is an old *Pink Panther* flick."

"First time I've seen a cash bar at a movie."

"Not much entertainment on the island, so the base does what it can to provide some fun social gatherings."

The lights dimmed, and Libby relaxed a little. Enjoying the antics of Inspector Clouseau, she worked her way out of the corner of the couch, and at one point even bent forward, laughing so hard she actually slapped Connor's thigh in shared amusement. Before she could snatch her hand away, he grabbed it and held it in his. Leaning in close, eyes on hers, he said, "You have a great laugh."

"Uh, thanks, I guess. My brother always said I sounded like a braying donkey. Hee-haw!" *God, he smells good.* She felt his thumb making circles in her palm, sending tingling sensations through her.

"No way! I love your laugh. It's spontaneous and kinda sexy."

Extricating her hand from his, she cautioned him that they were probably disturbing the others, and should be quiet. Although they were quiet throughout the rest of the movie, the heat rising between them was thick and palpable. Connor's thigh occasionally rubbed against hers. She tried to move her leg, but finding the contact enjoyable, she relaxed.

Thankfully, the movie ended, and Libby quickly jumped up. "Thanks, guys, for the evening. I'd better get home so I'll be prepared to face the urchins in the morning."

While the women made a pit stop in the powder room before leaving, Connor and Stephen chatted outside. "So, how do you think it went?" Stephen asked. "Do you think you maybe rushed her a bit?"

"Maybe," Connor conceded. "I just wish I could get that damn song out of my head."

"What song?"

"The Bellamy Brothers' 'If I Said You Had a Beautiful Body, Would You Hold It Against Me.' Anyway, by the way she jumped up like a jackrabbit at the end of the movie, I don't think she's expecting me to take her home. Guess I'll just take off."

"You've had a lot of girlfriends since I've known you, Connor, but I've never seen you quite like this, or moving quite so fast."

"What can I say?" And with that, he headed toward his Jeep, humming that damn song.

# CHAPTER
# FIVE

Libby sat in her usual spot in a back corner by a window at Books 'n' Brew, mulling over lesson plans and pondering the challenge of teaching such diverse students. Aimée had been right. The coffee shop had become a favorite hangout for her. Just seeing the red gothic letters painted on the picture window announcing *Dr. Shirlee's Books 'n' Brew* brought a smile to her face as she approached her destination.

Entering the door, she loved being greeted by the spicy aroma of flavored coffee brewing behind the counter to her left. Several mismatched tables and chairs were scattered throughout the large room. A few overstuffed chairs were positioned near the bookshelves lining the left wall extending from the counter, and along the back wall. Libby's favorite table in the corner gave her a bit of privacy if she was engrossed in schoolwork, while still giving her a view out the window, which was draped with red-and-white checked gingham curtains. She could also keep an eye on the doorway to monitor the comings and goings of the shop. She especially enjoyed it when Aimée joined her, and sometimes Dr. Shirlee herself.

Aimée had been right about her, too. Dr. Shirlee had quickly become a favorite. She was a softly rounded woman in her mid-to-late fifties, with faded blond hair showing definite signs of silver threads among the gold.

When Libby asked Shirlee why she was called "Dr. Shirlee," she had laughingly responded that she was like the Dolly Parton character in the old movie *Straight Talk*—a buxom broad dispensing lots of advice. Libby had learned from Aimée, however, that Shirlee had a PhD in English literature and education. A retired professor of teacher education in the United States, she had come to the Charlottes to find solitude, to indulge in her favorite hobbies of drinking coffee and reading books, and to write the Great American Novel.

Shirlee's expertise in teaching was just one of the many reasons Libby visited the shop. Sensing Libby's pensive mood, Shirlee opened the conversation. "So, how are things going with your young charges? Are you channeling their raging hormones into an appreciation for Shakespeare and John Donne?"

"Not yet," sighed Libby. "I have to grab their attention first."

"Just be aware of those adolescent boys, and what might grab their attention!" cautioned Shirlee.

"Oh, I know. We were warned about professionalism in teacher education. The director of student teaching was always harping on that—about our appearance and inappropriate dress, in particular. No butts, no boobs, no bellies!"

"Sound advice!" laughed Shirlee.

"Aimée seems to have established a rapport with them somehow. The first day of school, she was greeted in the halls with '*Bonjour, Madame Parker! Comment ça va?*' The students were eager to chat with her, and to go to her class. She's so bubbly and enthusiastic, it's no wonder she's loved. Aimée is an apt name for her. You know, it means 'beloved.'"

"Now, remember, Libby, you are not Aimée, and you have your own personality and talents. You have to find your own approach to working with the students. They can spot a phony a mile away! So, think about who *you* are, and think about who *they* are."

"That's the problem. They are so diverse in their backgrounds, and so different from my own. How can I reach them?"

"Diversity—unity in diversity. Perhaps therein lies your answer. What do they know about themselves and their own backgrounds? Maybe researching their backgrounds and sharing them would be beneficial."

"Of course!" replied an enthused Libby. "The base kids are from all over Canada. They love the Internet, especially now that it's just come to Masset. We don't get great service yet, but it might inspire them a bit to do some research, along with the library resources. The Haida students have a rich heritage, and they have resources in the elders to explore it right here. I remember doing an 'historical narrative of schooling' paper in one of my teacher education courses. I interviewed my grandparents about what school was like for them, and what was going on in society at the time. Then we had to make connections between the two."

She paused a moment, ruminating, then continued with enthusiasm. "I know! I could have them use the library, and maybe the Internet, to do their research for a writing assignment—something like I had. Then they could interview their older relatives to bring to life their research. I'm sure many of the base kids could be in touch with their own grandparents by email or telephone, or even by sending a questionnaire to them by regular mail, especially if their grandparents don't have access to the Internet or haven't embraced it yet."

"Great idea! I bet the grandparents would love to tell their grandchildren about their lives, too. That intergenerational connection is being lost in all cultures," replied Shirlee, coming to sit at the table with Libby. "You're capturing my imagination. It sounds like fun—and it's certainly worth a try with the students!"

"Now, how can I get them reading? This instant-gratification world of technology we live in is blunting any adolescent desire to read books."

Shirlee rose quickly and searched her shelves for a small paperback volume. "Try this. It's a fictionalized history of the two Haida clans, the Raven and the Eagle, and the near extinction of them and their culture by the Europeans' arrival in 1775. It's told in narrative form, intended for children, but certainly anyone could learn the history of this proud First Nation from reading this historical fiction account."

Flipping through the small book, Shirley pointed out some of the sketches throughout it to Libby, and explained, "Bill Reid demonstrates authentic Haida art in his illustrations for the events in the book. It's an engaging story, and it should instill pride in our young Haida. It might even give the other students greater insight into the culture they are experiencing while on the islands." She handed Libby the small volume *Raven's Cry* by Christie Harris. "I think this edition may be out of print, but it's been reprinted, and I can order copies for you."

"This is great!" Looking more closely at Bill Reid's Haida artwork, Libby exclaimed, "I've just had a brainstorm! I can involve the art teacher in the history of Haida art, and maybe we can have students work on some related art projects."

"Well, there has been a revitalization of Haida art. You may have seen some of the argillite carvings and button blankets in Raven's Nook. In fact, Willow Shaw, the owner, would be a good resource, and she could possibly be a guest speaker for your class. She knows Haida art and the history of it very well."

"Oh, I'm just so excited. I haven't been to the shop yet, but my mind is going a million miles a minute with ideas and plans! Thanks, Shirlee, for helping me work through this."

"Well, your enthusiasm will go a long way toward grabbing the attention of those youngsters."

At that moment, the door opened, and Connor Ferguson strolled in, a smug smile spreading across his face. "Afternoon, ladies. So, what are Doc and the Prairie Rose hatching up today?"

"Well, 'hi, Doc,' yourself!" responded Shirlee. "We've got a winner here, Connor. Those teenagers won't know what hit them with the plans she has for them. We ought to bottle and sell her enthusiasm. We'd be an overnight business success!"

At the sight of Connor, Libby immediately withdrew into herself. The man unnerved her, making her feel self-conscious, silly, and not in control of her body's reactions. "Oh, I don't know," Connor mused. "The Prairie Rose looks a little fragile to me."

That did it! "I'm not fragile, and I'll thank you not to call me a flower!"

"Whoa! I see the ginger in the hair coming through!" he teased. He turned then to Shirlee, who had returned to the counter and was smiling at their exchange. "Just here for my high-octane java, Shirl. I'm waiting on a small package to be delivered later tonight."

"Here you go, Doc. Your usual. Have you heard from Willow? You'll be glad to have her home again."

"Oh, she's doing her thing on the mainland, getting her cultural fix in Vancouver. I don't expect her back until sometime early in the new year. I'm lonesome without her, though," he admitted, looking downcast.

*Who is this guy? A renegade pilot who Shirlee called "Doc"? He's expecting a small package later tonight. Is he in pharmaceuticals? Maybe a drug dealer?* Libby had to admit though, that he struck an attractive pose while leaning against the counter, talking to Shirlee. *Stop it,* she told herself. *You're not interested in anyone these days, and least of all him. The man is insufferable. Besides, he seems to be attached to this Willow person, whoever she is.*

Libby took advantage of their preoccupation with discussing Willow to gather her papers and make her escape. At the sound of the door opening, Shirlee and Connor turned to watch Libby's retreating figure. *And what a figure it is,* thought Connor.

Reading his thoughts, Shirlee asked, "Attractive gal, isn't she? Is that a spark of interest I see in your eye?"

"Just wishing I was one of those young fellows in her class. They didn't make teachers like that in my day!"

"We were just talking about that. I bet there's more than one young lad with a crush on her. She really has some great ideas, though, and she truly wants to reach each of those kids. I'm sure she'll get to them."

"Well, she's getting to me. I don't know though, Shirl. I can't help wondering what she's doing here. There's something about her. Doesn't she seem a little sad? There's an aura of mystery tinged with sadness about her." Connor shrugged his shoulders, and, picking up his coffee, prepared to leave. "I guess only time will tell."

# CHAPTER
# SIX

L ibby reluctantly pulled herself away from reading *Raven's Cry*, which she found fascinating. Aimée had convinced her that, although her dedication to her students was great, she also needed a social life. Not wanting to explain why she really wasn't interested in a social life, Libby had finally agreed to attend the Oktoberfest with the Parkers.

When Libby had protested that there was not a lot of German heritage there to celebrate, Aimée had explained that the celebration was a joint effort by the base and the Masset community to encourage good relations between the island's cultural groups. Besides, it was an excuse to have a good time. Such occasions were limited in the semi-isolated environment. Aimée and Stephen would be there soon, and Libby had to get ready.

She'd sewn a colorful dirndl skirt out of brightly flowered calico, and had topped it with a white embroidered peasant blouse and a black-laced cummerbund. She brushed out her reddish-blond hair and applied a touch of makeup. She surveyed the results in the mirror. *That will have to do.*

In the car, Aimée was full of her usual bubbly enthusiasm. "I'm so glad you're coming, Libby. You'll meet more people. I especially want you to meet Maggie Davis, Gus's wife. Gus is the manager at the airport. I think you met him your first day. And, of course, Connor will be there . . ." Her comment trailed off.

Stephen looked at his wife sharply and shook his head with a crooked grin. Libby was struck again by the distinct contrast between Aimée and Stephen. Where Aimée was short, dark, and bubbly, Stephen was tall, blond, and quite reserved. *I guess opposites do attract.* She had heard that his patients appreciated his quiet demeanor and genuine concern for their welfare.

"I look forward to meeting Maggie, but I can't say Mr. Ferguson or I have any reason to care whether one another is there or not."

The Parkers cocked eyebrows at one another and drove on in silence.

The CFS Base Recreation Hall was decorated festively for the occasion, and the aroma of bratwurst and sauerkraut wafted toward the new arrivals. Beer steins clinked, and the "oom-pah-pah" pick-up band pumped out German ethnic music.

The Parkers and Libby joined the Davis couple at a large round table. Maggie was charming, and she was definitely beginning to show her blossoming pregnancy, which she readily acknowledged. "Yes," she informed Libby, "this is our third. We have two rambunctious boys at home, two and four, so we're hoping for a princess this time around."

Maggie and Aimée smiled at one another, watching Libby glance toward the bar where Connor was chatting with some of the guys and hoisting a stein to his lips. They were teasing him that he'd forgotten his lederhosen. *He is an attractive man,* Libby thought, noting once again those sinewy forearms emerging from the rolled-up sleeves of a plaid flannel shirt. The usual blue jeans fit snugly over his muscled thighs. At that moment, he turned to face her, raising his stein in salute and smiling that slow, amused, yet appreciative grin that made those crystal blue eyes twinkle.

Caught in the act of admiring this dark-haired Adonis, Libby felt herself blushing, and she immediately turned away, only to be confronted by her two new friends. "He cuts a fine figure, doesn't he?" commented Maggie.

Aimée added with a giggle, "Wouldn't you just love to run your fingers through his hair?"

"I don't know what you're talking about!" spluttered Libby.

"Oh, you never know what can happen at a dance. That's how Stephen and I met. My college roommates and I attended a base dance in Montreal," explained Aimée. "When I walked in, Stephen caught my eye, and it was instant attraction. I found out later that he had said to his buddy that he was going to marry 'that girl' someday. And here I am!"

Maggie added, "And like you, Libby, I came to the Charlottes to teach school, and I met Gus at a fish fry. His family is in commercial fishing. He still helps his brothers when he can, but the airport work is a better schedule for a family man. Long story short, here I am, settled happily on the island with two kids and one on the way."

"That's not likely to happen to me," Libby whispered somewhat wistfully. *They don't know my story.*

Just then, the band started up a rousing polka, and Connor was at her side. "I know a prairie gal like you knows how to polka." Before she could refuse, Connor grabbed Libby's hand, pulling her to the dance floor. Maggie and Aimée watched the couple twirling faster and faster around the floor. Libby, letting herself go, was laughing, her eyes sparkling.

"It's good to see her enjoying herself," said Dr. Shirlee, who had joined the group. "There's such a sadness about her at times. Do you know her story, Aimée?"

"No, she hasn't confided in me, but I know there's something there."

The polka was over, and the bandleader had announced they were going to slow it down a bit. Before Libby could escape, Connor swept her into his arms, and, holding her close, began a slow, sexy waltz, moving to the rhythm of the music.

With his strong muscled arms around her, he cuddled her against his soft flannel shirt. She could feel his rapid heartbeat, a residue from the fast-paced polka. Her heart was beating hard, too, but she wasn't certain it was from the polka. She had lost herself for a while. *This feels good. But it shouldn't.*

Too soon, the music ended, and Libby quickly excused herself and returned to the table. Rather than rejoining the guys at the bar, Connor also joined the group. These were his longtime friends. The rest of the evening was filled with much teasing and joking, the lighthearted camaraderie that is comfortable among good friends.

When the band started the last dance, Connor pushed back his chair and was about to claim Libby when a young officer who had had his eye on her all evening appeared at her side and asked her to dance.

He introduced himself as Matt, and, holding Libby uncomfortably close, circled the floor with her. She glimpsed Connor at the table, scowling unhappily. Libby wasn't very happy herself, but didn't want to let it show. She pushed slightly away and smiled at Matt, trying to make small talk. When the music stopped, Matt suggested he take her home, and while Libby was trying to think of how she could graciously decline, Connor appeared and said gruffly, "I'm escorting the lady home," and led her away.

She was somewhat relieved, but a little irritated, too, at Connor's unwarranted possessiveness and assumption that she couldn't take care of herself. They said their good-byes to the group and headed to Connor's Jeep.

An awkward silence ensued on the drive to Libby's cottage. Still fuming about Matt's cutting in on what he'd thought would be a pleasant finale to a lovely evening with Libby, Connor finally broke the silence. "Are you miffed about something?"

Sitting a little straighter on her side of the car, Libby accused, "What gives you the right to assume I needed your help or that I wanted to come home with you?"

Taken aback and somewhat chastened, Connor replied, "I'm sorry, Libby. It's just that Matt is such a player, and I just didn't relish the thought of your being taken in by him. Guess I overstepped some boundaries. I really am sorry." He hesitated. "And I guess I was hoping to bring you home all along."

Softening at this confession and his boyish demeanor, Libby relented. "OK. I didn't really feel comfortable going home with someone I'd just met, but don't ever think I can't take care of such situations myself. I'm a big girl."

They were now outside her cottage. "OK. Truce?" Connor asked.

"Truce," Libby replied. "And to show my good faith, why don't you come sit on my porch, and I'll make a cup of tea. It's a beautiful night."

Sitting on the porch, watching the moon make a glittering, rippled path across the bay, they shared more about themselves. Libby couldn't contain her curiosity any longer. "OK. I've heard you called 'Doc' several times since I've come here. What's the deal? Is it an inside joke—like you crashed into the 'dock' sometime on one of your wild flights? You have quite a reputation as a pilot."

Connor laughed. "Actually, I'm a doctor."

"A doctor? A PhD type like Shirlee?"

He snorted. "No, a medical doctor. I work for Northern Health at the clinic in the Haida village of Old Massett."

"But I thought you worked for TPA as a pilot."

"No," he laughed again. "I help Gus out once in a while when he needs me, but my first loyalty is to medicine. I learned to fly with my dad, who owned a small flight company, hauling cargo and sometimes people for the island. But I had a fascination for medicine and healing. I knew a doctor for the people was needed on the island so that they wouldn't have to fly off it for their health care or depend solely on the medical officers who are temporarily posted to the base."

"So the small package you were waiting on the other night was…? I thought maybe you were into selling magic mushrooms or something."

Connor almost choked on the tea he'd just swallowed. Totally losing his composure at that one, he laughed heartily. "Babies, Libby. The small package I was waiting to deliver was a baby— that's a big part of my practice. In fact, Stephen and I work a lot together on that. He sometimes comes out to the village clinic to give a hand with a walk-in on his weekends off. We share call, and cover for one another if one of us is away."

"Oops," Libby laughed at herself. "Guess my imagination got a little too creative. English-major alert! Do your parents still live here?"

He became quiet, then responded painfully. "No, unfortunately. Several years ago, Mum and Dad took a trip to Vancouver, and on their way back across the Hecate Strait, Dad's small private plane lost one of the engines and half the power. A plane can drop two hundred feet suddenly over the Strait, which usually isn't a problem, but when it loses its usual power, well…they went down and drowned before help could get to them."

"Oh, Connor. I'm so sorry." This man had suffered loss. Maybe he would understand hers. "I'm also sorry for my glib remark about crashing into a dock."

"That's OK. You had no way of knowing. Guess we're even for blunders tonight. Now, tell me about the prairies."

She talked about growing up with her mum, dad, and brother, Corbin, and the harsh winters, where snow blew horizontally in forty-mile-an-hour winds. Conversation came easily to them that evening. Later, Libby would realize they'd sat and talked for hours, covering several topics, but nothing too personal or revealing. The late evening passed into night; the moon crossed the sky and disappeared. Libby never mentioned Ben. Connor never mentioned Willow.

At the door of her cottage, she bid him good-bye. "This has been nice."

"Very nice," he said softly. Placing his hands on her upper arms, he leaned forward and gently brushed her lips with his. Libby felt a tingling all the way to her toes. Then his arms enclosed her, drawing her closer, and his mouth searched hers more urgently, awakening her core.

She responded to his kiss fully and unconsciously, then suddenly pulled away, saying, "I'm sorry...I can't."

"Why, Libby?" Connor asked, stunned by her sudden reaction.

"I...I just can't. Please go now, and thanks for the evening."

He turned, leaving her to watch him go. He didn't understand, but he thought once again that she was running from something, something he desperately wanted to help her face.

# CHAPTER
# SEVEN

*C*onnor dropped by Books 'n' Brew on his way to the clinic in Old Massett. Stephen Parker was holding a Saturday-morning drop-in clinic there, and Connor had paperwork to catch up on. The bureaucracy of a government clinic sometimes got to him, but maybe he and Stephen could go fishing when they were done.

"So, tell me, Shirl," Connor asked, since no one was in the shop, "What's with Libby? There seems to be something troubling her. Do you know anything about her background or why she's here? I figure if anyone can get someone's story, it's you."

"I'm afraid she hasn't confided in me, Connor. We have great talks. I've learned some about her family, and, of course, she says she's here because she wanted a new challenge, and we discuss teaching, but I agree. There's something more—a shadow that sometimes crosses over her."

"I know. It seems like she's running from something. I wish I knew what."

"Be patient, Connor. She's a great gal—there's depth to her. Someday she'll be ready to tell us."

Just then, the object of their conversation walked through the door, a stack of books and papers in her arms. "Oh!" she started at the sight of Connor. She hadn't seen him since the awkward ending to the Oktoberfest evening a week ago.

Smiling and acting like there had been no awkwardness, he greeted her. "Well, hello there. Shirlee, give the lady whatever she wants. I'm treating. You've got quite a load there. Teachers' work never done?"

Relieved, she replied, "Thought I'd get some papers graded, and the walk downtown was refreshing. I'll have my usual almond roca mocha, Shirlee. Thank you, Connor; will you join me?"

"For a bit," he replied, then explained his plans also for paper-work and possibly fishing with Stephen later. "Have you been out to the Tlell River yet? It's a wonderful place to relax, and it has great steelhead and coho salmon fishing."

"No, I haven't ventured that way yet, but I have been hunting for agates at Agate Beach. I can't believe what beautiful jewelry some of the…uh…'homesteaders' make with the rock."

Connor laughed. "You mean old hippies. After they gave up the magic mushroom trade, some of them who settled here as squatters took up crafts and organic gardening. I guess they found out they needed money to live on."

Libby smiled. The conversation was light, and she relaxed. They chatted for a few more minutes, and then she asked, "I've been wondering, Connor, after hearing about the loss of your parents in an airplane accident, how you are still able to fly. Hope I'm not prying."

"No, that's fine." He took a breath before continuing. "I grew up flying. Dad was a great teacher, and I was often with him on his cargo trips, so it's second nature to me. He would be the first to tell me not to let their accident hold me back." He took a sip of his coffee and met her eyes. "You know, Libby, sometimes we have to face our demons."

"Maybe," she replied quietly.

She was relieved when he switched to lighter topics and then left on a friendly note. "See you next time, Libby—the paperwork won't do itself." She was glad that it seemed they were still friends. But did she want more? Was she ready for more?

Watching, Shirlee nodded with approval at Connor's gentle approach. *Best not to overpower or push this one,* she thought. *She will come around, if that's what he wants, and I'm sure that's what he wants. They both need some happiness. I hope they can find it together.*

After Connor's departure, she and Libby started discussing school, their favorite topic in common. "I hear from the principal you are getting a great response from the kids about their heritage projects. Keeping them busy with meaningful work keeps them from making trouble in the classroom." Taking a break in the momentary lull in customers, Shirlee brought over some cinnamon-raisin scones to join Libby at the table.

"I've always believed that, too. I have one particularly challenging class. The kids seem to think they aren't smart enough to do the work I assign, but I believe they need challenges and interesting assignments, just like the university entrance classes, and I think they are surprising themselves," she explained proudly, taking a bite from her scone.

"I have, however, faced my first major discipline problem. There's this one student in my upper-level class who has needled me since day one. It's not really a serious problem, but he was just getting under my skin, so to speak. One day, I'd had enough, and I let him have it! Of course, he sat back in his desk, crossed his arms, and smiled at me with satisfaction. He had gotten to me, and he knew it! I said to myself, *Oh shit, Libby! You know better than that!*"

Remembering the incident, she sucked in her breath and continued. "I immediately composed myself and asked to see him after class. That stunned him. While we discussed his behavior away from his audience of the other students, he was rather sheepish. We got to the root of the problem, and he really hasn't been one since. I'm glad, because he's very bright and could become a positive leader in the class rather than a distraction." Libby sipped her coffee and took another bite out of her scone.

"Good for you. Yes, you committed the cardinal sin of 'losing it' in front of the students, but you rectified the situation immediately. I'm sure it will have an impact on the others, too."

Changing the subject, Libby asked, "Connor mentioned the Tlell River. Is it far from here?"

"Nothing's far from here, Libby. The island is only seventy miles long. No, just head out on 16—that's the highway toward Skidegate at the southern end of the island—and watch for the signs. It really is a peaceful place to walk, though sometimes families are there having picnics, and, of course, the fishermen. The mornings and evenings are starting to get foggy now, so afternoon is the best time to go. And don't wander away from the shore, off into the wilderness areas."

Turning her back to put some items away, Shirlee casually added, "Connor lives on the Tlell. He's built a log home out there."

"Oh, really? I may have to take a drive out there some weekend. I could use a peaceful walk. It could be just the ticket."

*There it is again,* thought Shirlee. *She's looking for some peace. But I have a feeling that if she's attracted to the Tlell because of Connor, it won't be peace she'll be looking for—or finding.*

# CHAPTER
# EIGHT

*L*ibby hadn't seen Connor in a couple of weeks, but she hadn't been able to get him out of her mind. There was certainly a physical attraction she knew they both felt, but there was more to him than she had originally thought. He seemed to be getting under her skin, too, but in a decidedly different way than her troublesome student. *I guess he's troublesome for me, too!*

So on that cold Saturday, Libby finally made her way down Highway 16, the only paved road on the island, to the Tlell River. Giant spruce lined the narrow road like sentries. She quickly hit the brakes as two deer jumped out in front of the car to cross the road. They were much smaller than those on the prairies.

Finally, she pulled into a makeshift parking lot surrounded by tall red cedars and Sitka spruce that were almost blocking out the sky. Hearing an unfamiliar, high-pitched bird's cry, she looked through the majestic trees to see a bald eagle soaring regally above in the patch of blue sky, seemingly in search of small prey.

Once again in awe of the raw natural beauty of the islands, Libby followed a worn path and emerged onto the rocky riverbank dotted with driftwood, sand dunes, and a few larger outcroppings of rock. The tide was going out, so the river was calm, and a gentle breeze whispered among the spruce and cedars. She was glad she had donned her Irish fisherman knit sweater and her all-weather jacket. There was a damp chill in the November air. If she were at home on the prairies, she would probably be experiencing the first snowfall. There apparently was little snowfall on the islands, and what little snow that did fall melted almost immediately. But the cold here was damp, and it chilled her right through to the bone.

Unsure exactly why she'd come, Libby walked along, head down, beach-combing for agates, Japanese glass floats, or other artifacts that folks often found along the river, having been brought in by tidal waves. Coming around a bend in the river, she looked up and recognized the unmistakable figure of Connor, who was fishing several yards ahead. Catching her breath in anticipation of their meeting, she pressed on. *He's the reason I'm here.* She was startled when that dawned on her.

Noticing her approach, that slow grin spread across his rugged face, and his sky-blue eyes twinkled above his chiseled cheekbones. She was pleased at this friendly welcome. "Hi, there," she said. "Thought I'd take your recommendation of a walk along the river. You were right. It is peaceful. Are you catching anything?"

"Yeah, I got a couple of beauties. A nice steelhead that I released back into the river. Need to preserve our resources if I'm not going to use it. But I also got a huge coho that will make a tasty supper. Glad you made it out here. It's nice to find a little spot of peace, quiet, and solitude."

"Oh, I'm sorry I interrupted your solitude," she apologized, realizing he may not want company.

"No, no! I didn't mean that. Sometimes solitude is best shared by two." He smiled down at her.

They chatted for a while, and Connor shared his thermos of hot chocolate. Sitting on a rock together, the close proximity once again made Libby squirm in a delicious kind of way. The sky was losing its afternoon light, however, and Libby knew she needed to be leaving soon, though she hated to go. *Maybe he'll invite me to stay for supper.* "Guess I'd better be getting back to town."

Wanting to keep her there, but remembering Shirlee's caution about not pushing, he reluctantly replied, "Yes, you will want to get back before the fog starts rolling in, especially since you're not used to the road in such conditions."

Disappointed, Libby sighed. "Yes, well then, I'll see you around sometime." With regret in his eyes, Connor watched her turn and quickly stride away, not knowing what to say to make her stay.

Blinking back tears and having no idea why they were stinging her eyes, she started to jog to disappear as quickly as possible. With the tide having retreated further, the sand was wet and slippery, making her shoes the same. Rather than going around a small outcropping of rock, she scrambled over it. The mist in the air had made the rock slippery. Before she knew what had happened, she slipped between the jagged edges and caught her foot, painfully twisting it in a crevice. Involuntarily, she emitted an anguished cry.

Having continued to follow her progress down the shoreline, Connor saw the accident and broke into a run, calling, "Libby!" He was by her side in minutes. "Don't move," he ordered. "I'll try to get your foot loose with as little discomfort as possible." He unlaced and loosened her walking shoe, then gently pulled her foot from it. "We're going to have to get you a pair of good hiking boots. These ones aren't meant for walking over slippery or rugged, uneven terrain. Why did you run?"

"I…I don't know," she lied, choking on the words and the pain. How could she explain her disappointment at his not encouraging her to stay?

He helped her up, but she could put no pressure on her foot. "You've probably sprained it, but we can't rule out a fracture. We'll hope for a sprain. My place is only a quarter of a mile downriver. We'll go there so I can check it out." With that, he scooped her into his arms and began carrying her.

"You can't carry me that far!" she protested. "I'm not exactly a featherweight."

He looked down directly into her hazel eyes. "I could carry you forever."

"Forever is a long time," she replied, eyes downcast and tone suddenly wistful. When she thought of forever, she invariably thought of Ben and how she had believed they would be together forever.

"Just be quiet now! Doctor's orders," he said with a grin. "Rest your head on my shoulder, and we'll be there in no time." She obeyed, nestling against his broad chest. *Maybe I could do this forever.*

They soon arrived at his home, which was built of red cedar logs. He wound around the path from the riverbank to the veranda that encircled the lodge. Comfortable log rocking chairs and benches invited visitors to while away some time, enjoying the view. Still carrying her, Connor managed to open the door and step inside.

Libby suddenly remembered, "What about your fishing gear? You left it on the bank."

"Don't worry about that. I'll check your ankle first and get you comfortable here, then I'll fetch my gear and your car." He set her in a padded log rocking chair and brought her a Haida-designed blanket to keep her warm while he examined her ankle.

Connor asked her to point to the spot where it was most tender. Libby indicated the outer part of her ankle. He palpated her foot for other tender areas, and she winced each time he touched the outer part of her ankle. He asked her to flex her foot through its normal range of motion, and then physically moved it himself, asking her throughout the procedure if each movement increased or decreased the pain, or if it remained the same. Whenever she twisted her foot inward, there was more pain.

Finally, Connor leaned back on the footstool and concluded, "I don't think it's broken, Libby. I suspect you have an inversion sprain and have strained the ligaments around the outside of your ankle.

There's no bruising yet, but there is some puffiness beginning, and I think you'll experience both before long. We will need to get it x-rayed to be sure there isn't a fracture. In the meantime, we'll keep it elevated, and I'll apply some ice. You will need to rest it and keep off it, at least for a while."

He disappeared briefly. "Here, these will help you get around," he stated, producing a pair of crutches, "and the bathroom is just down the hall, should you want to…uh…freshen up."

"You have crutches? You're prepared for everything—a regular Boy Scout, aren't you?" she teased.

Connor ignored her. "OK, I'm going to start a fire in the fireplace and give you some hot tea to drink while I go and get the fishing gear and your car. You can't drive this evening in discomfort and with the fog rolling in, so I think it's best you stay here tonight. I'll drive you back in the morning, and we'll get an x-ray of that foot."

"Oh, I can't impose like that!" Libby protested, not a little unnerved, but strangely excited by the prospect. "What about my car? How will I get it back?"

"Tomorrow is Sunday, so I can get Stephen or Gus to come back with me and drive your car to town. Aimée could possibly stay with you while we're gone and get you settled into your cottage. I can bring you any supplies you may need when we get back with your car." He said this all matter-of-factly and in a tone that was not to be questioned.

"Well, you seem to have it all worked out!" Libby said a little huffily.

"There you go getting miffed again. I'm not trying to boss you around, little Miss I-can-take-care-of-myself!" he chided, then added a little more softly, "This is a minor crisis, and I'm just a friend trying to help out."

*Only a friend?* Libby wondered, disappointed, but she smiled and said, "I'm sorry. Guess I am a little touchy. I'm grateful for your help, but I don't have any overnight things with me."

"Not to worry. You'll find a few things you might need, including sleepwear, in the guest bedroom."

"Oh, you have many female guests for sleepovers?" she responded, again a little testily.

"I won't dignify that with a comment. You said it earlier; I'm just a regular Boy Scout—always prepared."

He helped her to the comfy sofa with deep pillows, covered in a woodsy-themed tapestry. After wrapping her ankle with a cold compress, he again covered her with the blanket and brought her the tea that had been steeping. "I'll go now to get my gear and your car. Shouldn't be more than half an hour, and then we'll have that fresh salmon I caught for supper. Do you need anything else before I go?"

"I'll be fine," Libby said. "How will you get back so quickly?"

"Well, I won't be carrying a burden for one thing," he teased.

Libby decided to let that one go, and laughed in response. "A burden, eh?"

After he left, Libby snuggled into the sofa, sipped her mug of hot tea, and began taking in her surroundings. It was a beautiful log home with a spacious openness. Like the house, the furniture was also hewn of logs from island trees, and beautiful area rugs woven in Haida motifs were scattered on the hardwood floors. The stone fireplace that ran from floor to ceiling was obviously constructed of natural materials from the Charlottes.

The house definitely had a masculine feel; however, looking around, Libby was surprised at the number of art pieces throughout. Carvings in argillite decorated end tables. Prints of orcas, ravens, and eagles in Haida artistic interpretations adorned the wall, along with a single cedar bark woven hat that ancestral Haidas wore.

Reed baskets were grouped in nooks, and, of course, the popular button blankets were draped over chairs and benches. Connor obviously had an eye for art and an appreciation for the Haida First Nation culture.

After surveying her surroundings, the warm fire and hot tea began lulling Libby into a cozy sleep. Just before dropping off, she noted through her sleepy haze a framed black-and-white photograph on the mantle of a handsome couple, possibly in their forties or early fifties. The man had rugged good looks, with greying hair and happy eyes that looked vaguely familiar. He had an air of strength, making observers feel they would be safe with him. The woman had long, dark, straight hair streaked with silver, and dark kind eyes. *Attractive in maturity,* Libby thought drifting into sleep, *she must have been gorgeous in her youth.*

Hiking back to the scene of the accident, Connor pondered his good fortune at having Libby in his home, yet he knew it presented a dilemma. He wanted to run his fingers through that reddish-blond hair, stroke her cheek, her neck, and other more private nether places. The thought of touching her made him long for her, and he could feel his body responding to that longing. Yes, there was that strong desire that Libby aroused in him, but he still sensed a fragility about her for all her brave talk. He had never felt this emotional about a woman before, and he didn't want to ruin any possibility of a meaningful connection with her. He'd have to tread carefully.

Libby awoke to the tantalizing smell of salmon being grilled, and hot coffee percolating on the stove. "I never heard you return. You should have woken me up."

"You looked far too peaceful, and I think you needed the rest after your afternoon adventure. Supper will be ready soon," Connor responded.

"Oh, what can I do to help?" she replied, attempting to get up, but having forgotten about her ankle, she soon fell back on the sofa in frustrating pain.

"Just relax," he said. "You can help next time." She smiled to herself at the possibility of a "next time."

They ate companionably, without the usual tension and barbs. She then asked, "I've been admiring your wonderful collection of Haida art. Are you a connoisseur of art, or mainly interested because it's local? It certainly adds to the natural beauty of your home."

"Thank you. I guess my interest is in its beauty, definitely, but it's also personal. It represents my heritage. I have Haida blood running through my veins."

Libby was surprised. "Really? With a name like Ferguson and those bright blue eyes?" He did not look like the few Haida she had met so far on the islands.

"Are you stereotyping, Miss Campbell?" he asked, an amused smile pulling at the corner of his mouth.

"Oh, no!" she proclaimed, feeling the heat rise to her cheeks. "I…I didn't mean anything like that! I…I . . ." she stammered, embarrassed.

He laughed at her discomfort, and relieved her of it quickly. "I was teasing you, Libby. With everything I know about you and what you've been doing for all the students at the high school, including the Haida ones, I know you have no biases."

While she collected herself from her faux pas, he continued. "Let me explain the name and my bright blue eyes, as you called them." He said the latter with an obvious twinkle in them. He just couldn't help teasing her. "My mother was full-blooded Haida. My father's family had Haida connections also, but several generations back. If you recall from your reading about the Haida, when the Christian missionaries came to the islands, they attempted to stamp out a lot of the indigenous culture in their Christianization of the people. That included changing many of their names, so many of the families took the anglicized names of missionaries. My family must have taken one from a Scot."

"My blue eyes," he continued, "come from the intermarrying of the Haida Fergusons with Caucasians who came to the islands over the years. For example, my Ferguson grandmother was a McIntyre, and she looked very much like you—strawberry-blond hair and sparkling hazel eyes. It's possible she was a distant relative or descendant of Captain McIntyre, for whom the McIntyre Bay is named. And that, Miss Campbell, is your heritage lesson for the day!"

Libby flushed slightly at the reference to her looks, but responded with a new, keener appreciation for Connor. "That was a very good lesson, Dr. Ferguson, and quite fascinating. Thank you for it and for this delicious supper."

He cleaned off the table, and they retired to the sofa with their coffee. After placing a small stool under Libby's foot, he put more logs on the fire and prodded it into a warm blaze.

They chatted comfortably, Connor resting his arm on the back of the sofa. Eventually, he began stroking the back of her neck gently. She neither stiffened nor refused this attention, but her heart began pounding a little more insistently. There was definitely something about this man that was breaking down her resistance. Could she be falling in love in spite of herself?

Soon, his arm slid around her completely, and he pulled her to him, careful not to disturb her foot. Brushing back her hair, he kissed her forehead and cheek. Then tipping her chin with his index finger so that her eyes were raised to his, he covered her lips with his. She responded in kind, and their tentative kisses grew more urgent. His tongue ran around the inside of her lips, thrilling all her senses so that her mouth quickly drew his tongue in to dance with hers.

Sliding his hand down her shoulder, he gently caressed her breast. When she didn't protest, he slid his hand under her sweater and around her back to release her breasts from her bra. Cupping and stroking her soft, supple flesh, he eventually raised her sweater and bent his head to a nipple, taking it into his mouth and running his tongue around it.

*Oh God, there must be a direct line from my breast to my core.* Responding to the tightening of her core, Libby squeezed her thighs together and moaned, "Oh, Ben."

Connor immediately drew away and sat upright. "Ben? Is there another man in your life?" he accused.

"No, Connor. I can explain," she implored.

He was standing now, drawing himself to his full height, and looking down at her intensely. Letting pride overcome clear thinking, he retorted, "No need to explain. I know all I need to know, and I will not be compared to another man, nor called by his name. You will find what you need for the night in the guest bedroom, and I trust you can get there on your own. You have the crutches. We'll go to town first thing in the morning. Right now, I need to chop some firewood." With that, he left, banging the back door behind him before Libby could respond.

She heard the angry, incessant striking of an axe upon the firewood. There would be no explaining to him tonight—and just when she thought she might be able to open her heart to love again.

She gathered up her crutches and, confused, hobbled to the guest room. There on the bed was a long flannel, yet feminine, nightgown laid out for her use, along with toiletries on the dresser. *Whose possessions are these? Willow's? He has a lot of nerve being angry with me while expecting me to wear another woman's nightgown!*

Picking up the toiletries from the dresser, she noticed another framed picture, this one a candid shot of a young couple walking along Agate Beach. She noticed Tow Hill in the background. Though the figures were in the distance, she recognized the teenage image of Connor with his head thrown back, laughing. The young girl was in profile, but she had a lithe body, and flowing dark hair blowing in the wind. She clutched Connor's arm, laughing up at him with adoration in her eyes. It was clear these two loved one another very much.

Libby felt a pang in her heart. Seeing the two reminded her of her and Ben's young teenage love, and it made her wonder if Connor, too, had had a longtime love. Was this lovely young girl Willow? Pride and instinct for survival overrode her sadness about her and Connor's misunderstanding, and having no other choice, she angrily grabbed the nightgown and headed for the bathroom.

Outdoors, Connor fumed. Swinging the axe with a vengeance stroke after stroke, Connor chastised himself. *What's with the macho attitude, Ferguson? So much for taking it slow. But who the hell is Ben? What's their story? Is this what makes her hold back?*

After the physical activity released some of his pent-up emotions, Connor realized he'd have to back off and wait, wait for her to tell him and respond to him fully. And yes, she was worth the wait.

# CHAPTER
# NINE

*I*t was Christmas Eve morning. Libby strolled along the road toward downtown to get her mail at the post office and maybe a cup of coffee at Books 'n' Brew. Had she made a mistake by not going home for the holidays? She had talked to her parents that morning, and the conversation had probably made her nostalgic and a little wistful. Her brother, Corbin, would be home, bringing, once again, a new girlfriend. She was reminded of the family joke, wondering each time if it was worth remembering "this one's" name.

Though she wanted Corbin to be happy, she wasn't sure she could take all that lovey-dovey stuff of new love since she had lost her old one, and probably any possibility of a new one, too. She hadn't seen Connor since their ill-fated encounter at his home on the Tlell. The trip home would have been long and expensive, too, so it was probably best to spend the holidays curled up with a few good books and lesson plans for the new semester.

Sorting her mail, she opened the door to the coffee shop. She'd received several seasonal greeting cards and the usual fliers and bills. The aroma of cinnamon-spiced coffee and mulled cider greeted her, along with Dr. Shirlee's, "Merry Christmas, Libby! Can I pour you something festive, or do you want your usual mocha?"

She was about to respond when suddenly her face clouded over and a lump caught in her throat. Shirlee immediately asked, "Libby, what's wrong?" Libby stood still, staring at one of the envelopes in her hands. It was postmarked Crocus Plains, Manitoba, and the return address said "Patricia Warren." Ben's mother. She couldn't open this letter here. She suddenly didn't even want to be here.

"Libby," Shirlee tentatively began again. "Is anything the matter?"

"Oh, oh…uh, no," Libby stammered, visibly shaken. "I'll take my mocha to go, please."

Not wanting to pry further, and staying on a safe topic, Shirlee commented while preparing the beverage, "I suppose I'll see you at the Parkers' annual gathering tonight. They do it mainly for all us single folk. Aimée really gets into the French Canadian thing, with a huge meal at midnight after mass. She makes homemade *tourtière*, a traditional meat pie, and everything."

Still distracted, it took Libby a moment to register what Shirlee had said. "Uh, no. I think I'll pass."

"Aimée will be disappointed. She's become very fond of you—like a sister. She misses her big family back in Montreal." Shirlee handed her the mocha, saying, "It's on the house—Merry Christmas."

"Yes, thanks," Libby replied absently. Opening the door, she left the shop, leaving Shirlee frowning with concern for her young friend.

On her way home, Libby puzzled over the letter from Ben's mother. They hadn't been in touch since she'd left Crocus Plains. In fact, they hadn't had much contact even before that. It had been too painful for both.

Entering the cottage, she set the mail on the table. She opened all the envelopes except Patricia's letter. After puttering with minor tasks, she finally picked up the envelope and took it out to the porch. Her rocking chair on the porch with the peaceful view of the bay was her place of solace. She hoped it would give her the strength to face whatever was in the letter.

She unfolded the single sheet of paper and read the beautiful script of Patricia's hand.

*Rosemary Vaughn*

*Dear Libby,*

*I know we haven't kept in touch, but I thought during this holiday season, which is so often fraught with pitfalls and great sadness for those of us who have experienced tragedy in our lives, it was time to break the silence. I spoke with your father in the grocery store the other day, and he and your mother are very proud of the accomplishments you are achieving as a teacher, but they are also very concerned about you.*

*I'm sure folks are telling you to go on with your life, but we both know it's not that simple. Ben was your true love, your soul mate. I loved you like a daughter, and thought someday, when you two were married, you would be one to me. You thought that your love was forever, and that you and Ben would be together forever. Life, however, doesn't always follow what we think. But, Libby, you must know that your love for Ben will be forever, living on in your memories and your heart. But in life on Earth, we never know how long forever will be. Each day we begin a new path toward a different forever. So Libby, it is not a betrayal to Ben or your memories and love for him to begin each day looking toward a new forever. Though the path is difficult for us, we both must take it.*

*I wish you all the best as we look toward a new year and, perhaps, a new beginning.*

*Forever yours,*

*Patty*

It all came flooding back: the memories of Ben and the life they were to have shared. They had been high school sweethearts, had gone on to college together, and had planned to marry and settle down in a small town to raise a family. Those dreams had been shattered when an accident took Ben's life. She had tried to go on, completing her degree and teaching in her hometown of Crocus Plains. But watching the young adolescents with their crushes and blossoming young loves just brought back too many memories of her and Ben's young love. It was just too painful. The memories haunted her, and she had had to get away. Everyone had said, "You're young, Libby. You'll find another love." But they just hadn't understood. Feeling she'd never recover, indeed, she had run away.

The tears began slowly, then came in torrents, releasing an anguish Libby had not truly faced since Ben's accident. She hadn't realized how much had been bottled up, but after the storm had ebbed, a tranquility and calm fell over her. Patty's words had been a balm to an open wound. She was so grateful to Patty for her words and selflessness in reaching out to her. She knew it would still take time, and she'd never forget Ben, but at least now she felt that facing forever really was a possibility.

Exhausted from her purge of emotions, and with a slightly lighter heart, she began rereading some of her other Christmas greetings that she'd only given a cursory review before. She was smiling at a friend's account of her camping trip with three teen-agers when the phone rang.

It was Aimée. Without letting Libby know Shirlee had called her with concern, she greeted her friend with, "*Bonjour—Joyeux Noel!* Just checking in with you. Are you all set for the best time of your life at my blow-out *soirée* tonight?"

Libby laughed at her bubbly friend's infectious enthusiasm. Sighing, she thought that now was probably as good a time as any to begin looking forward, and replied, "Merry Christmas to you, too! Yes, I plan to be there with bells on!"

Not expecting this kind of response after Shirlee's warning, it took Aimée a moment to respond. "Great! Great! *Mon amie.* We'll see you at seven sharp, and bring a big appetite. You won't believe how much food I've prepared!"

"I'll be there on the dot!" replied Libby, hanging up the receiver. The next problem was, of course, what to wear. Her thoughts turned to Connor. Thanks to Patty's generosity, she could now open herself up to possibilities and no longer rebuff his attentions because of guilt and sad memories. She knew Ben would not want her to mourn forever. Though it had been and would continue to be a long journey, tonight was a beginning. Smiling wistfully, she searched her closet for just the right outfit, with a hunky young doctor/pilot in mind.

# CHAPTER
# TEN

imée opened the door to the Parkers' PMQ and welcomed her friend with a big hug. She was so glad Libby had decided to come. Aimée had watched Libby become increasingly introspective at the approaching holidays. Hoping it was just the result of missing home and family, she vowed to make this party a gala evening for her friend. She also knew there was a very concerned and handsome man in her living room hoping to do the same thing.

Entering Aimée's living room, Libby was warmly greeted by her friends, including Shirlee, Maggie, and Gus. Even though shopping on the Charlottes was somewhat limited to mail order catalogs, the room was gaily decorated in chintzy but festive Christmas decorations. Her friends were also dressed in gaudy yet charming holiday gear: reindeer sweaters, flashing earring globes, and jingle bells tinkling on their shoes. *Hmmm. Maybe I made the wrong choice for my outfit. I don't quite fit in with this jolly, festive group.*

Libby had brushed her strawberry-blond hair out to a fluffy fullness that framed her face and rested gently on her shoulders. Her soft cashmere turtleneck sweater in a shade of coral highlighted her peaches-and-cream complexion. The sweater topped camel-colored wool slacks that skimmed her slender yet curvy hourglass figure. She had a light touch with her makeup, just enough to enhance her hazel eyes and bring out their sparkle. Lifting those eyes to survey the room, it became obvious that there was one person for whom her choices were perfect.

Across the room, Connor leaned against the fireplace mantle with one arm and held a glass of merlot in the hand of the other. His stance seemed casual, but he was otherwise mesmerized. His blue eyes met Libby's hazel ones, signaling his charmed approval. Eyes sparkling, she smiled slowly and shyly at him. That's all it took, and he was across the room, declaring, "Libby, I'm so glad you came!" With their friends looking on approvingly and smiling at one another knowingly, Connor drew Libby to a cozy loveseat near the fireplace, giving them a bit of privacy.

"I've been wanting to talk to you ever since . . ," he hesitated, taking both her hands in his, then continued, "ever since I acted like such a jerk. I want to apologize, because I had no right to act like a jealous tyrant."

Libby smiled, pleased at the thought of his being jealous, but quickly assured him, "It's all right, Connor, and I can explain."

"No, no, Libby," Connor interrupted. "I jumped to too many conclusions, and it's none of my business what's in your past. You have no need to explain anything to me. I want us to start over with a clean slate."

She wanted to tell him about Ben—she *needed* to tell him about Ben—but perhaps this was neither the time nor place. Maybe for now she could just savor this wonderful moment and perhaps the beginning of an even more wonderful future. "I'd like that very much, Connor." Heads together, they chatted for the rest of the evening, barely noticing their friends' banter or the delicious delicacies being passed around and devoured.

Suddenly, Aimée clanked her wineglass for attention and announced with an impish twinkle in her eye, "OK, gang, it's 11:30. It's time for all you Catholics, and any heathens who'd like to tag along, to go to the traditional Christmas Eve midnight Mass.

I promise you a wonderful feast upon our return. Remember, *mes amis*, I make the best *tourtière* on the island!" to which she received friendly chiding of, "You're the *only* French Canadian on the island!"

Laughing good-naturedly, Aimée looked slyly at Connor and Libby in their cozy corner and said, "It would be really helpful if a couple of you would stay behind to make sure the house doesn't burn down and to put the final touches on the table while the rest of us pray for your souls." Taking their cue, Connor and Libby volunteered.

Closing the door on the boisterous group, Connor turned to Libby, and looking up, discovered that Aimée had strategically placed mistletoe in the entrance. "Thank you, Aimée," he smiled. Libby looked at him quizzically. He continued, "Not that I needed an excuse, but Aimée has provided me with a reason to do this." He drew Libby to him and gently kissed her. Libby's arms automatically went around his neck, responding eagerly.

His grip tightened, and her body molded perfectly to his. Libby's fingers crept into those dark curls at the nape of Connor's neck. He groaned as her lips parted to receive his kiss more fully. Realizing it wasn't only his mouth that was responding to her kiss, he unwillingly pulled away and said, "I don't think the Christmas Mass is very long, Libby." Her hand caressed his cheek, and slowly and reluctantly, she drew her arms from around his neck. He smiled down into her face and said, "I have something for you."

Going to the coat closet, he pulled a small box wrapped in gold foil paper from his jacket pocket. "Merry Christmas, Prairie Rose."

Stunned, she stammered, "But, Connor, I have nothing for you. We didn't exactly part on friendly terms, and I frankly was unsure how tonight was going to go. How could you know?"

"I had hope, Libby, and you once said that I'm always prepared like a Boy Scout, so just in case," he grinned. "Open it."

Libby unwrapped the small square package and opened the lid and gasped at the sight of a beautiful copper bracelet lying inside. It was carved with a raven's head in the Haida tradition, and the Haida carver's name was etched on the inside of the bracelet. "Oh, Connor, it's gorgeous. But how can I accept it? I have nothing for you."

Putting the bracelet around her wrist and assessing it, Connor teased, "Hmmm. Ferguson, not bad! You have great taste. The copper complements your outfit and dazzling hair." Looking into her eyes deeply, he said more seriously, "The Raven represents my mother's family. And Libby, you have just given me everything I dreamed of for Christmas."

# CHAPTER
# ELEVEN

After a huge feast, much wine, and jolly fellowship, the Christmas Eve party at the Parkers' broke up. The single folk, like Shirlee, went home to empty houses, remembering Christmases past with their families. Others, like Gus and Maggie Davis, went home to prepare the surprises that a visit from St. Nicholas would be leaving for their children's Christmas morning. Connor followed Libby home, ostensibly to ensure her safe arrival at that late hour.

He escorted Libby to her door, and after she unlocked it, she surprised him when she turned to him and said, "Do you have plans for Christmas morning, Connor? Do you need to be anywhere? Expecting Santa Claus, perchance?"

"Uh, no, I don't. The Davises invited me to join their circus for Christmas dinner later in the day, but nothing until then. Why?" Dare he hope this evening hadn't ended?

"I just thought that since it's almost morning anyway, and since we're both alone, perhaps you would like to spend it with me," she suggested cautiously.

He once again looked deeply into those hazel eyes and asked, "Are you sure, Libby? Really sure?"

Thankfully, remembering Patty's letter, she replied confidently, "Yes, Connor, I'm sure. Very sure." She took his hand and drew him into her homey little cottage. After shedding their jackets and hanging them in the small closet, she said, "Aimée put on quite a spread. I'm assuming you're as stuffed as I am, but can I get you anything?"

Connor brushed a lock of hair away from her temple with one hand and slid the other around her waist, drawing her close. "My eyes are drinking in a feast before me, and I'm looking at the only thing I could possibly want at this moment."

Their kisses grew from gentle caresses to passionate urgency. Connor's hand slipped under the edge of Libby's sweater and slid deliciously up her back. Moaning softly, Libby let herself melt into the moment, and this time, there was no mention of Ben escaping her lips.

Knowing there was no turning back for him now, Connor resumed his sometimes-masculine assertiveness by whisking her up into his arms and moving toward the bedroom. Used to being a man in charge, he suddenly remembered the fragility of his prairie rose, and asked once again, "Are you sure, Libby?" In response, she pulled his head toward her until his mouth met hers.

Setting her gently on the edge of the bed, Connor slipped her sweater over her head, and admiring the soft mounds peeking out of her peach-colored, lacy bra, soon had them released from entrapment. He knelt on the floor before her, and cupping her breasts, he began the slow sucking on her nipples as he had done once before. Her core muscles tightened also as they had before, but this time she murmured, "You're making me crazy," and dug her fingers into his curly head to draw him closer.

"I hope so," he said, grinning, and encouraged, began flicking his tongue action down her torso as he slipped his hands inside her slacks and panties to slide them down. No longer able to be a bystander, she grabbed the back of his sweater and tugged at it. He sat back and pulled it over his head, never taking his eyes off her. Noticing the impressive bulge in his pants, she leaned forward.

Tucking her hand inside his belt and waistband, she pulled him toward her with one hand and, with the other, began to release his mound just as he had her girls. He couldn't help grinning again and teasing her. "In a hurry, Prairie Rose?"

She grinned back. "Stop with all the talk. Get those clothes off and take me to bed." He didn't have to be asked twice, pausing only once to add a layer of protection, with which she gladly assisted.

After tender yet fervent lovemaking, in which they explored their bodies, which seemed to be meant to cleave perfectly together, Libby and Connor slept peacefully—though briefly—in one another's arms through a shortened night. Libby awoke first and looked at this strong yet gentle man. *He's going to become the center of my being. Now I have to tell him about Ben and why I escaped to the Charlottes.*

Connor began to awaken then. He ran a finger down her cheek and pulled her close, saying, "Mmmm. This is nice. Merry Christmas, Prairie Rose." Before she had a chance to say anything, he kissed her deeply and awakened her thoroughly with early-morning bliss.

After a quick shower, Libby made coffee and brought it to the porch, where Connor was waiting for her. They sat wrapped in blankets against the morning chill, rocking in the wicker chairs and watching the gentle waves lapping the dock on the bay. Spending a leisurely morning so comfortably together gave Libby the opportunity to talk openly with Connor, but before she could broach the subject, the phone in the kitchen rang. After answering it, she brought the portable receiver out to Connor. Looking at him quizzically as she handed it to him, she said, "It's Gus."

Taking the receiver, Connor turned to her, saying, "I'd better take it. Sometimes he has an emergency at the airport." He excused himself to take the call indoors.

He returned, laughing. "No emergency, just some impertinence from some nosey but well-meaning friends. According to Gus, it was apparent to everyone that we were making a connection last evening—to everyone's approval, by the way. Anyway, Gus was wondering if there was anyone I might like to have join the Davis crew for Christmas dinner today. I told him I didn't think anyone was ready for that crew, but I would ask. What do you think?"

"Oh, they have lovely boys! It would be nice to be around children at Christmas. If you really want me to go with you, I'd love to." Frowning, she added, "But how did he know to call here?"

"When I didn't answer my phone at home, he deduced from last evening's observations that I might be here." He laughed, then added emphatically, "And by the way, I would want you to go with me anywhere." Leaning down to kiss her, he pulled her to her feet and enveloped her in his arms, crushing her to his chest.

"None of that now, Mr. Boy Scout. I hope this is one time you really are prepared. We can't go empty-handed. We'll have to put together some little gifts, and I'll have to make something to contribute to the dinner."

Indeed, Connor was prepared. He already had gifts for the boys in his Jeep. Libby wrapped them, and they signed the tags from them both. Like her mother, Libby always had a little gift drawer with items handy for such occasions, so she was able to contribute a nice hostess gift for Maggie. Looking in her fridge, she found the ingredients to make a festive salad, and with a bottle of wine from Connor's collection, they were all set. Libby once again postponed her revelation. *Ah, well*, she sighed to herself. *It is Christmas, and it can wait until after the holidays.*

She was a little nervous on the way to the Davis home. She liked Gus and Maggie, but she didn't know them that well, certainly not like she did the Parkers, and this event would be their debut as a couple. She needn't have worried. They were welcomed with delight and open arms. The boys, Jacob and Dixon, immediately tackled Connor. They all tumbled to the floor, where they commenced their usual wrestling match.

"The boys just adore Connor," Maggie commented, leading Libby and her salad to the kitchen, where they would put the finishing touches on dinner. Smiling, she added, "I'm so glad you two have found one another. Connor is special to us all, and we so want him to be happy."

"Thank you," said Libby, not knowing what else to say. Everything was so new, and perhaps Maggie was being presumptuous, or at least a little premature. Noticing Maggie was rubbing her back, Libby was able to change the subject. "How are you feeling? The time is getting close, isn't it?"

"Yes, it is," agreed Maggie. "Probably in early February, and I'm more than ready! I'm feeling very much like the Goodyear Blimp these days."

"Oh, no, Maggie. You truly have that glow about you. It's obvious that you are a wonderful mother to your boys, too. What do they think about having a baby in the family?"

"Oh, they won't admit it, but I think they're excited and ready to be big brothers. They'd probably like a little brother to harass, but if it's a girl, I think they'll be pretty protective of their little princess. Guess dinner is ready. We'd better call in the troops!"

They enjoyed a delightful family dinner, and Libby was so glad she'd come, even though it reminded her of family and Christmases on the prairies. The boys were tickled by her stories of her and her brother, Corbin's, searching for presents before the holiday, and they marveled at her description of how, after dinner, they would all go skating on the pond or make snowmen if the snow was just the right consistency. How the boys longed to be able to ice skate like Libby and her brother had!

All in all, it had been a successful evening, and Libby and Connor left basking in the warm, happy glow of fellowship with good friends. He drove Libby home, and kissing her goodnight, he whispered, "Tomorrow and tomorrow and tomorrow . . ."

"Are we starting to quote Shakespeare, Dr. Ferguson? Macbeth is a little ominous in that speech," teased Libby.

"No, my Prairie Rose, just thinking about the promises that tomorrows bring."

# CHAPTER
# TWELVE

*A*nd the tomorrows were wonderful. Libby and Connor spent much of the holiday season together. He had clinic hours and on call duty, while she had lessons to prepare for the new semester, but whenever it was possible, they were together. The new year promised to be, well, just that—promising.

They walked Agate Beach, climbed Tow Hill, fished the Tlell River, and dug for clams on North Beach. If weather permitted, they cooked the fish or clams over an open fire on the beach or the river's shore. Not that the weather really mattered. Wherever they were, they'd bundle together and find ways to keep warm. Other times, they spent quiet evenings and weekends at one of their places, reading, talking, and generally getting to know one another better and becoming closer.

Time passed pleasantly, and it became more difficult for Libby to bring up Ben, her past, and her fears of loss. *Maybe it doesn't really matter. Things are great right now. Would it make any difference?* Occasionally, however, a shadow would cross Libby's countenance, but those times became less and less frequent. If Connor noticed these times, he respected her privacy, thinking if she needed to tell him something, she would.

When Libby returned to school after the Christmas break, it seemed like all of her students had contracted wretched colds. Soon she was coughing and sneezing herself, and she discovered, to her delight, that Connor could be an excellent nurse. He was very solicitous, bringing her magazines, making her soup and hot toddies, and tucking her into her rocking chair or bed with cozy blankets. She recuperated slowly from most of her symptoms, but had developed a severe earache.

Resisting giving in to the pain, she entered Books 'n' Brew to get her jolt of java and maybe have a chat with Shirlee. She noticed the Parkers sitting at a corner table and having a cozy têteà-tête this damp Saturday morning. She chatted with Shirlee while waiting on her mocha, but she couldn't help overhearing snatches of their conversation.

"Willow should be coming home soon, shouldn't she?" Stephen asked, his mouth full of a cinnamon-raisin scone.

"Haven't heard specifically, *mon cher*, but it's usually sometime in February or March. You've got a crumb on your upper lip," Aimée added, reaching up to flick it off with an affectionate gesture. "Connor must be so anxious to see her. They're so close, and have been ever since they were little ones growing up together."

*That's a name I haven't heard in a while*, thought Libby, her heart sinking a little. *I wonder why no one ever talks about her when I'm around. What is her and Connor's relationship, anyway?* Libby felt she couldn't leave without acknowledging them, so she wandered over with her coffee drink to their table. Was it her imagination or did they immediately clam up as they saw her approach?

Libby mustered a casual greeting. "So, what are you two up to this drippy Saturday morning?"

"Oh, we're just having a *petit déjeuner* together before Stephen covers the clinic out at the village while Connor's at that symposium at the hospital in Queen Charlotte City. How's your cold? You still look a little peaked," inquired Aimée, her voice tinged with concern for her friend.

"I'm not coughing and hacking so much," Libby replied, "but I can't seem to shake this earache. Guess it's all a part of the virus."

"You can't be too sure, Libby," replied Stephen. "It could be an ear infection. Come on out to the clinic this afternoon and I'll take a look. You might need an antibiotic."

After a little idle girly chitchat about Maggie's impending due date, Libby took her leave, promising to see Stephen later that afternoon.

Libby drove the short couple of miles down the road that ran along the inlet to Old Massett, catching a few glimpses of the waves breaking on shore until she turned off onto the street that would take her to the clinic. While waiting for Stephen to see her, she admired the small Haida children playing with the well-worn toys while they waited with their mothers to be seen by the doctor.

Driving back the way she'd come, Libby thought a bit wistfully about the little children at the clinic, reminding her that she and Ben might have had a little one of their own by now. Shaking the thought off, she was glad she'd carried through with her promise to Stephen to check in with him. She did indeed have an infection, and he immediately put her on an antibiotic.

Knowing Connor would be gone most of the weekend, Libby concentrated on grading papers and making plans for more activities and speakers on Haida culture and history for her students. The name Willow came to mind. Shirlee had mentioned that she was an expert resource on Haida art. She owned an art store in town called Raven's Nook. It featured works of Haida artists and artisans, especially those from the islands.

Libby had never gone into the store. Willow had been away anyway, and it being the off season, her assistant only opened it a few days a week. Libby wasn't sure she could bring herself to go, even upon Willow's return. There was something about her name always being linked to Connor's that made Libby uncomfortable and uncertain about her own happy future.

By Sunday evening, the antibiotics had taken effect, and she was feeling much better. She was thinking about getting into her pajamas and reading in bed for a while before falling asleep when someone rapped at the door. Wondering who it could be, she opened the door, and Connor stepped forward. Pulling her into a big bear hug, he covered her mouth, that was open in surprise, with his own. When she could catch her breath, Libby gasped, "I wasn't expecting to see you this evening."

Still holding her close to his chest, he said, "The symposium got finished early, so I was able to leave Queen Charlotte City early, too, and drove home as quickly as I could to see you."

"Well, that's a pleasant surprise! I was just thinking about going to bed."

"An excellent idea," he responded eagerly, seeking out her mouth again, first caressing her lips with his, then running his tongue gently over them and inside them, and finally probing to find her own responding tongue. Libby's knees weakened, giving in to the throbbing connection the kissing brought to her loins. Connor scooped her into his arms, repeating the gallantry he'd done many times since Christmas Eve, and carried her to her bedroom.

"You're looking much better," he said. They lay together, open and exposed to one another. Before she could respond, he turned her on her tummy and began seductively massaging her back. He added with a grin, "You feel great, too." Rolling her back to face him, he bent to suckle her hardened nipple. "Bet you taste yummy, too."

She had been going to tell him about her earache, but his tongue flicking her nipple and his hand sliding down to her trigger spot put it completely out of her mind. Besides, Stephen had taken care of it with an antibiotic.

Leaving her taut nipples, his tongue slowly made its way down to meet the hand that was massaging her essence. Writhing, her breath caught and quickened, and she began pulling him frantically toward her. He stopped suddenly. "I haven't protection with me. I don't usually carry condoms to symposiums," he joked feebly.

"And I'm glad you don't have that habit!" She smiled. "I usually leave that end up to you, so to speak. I'm afraid I don't have anything either. I did get on the pill, though, and had a thorough physical before I came in August, so I'm pretty sure I am very healthy."

"Me, too," Connor said, relieved. "In our business, we have to get tested every time we prick ourselves in a procedure. I've never had a problem. Shall we proceed, my Prairie Rose?"

And proceed they did.

# CHAPTER
# THIRTEEN

*L*ibby bustled into the George M. Dawson Secondary
School, a typical February early-morning fog envel-
oping her. Shedding her coat as she went, Libby headed toward
the teachers' lounge, more rushed than usual that day. She'd felt
a little queasy that morning, and she hoped she wasn't getting a
stomach bug on top of the cold and earache she'd finally shaken.

Hanging up her coat, she glanced over her shoulder to greet
Aimée. She was startled to see her friend pacing around the room,
clasping her hands to her breast, and saying to herself, "*Mon Dieu,
mon Dieu!* Let them be safe."

"Aimée, what's the matter?" Libby grabbed her by the shoulders and willed Aimée to look at her. Fortunately, the other teachers
had gone to their classrooms, and Libby and Aimée had the first
period as a prep that day.

"Oh, Libby! It's, it's…Maggie, Gus, and Stephen, and Connor,
too. I'm so worried."

Giving her a little shake, Libby implored Aimée to explain.
Taking a big breath, she began, "Maggie went into labor last evening, and Stephen is looking after her, but she didn't make the
progress she should have. He finally concluded that she was in a
transverse arrest."

At Libby's blank look, she explained, "The baby was stuck
in the second stage of labor. Maggie was getting exhausted, and

Stephen felt a C-section was the best option, but the surgeon at the Queen Charlotte Hospital is away at a conference, so they had to get her to Prince Rupert. They can't fly across the Strait in the Goose at night, especially in this fog, but they took off anyway while it was still dark, hoping to time it so they'd be able to land at sunrise." Aimée stopped, out of breath.

"Who took off? How does Connor figure into this?"

"Gus wanted Connor to fly the plane because he's the most skilled pilot and the only one who'd dare to fly in these conditions, and Stephen wanted him along to assist medically if needed. They should have reached there by now, but I haven't heard anything. Libby, I'm so worried."

Libby sucked in her breath to calm herself, then tried to assure her friend. "I'm sure everything will be all right. I understand Connor is a very skilled pilot, if somewhat daring. They'll be fine."

"You don't understand, Libby!" Aimée cried. "It's too dangerous. This is logging country. There are log booms in the bay waters near where they should land, and in this pea soup, they can't see what's below them. If Connor misjudges on their descent, they could hit a log and . . ." She couldn't continue.

Libby paled and sat down abruptly. With her elbows on the table, she held her head in her hands. It was Aimée's turn to ask what was wrong. Images of Ben's accident came flooding back to her. While in college, they had worked summers at resorts in Clear Lake, a hot vacation spot in northern Manitoba and a good source of employment for high school and college students. It was their last summer before their graduation year when a freak boating accident took Ben's life and, along with it, the dreams of her life with her soul mate.

She had at last found some happiness. She was letting herself go and maybe even falling in love. She couldn't lose another love, especially to water. Pulling herself together, she told Aimée the whole story and why it had sometimes clouded her happiness. "I can't lose Connor now, Aimée. I've just found him."

"Oh, Libby. How horrible. Why haven't you shared this with us? You absolutely must tell Connor. It will explain so much to him. We've all felt you were running from something. And now I know it's pain you're running from. He's a compassionate man, Libby. He will understand. He's had losses himself. You know about his parents. He won't expect you to forget Ben, but he will want to make you happy in the present."

Libby smiled weakly. "He *is* a caring man, and to think when we first met I thought him so arrogant and full of himself. You're right. I must tell him. That will clear a path for us. Shoot, look at the time. We have to get to class. Please let me know as soon as you hear anything!"

Libby could barely focus on the book reports her sophomore students were giving. When the bell rang for the change of classes, she was relieved to see Aimée smiling at her door.

"They're fine. Everyone is fine. Stephen couldn't call right away because he was assisting with the surgery, and Gus was a mess, so Connor kept him company. Light was barely breaking when they reached Prince Rupert, but Connor brought them in safely. He's flown that route hundreds of times."

She sighed in relief before continuing. "Gus and Maggie have a beautiful little girl—just what Maggie wanted! They're calling her Sadie, and she was a whopping nine pounds. She'll be able to throw her weight around with those big brothers!" Aimée laughed. "Connor and Stephen are flying back this afternoon, bringing a few passengers. They should land about the time we're leaving the school. Why don't we go to meet them?"

"Oh yes, let's!" agreed Libby. Now that she had let go of her past and had decided to tell Connor about it, she could hardly wait to begin looking forward…with him. "We'll take my car. I imagine they left theirs at the airport." Students for the next class were streaming in, so they could no longer chat, but Libby was relieved to be able to greet this class with a smile.

Later, Libby pulled the car into the parking lot, and noting the passengers walking across the landing, commented, "Looks like we got here just in time." Aimée spotted Stephen immediately, jumped out of the car, and ran to him. Libby started to do the same when she spotted Connor's dark, curly head, then stopped dead in her tracks.

That dark, curly head was bent toward a beautiful upturned face. His arm hugging the woman to him, Connor gazed adoringly into her eyes and squeezed her tighter. Libby had thought those gazes were hers alone. Then this picture became suddenly familiar. She had seen a photo at Connor's of a much younger couple in a similar pose. She thought the young boy had been Connor, but she'd been afraid to ask him about the photo and the girl in it. This beautiful woman with the flowing black hair, wearing a long multi-colored broomstick skirt covering knee-high leather boots that matched her soft suede blazer, must have been her. And she must be Willow.

Taken by surprise and not knowing what to do, once again Libby ran away, getting into her car and driving to her cottage. Through tears, she vowed, *I can't do this again. I can't lose another. I may not have lost Connor to the Hecate Strait, but I may lose him to someone who appears to be a very beautiful Haida princess.*

Back at her cottage, she paced the floor, sat down in the rocking chair, got up and paced again, put on the kettle, took it off, went onto the porch, and came back in. What was the matter with her? She was full of jitters, and couldn't settle down. She hadn't felt well that morning, and now she had all of this to think about.

*What will he do now that she's back? Will he ignore me? How will I handle that? What do I do now? Why did I let myself let go? Why did I let myself fall in love? Love—yes, that's what it is.* Shocking herself at the realization, she dissolved in tears. Then, pulling herself together, she resolved, *I can't let him see how head over heels I am about him. I have some pride, and he can't treat me like this, keeping this other person secret from me.*

She'd just bolstered her courage when there was a knock at the door. *It's probably Aimée wondering what happened to me,* she thought, reaching for the handle. But it was Connor on the doorstep, frowning and not looking any too pleased. "What happened to you?" he demanded, but not letting her answer, he continued. "Aimée said you'd come to meet us at the plane, but when we looked around for you, you'd disappeared."

She opened her mouth to say something, but he went right on. "Look, Aimée told me about Ben. I understand a lot now, and I am truly sorry for what you must have gone through. But I thought we had grown close. I don't know why you didn't trust me enough to tell me."

He had come to her, and she had been ready to talk about Ben and ask about Willow. Now this affront about trust threw her over the edge. "Trust! And you have no secrets that you hesitate to share?"

"Me? I have no secrets. My life's pretty much an open book." Still no mention of Willow.

"I saw you get off the plane and walk across the landing, and I . . ." She hesitated. If he wouldn't bring Willow up, she couldn't either. She changed direction. "I couldn't help but think of Ben. I had been so worried that you'd be lost to the water, too, and I couldn't take it. Ben was my whole life, and we were to be together forever."

"I see," Connor interrupted, shrinking a little. "So, it will always be Ben." He drew himself up again and walked to the door. Pulling it open, he turned and said sadly but firmly, "I'm sorry, Libby, but I can't compete with a ghost." And he was gone.

Stunned, she couldn't run after him. She had only meant to deflect the conversation from her appearing to be a jealous, little woman by asking about Willow. She had been prepared to tell him how the danger he had been in had really affected her, and that she couldn't bear the thought of losing him, but it appeared she'd lost him anyway. Forever.

While Libby agonized over the thought of losing Connor, he berated himself as he stalked to his car in agitation. *Hothead. What is it about that woman that makes me go off half-cocked? She makes me crazy.* He smiled at that, remembering her saying the same thing about him when he made love to her. *And it was love I was making. Not just great sex.* There, he'd said it. He was in love with her. But could she ever truly love him? Would Ben always be hovering in the background? It seemed so.

# CHAPTER FOURTEEN

*W*ith parent-teacher conferences, staff meetings, and supervision of the yearbook committee, the week passed without Libby having the opportunity to talk with Aimée about what had happened with Connor. She knew Aimée and the gang probably expected she would be at the Base Valentine's Day Dance on Saturday with Connor. *Oh well, they'll figure it out.*

As she walked home after school on Friday, a car slowed as it neared her, and a voice called out, "Hey, sweet cheeks, how's it going?"

Turning toward the car, she shook her head and smiled indulgently. "Oh, hi, Matt. How's it going yourself?" It was the young—and a little immature—lieutenant who had danced with her at Oktoberfest. Since then, of course, she and Connor had become an item, and while Matt had respected that and never crossed any lines, he did take every opportunity to talk to her and innocently flirt with her. There simply weren't enough women for the young servicemen stuck on these semi-isolated islands for a tour of two years, so they longed for female companionship.

"Hop in; I'll give you a ride home." Libby hesitated for a moment, but finally thought, *Why not?* "I suppose you're going to the big dance with your Valentine tomorrow night," Matt stated matter-of-factly.

Why hadn't she foreseen the direction this conversation might take? "Well, actually, no, I'm not going at all. Just want a quiet evening at home," she responded, hoping that would satisfy him without further explanation.

"Oh, I get it! A more private, hot celebration of the holiday with your sweetheart!" He winked.

"Uh, no. Actually, I'll be spending it alone," she paused, but then thought she might as well let the truth be known. "I no longer have a sweetheart."

Incredulous, Matt asked, "What? I don't believe it! What happened?"

Libby wasn't about to confide her story with Matt, so she just said, "I guess some things are just meant to be—or not meant to be, in this case."

Not quite believing his good fortune, Matt blurted out, "Well, he must be a fool, and a hot babe like you can't sit home alone on Valentine's Day." A little more gallantly, he continued, "Please, Miss Campbell, let me have the honor of escorting you to the Valentine's Ball tomorrow evening."

"Oh, no, Matt. I really don't feel like it. I'd just be a wet blanket on your evening,"

"Hey, a wet blanket is better than no date at all on Valentine's Day!" he reasoned.

He finally wore her down, and she accepted his invitation. Connor probably wouldn't be there anyway, and if he were, he would see that she wasn't just sitting home pining for her loss.

The next day, she wondered if she'd made a mistake. She'd spent the morning in the bathroom "tossing her cookies" as her students would say. She had almost called Matt to say she wouldn't be able to go, but then the nauseous feelings passed. She got dressed, choosing something attractive and appropriate for the dance, but not suggestive. She didn't want to give that young lieutenant any wrong ideas.

She and Matt entered the Mess Hall, which was an effusion of red, pink, and white hearts, streamers, and balloons. All eyes swiveled to note and recognize the proud young officer escorting the beautiful strawberry-blond in a teal cashmere sheath that flattered her body without clinging. At the last moment, Libby had added the copper bracelet that Connor had given her.

She was relieved that none of her friends were there. Maggie and Gus, of course, were getting settled in at home with baby Sadie. She hadn't had a chance to talk to Aimée, so perhaps Stephen was on call. And who knew what Connor was doing and with whom.

Matt and Libby joined a table of his friends. She was just getting acquainted when Aimée and Stephen walked in. When Aimée's eyes met Libby's across the hall, they grew very large, and she tilted her head, asking a silent question. Libby shrugged and mouthed, "Later."

Frowning, Aimée sat down at a table Stephen had picked. Stephen had said Connor would be joining them, and Aimée had assumed it would be with Libby. She immediately began nattering at her husband, who pleaded complete innocence as to what was transpiring between their friends.

They didn't have long to await Connor's arrival. He soon came in with the elegant Willow on his arm. She wore a stunning scarlet dress that draped gracefully to mid-calf. An intricately designed silver pendant rested just above her bosom, where her dress's V-shaped neckline exposed her neck and cleavage. Matching large teardrop earrings dangled from her ears. She and Connor were warmly greeted by the Parkers, but Aimée immediately attacked Connor as to what had happened between him and Libby.

"You're not in a need-to-know situation, Aimée," Connor replied rather curtly, which was out of character for him. Willow looked at Aimée, raised an eyebrow, and shrugged her shoulders, implying, "What can I say?"

Matt and Libby had just taken to the dance floor when she spotted Connor and Willow joining the Parkers. She turned pale and tripped over her own feet. "Whoa, babe!" Matt exclaimed, then following her gaze, asked, "Hey, who's the gorgeous babe with Ferguson? At least you got ditched for a knockout!"

"That was a little insensitive, Matthew, and her name is Willow Shaw. I have no idea who she is or anything about her."

"Oh, sorry about that, sweet cheeks," he said, and he pulled her a little closer.

Finally noticing Libby and that last little gesture of Matt's, Connor glowered, a thundercloud clearly floating over his head. He grabbed Willow's hand and they began to dance, immediately in a rhythm with one another as if they'd been dancing together all of their lives. Connor kept taking furtive glances at Libby, and when the strobe light picked up the reflection of her copper bracelet, he wasn't sure whether to be angry or heartened. Mainly, he was overwhelmed with sadness.

Sensing his mood, Willow broke into his reverie. "She's lovely, Connor, and you're obviously smitten. Don't let a little tiff spoil things. I'd love to meet her. Why don't you use the opportunity of introducing me to break the ice?"

"It's more than a little tiff, Willow. It would be pretty hard to crack that ice. It goes pretty deep, and you wouldn't understand. Let's just dance." And dance they did—polkas, two-steps, old-time waltzes, and the jive.

Her heart sank even further watching them. Libby recognized a longtime relationship of a couple totally in tune with one another. She excused herself, telling Matt she was going to use the powder room. "Good idea," Matt said. "Think I'll use it myself.

Well—maybe not the powder room." At least in his youthfulness, Matt could always make her smile.

Seeing Libby head for the ladies' washroom, Aimée took the opportunity to follow her. "*Mon Dieu, ma cherie!* What is going on? Why haven't you called me?" Aimée exclaimed, oblivious of two other women in the room washing their hands.

"Uh, maybe it's not the time or place, my friend." Coming closer to her friend, Libby whispered almost the same words she had used with Matt. "Some things are not meant to be. Nothing lasts forever. I learned that a long time ago."

"You can't mean that, Libby. You two are meant for each other!"

"You are a romantic, Aimée. We'll talk one of these days." She gave her friend a hug and went back to her table.

Meanwhile, Connor had also followed Matt into the men's room, and he stood at the urinal next to Matt. "What are you doing with Libby?" Connor demanded.

"Uh, dancing, maybe?" Matt replied glibly.

"Don't smart-mouth me, you little punk. You'd better treat her right."

"Hey, man! Is this becoming a pissing match?" Matt inquired, never quite realizing when his sense of humor and play on words might be inappropriate. He continued while washing his hands, saying, "I will treat her right, Dr. Ferguson—not that you did. Quite frankly, you have no right to interfere with anything about Libby." With that, he left the room, leaving Connor fuming and a little stunned as to what he meant about his not treating Libby right.

When he reached the table, Libby asked Matt if they could leave. "Sure, doll," he said, and they walked out to his car.

When they reached Libby's cottage, Matt walked her to the door. He put his arms around her and pulled her closer, leaning in for a kiss and hoping more might follow. Libby put her hand to his lips and said gently, "No, Matt, I'm sorry, but this is not the beginning of anything. If you want a friend to have coffee, go to dances, or simply talk, I can do that. But it can never be anything more than that." She kissed him on the cheek, then unlocked the door and went inside. Before closing the door behind her, she said, "Thank you for getting me out of the house this evening, Matt. Good night."

Dance was bad for
Both Coupler.

# CHAPTER
# FIFTEEN

*D*riving back from Queen Charlotte City, Libby tried to focus on planning the next stage of her life. She had been having a lot of nausea, her breasts had been tender, and then she missed her period for the first time. Her suspicions were aroused. When she'd missed the second one, she made an appointment with a doctor at the clinic in Queen Charlotte City, not wanting to go to the local military clinic. And she couldn't possibly go out to the Haida clinic to see Connor. Today, her suspicions were confirmed. She was pregnant.

After they'd become intimate on Christmas Eve, Libby realized she should have more protection than just relying on Connor's being prepared. In her hasty departure from the prairies, she'd tossed everything from her medicine cabinet into her toiletries bag, including the last month's supply of birth control pills she'd been taking with Ben. Somehow, using them hadn't seemed right, but she'd begun taking them until she could make an appointment with the new military doctor who had arrived to work with Stephen.

So, here she was, driving along the lone—and now lonely— road back to Masset. She couldn't imagine how this pregnancy could have happened, but it had, and she knew Connor was the father. There had been no one else. Since he had rather emphatically walked out of her life, she couldn't tell him. She hoped the clinic staff in Queen Charlotte would professionally honor confidentiality, but it was a small island, and the medical community was a pretty close-knit group, too.

Libby figured she wouldn't be showing much by the time school concluded, and she could camouflage the slight baby bump with oversized tops. She would resign her teaching position even though the principal had been pleased with her work and had personally encouraged her to stay. If she stayed, what kind of a role model would she be to the students?

No, she'd have to go home to Manitoba and have the baby. Her parents would be disappointed, but she knew they'd be supportive. She had a reputation as a good teacher, so she was fairly certain her former school would overlook her being an unwed mother, and she'd be able to get her old teaching job back to support herself and the baby. She should have known she couldn't run away forever.

Wistfully, she patted her not-yet-showing tummy and said aloud, "It's just you and me, babe." With that thought, she had a new resolve to do her best by this new life. After all, he or she had been conceived in love.

Having taken a sick day to go to the clinic, she knew Aimée would be wondering where she was and what was going on. Libby had still avoided talking much about Connor with her friend, but now she probably needed Aimée more than ever. But she hoped Aimée would keep Libby's confidences. She stopped in at Books 'n' Brew, knowing she'd probably have to change her drink of choice to avoid too much caffeine.

Taking a deep breath, Libby swung open the door. Shirlee immediately greeted her cheerily. "Well, there's my favorite English teacher. The usual?" she asked, reaching for the coffee to tamp into espresso for Libby's almond roca mocha.

"Um, I think it's time for a change, Shirlee. There's a little nip in the air. How about a hot chocolate?"

Libby had never changed her order before, but Shirlee obliged, saying, "Well, all right then. Hot chocolate it is. And here comes your sidekick now." The bell over the door tinkled, and Aimée, having seen Libby's car, rushed in.

"So, playing hooky are we?" Aimée got right to the point.

"Oh, I had an appointment I had to take care of on a weekday, and I've hardly missed any time, so I decided to do it today," she stated with enough off-handedness she hoped would stymie any further questions.

Preoccupied with thoughts of her own, Aimée never noticed the brush-off and rushed on. "We have to talk. It's been so long, and I have so much to tell you."

"It has been a long time," Libby agreed. "If you're free this evening, come by the cottage and we'll have a gabfest. Right now, I have to go down to Raven's Nook and speak to Willow Shaw. My students are nearing the end of their cultural heritage projects, and since you have all spoken of her so highly as the local expert on Haida art, I thought I'd ask her to be a guest speaker." She had been postponing this idea, but she had swallowed her pride because she always made her teaching decisions with the best interests of her students in mind, regardless of the cost to herself.

"Fantastic idea," Shirlee agreed. "I was hoping you would enlist her help. You've done so much to affirm the kids' heritage, and she will be a perfect complement to your project."

"She will be great, and she's such a cool person. You will just love her!" Aimée added.

"Yeah right," Libby replied, less than enthusiastically, as she opened the door to leave. The two women she left behind looked at one another, wondering what had just happened.

"Libby's been a bit off lately," Aimée complained, "and I feel like she's been avoiding me. The secretary at school said she'd taken a sick day today. She seems to have had a lot of queasiness lately."

Feeling a little queasy herself, she looked at Shirlee, "You don't suppose . . ."

"I suppose anything is possible, but I've always given Libby more credit than that. God, let it not be that little twerp Matthew!"

"Oh no! Connor would be devastated!"

"Well, let's not jump to conclusions." Shirlee's elder perspective prevailed. "Whatever the situation, we must be there for her."

Meanwhile, Libby was marching determinedly down the street, trying to reinforce her nerve to meet this Willow person. She did not want to betray her inner emotions, but she really didn't want to ask a favor and be beholden to someone who had clearly usurped her happiness.

Taking a deep breath, she opened the door to Raven's Nook. Willow's dark head was bent over some artifact on the counter. Libby spoke tentatively. "Ms. Shaw?"

Willow looked up from her work, and when she spotted Libby, her face broke into a radiant smile and she quickly came out from behind the counter. "You must be Libby! I've so wanted to meet you. Connor has told me so much about you."

Stunned, Libby stammered, "Connor has talked about me to... to you?"

"Oh yes. I was so disappointed things didn't seem to be working out. My brother is crazy about you, and now, sadly, heartbroken."

"Your brother!" Libby grabbed the counter to catch her balance. She was incredulous. "But how can that be? You don't even have the same last name."

"Well, technically he's my half brother. My father died before I was born, and when I was a year old, my mother met and fell in love with Sean Ferguson. They had Connor a year after they were married. So, yes, Connor is my baby brother." She laughed, then frowned and asked, "You didn't know?"

"No. No one ever explained it to me. Everyone kept saying how Connor adored you, but never explained your relationship, not even Connor. I saw that picture of you as teenagers on the dresser in his guest room. I suppose it was your nightie that I wore the night I sprained my ankle. Then when you returned in February on the Goose and I saw you clinging to one another, I thought . . ."

"Oh my God, Libby! You didn't think we were lovers!" It was Willow's turn to be incredulous. Libby nodded her head sheepishly. Willow exclaimed, exasperated, "That bonehead of a brother! How could he not realize you wouldn't or couldn't know? Everyone else probably assumed he'd explained our background, so didn't think to enlighten you."

The shock of this revelation and a lack of food that day plus the pregnancy all combined to make Libby feel a little dizzy and faint. She was probably slightly hypoglycemic. "Excuse me, but I think I'm going to have to sit down. I think I forgot to eat today."

"Of course," Willow responded quickly, bringing her some juice and a shortbread biscuit. "I'm sorry, I don't keep much at the store, but you look a little done in."

"Well, I haven't felt well lately. I seem to keep battling a touch of stomach flu. This will hit the spot," said Libby, hoping to deflect any curiosity. But Willow's eyes narrowed slightly as she scrutinized her.

"Anyway," Libby went on, "I understand that you are the resident authority on Haida art, and since I'm doing a writing project with my students on their own cultural heritage, or the Haida culture here where they are currently living, I was wondering if I could impose upon you to give a presentation to my classes. Your store is full of beautiful art and crafts!"

"Thank you, and I'd love to. Both Connor and Shirlee have told me about the work you're doing with the students. I'm so impressed. Everything I know about Haida art and culture I learned from both of my grandmothers, but especially my Grandma Shaw. I would be delighted to share it with your students. I named my store in honor of my mother's clan, the Raven. My father's clan was the Eagle."

"I understand you spend a lot of the winter months in Vancouver and Victoria. Why is that?"

"I love to visit the museums and galleries in Vancouver and Victoria. I especially enjoy the displays of Charles Edenshaw's work. He was a great carver during his time. In fact, his name is often linked to the golden age of Haida art. He followed his mother's moiety, the Eagle, in the Haida tradition. I think Shirlee said you had the students read *Raven's Cry*, which explains the clans and lineage along the maternal side."

After a moment's thought, she added, "I've often speculated if my father's last name, Shaw, perhaps had a connection to the Edenshaw family at some point. I suppose I even hoped it did. Guess I'll never know. I never thought to ask my Grandma Shaw, and she never brought up the subject."

Libby smiled for the first time. "I can tell you have a lot to share with my classes. I am so grateful."

"And I am grateful to have finally met you. I'm glad we've had the chance to clear up this misunderstanding. I'm annoyed with Connor. Just like a man to assume things. But I am hopeful now that you and my idiot brother will get back together. I am going to do what I can to help that along."

"Thank you, Willow, but it's too late for that. It has become very complicated, and I plan to return to my home province when the school term is over."

"I hope that isn't so, Libby," Willow implored, vowing to herself to speak to Connor at the first opportunity. In fact, better sooner than later, and after Libby left the store, she dialed Connor's number to invite him for supper.

# CHAPTER
# SIXTEEN

*I*t was a beautiful evening, so Libby and Aimée opted to sit on Libby's back porch to watch the sunset over the water. They sat in sisterly intimacy, sipping hot cocoa, ready for some girl talk, which they had both missed. Libby was surprised when Aimée refused a glass of wine, but she was happy that she didn't have to launch immediately into why hot chocolate was her own beverage of choice that evening.

"I have quite a bit of news to tell you, Libby." Aimée grinned impishly, like the proverbial cat who'd swallowed the canary.

"OK. Spill it."

"Well, you know that when Stephen finishes his tour here in Masset this summer, his commitment to the Forces is also completed. He's been trying to decide whether to re-enlist or join a practice back on the mainland." Aimée took a sip of her hot chocolate.

"He has so enjoyed working with Connor out at the clinic at the Haida Village on his off days, and coincidentally, Connor has been thinking about taking on a partner and expanding the clinic. He's certain he can get Northern Health's OK, especially now that the military docs won't be here. He's been quite busy and feels he can serve the Haida as well as the fishermen and other locals better with help. So-o-o, he's invited Stephen to join him." She smiled. "They get along so well, and after Stephen thought about it and we discussed what it meant for us, he has accepted his offer. So we're staying on the islands."

"Oh, Aimée! How do you feel about being so far from your family? You talk so often about them, and it seems you're all very close."

The impish smile returned. "Well," said Aimée, "we've made so many friends here, and the community's become like a family to us, so we thought it was a good place to raise our son or daughter." She stopped and looked meaningfully at Libby.

"Aimée, are you pregnant?" Aimée nodded her head in the affirmative, and both young women squealed, jumped out of their chairs, and hugged one another. "I'm so happy for you. You will be a terrific mother!"

"And with Auntie Libby here to help me, we'll have such fun!"

Libby's face fell, the happiness gone for the moment. "Oh, Aimée, I have something to tell you, too. I won't be staying, and I'll be handing in my resignation tomorrow."

"But why ever not? The students love you. They're learning so much, and I'll miss you! You're like a sister to me."

Taking a breath, Libby continued. "I'm afraid, Aimée, I'm pregnant, too. I can't stay here in this condition and work with young people. What kind of a role model would I be?"

Her suspicions confirmed, Aimée said, "It crossed my mind that you might be, Libby. Does Matt know?"

"Does Matt know? Why would I tell him?"

"Well, you've been spending a lot of time with him. I just thought maybe . . ."

"Well, you thought wrong! I have been spending time with Matt just as a friend. Everyone needs a little companionship, and I told him right from the beginning it would never be anything more."

"Then who? Connor?"

"Yes, I'm afraid so," Libby confirmed a little wistfully.

"Afraid! Why, Libby, it's perfect! You and Connor belong together. You'll get married, and we'll raise our babies together!" Aimée bounced with her usual enthusiasm and excitement.

"I wish it were that simple. Oh, Aimée, I've made such a mess of everything." She told her about her afternoon conversation with Willow and how she had just found out that Connor was Willow's brother.

"How could you not have known, Libby? Everyone knows that. Surely Connor told you when you asked."

"He told me about his parents, but he never explained about having a sister. So, just the way things evolved, I never asked. It seemed that she was like some exotic secret that everyone was in on except me."

"Now that you know, it can all be fixed, and we'll all live happily ever after!" Aimée enthused.

"No, Aimée, you don't get it. By my avoiding asking about Willow, I inadvertently led him to believe the memory of Ben was an impediment to our relationship. How could he believe that I truly love him now? He will think it's just because of the baby, and he'll feel trapped. I know he would want to do the honorable thing, but I can't put him in that position. So," she sighed, "it's best I go back home and start planning for a future as a single mum. And Aimée, you must promise me that you will tell no one. Especially Connor."

Wondering how this could have happened with Connor's medical background and Libby's level-headedness, Aimée let it be—for now, anyway.

\* \* \*

Out in their childhood home on Tow Hill Road, Willow and Connor sat sipping a cup of tea after the light supper Willow had prepared for them. She didn't quite know how to approach the subject, but finally she plunged right in. "Why didn't you tell Libby I was your sister, Connor?"

"What? Of course she knows you're my sister. What are you talking about?"

"Well, little brother, she apparently doesn't or didn't until this afternoon. You never explained it, and I assume everyone else thought you had, so it never came up in conversation. And because of this," Willow hesitated and drew a breath before she continued, "she had put two and two together and concluded that you and I were a couple."

"Oh come on Willow! Pardon me, dear sister, but ew! How could she possibly think that?"

"It doesn't matter how or why, she just did. I think that has played a large role in your being with your 'ew' sister tonight instead of her. Better straighten it out before it's too late."

"But there's the other complication of her former fiancé. I can't compete with that."

"Well, Connor, I see how unhappy you are without her. If she's worth it, you will find a way around all the complications, especially since it seems she's planning to return to Manitoba after school is out for summer."

"Guess that's why you're the older and wiser big sister. It's a lot to process. I'll have to work through all of this."

"I know you're a little shell-shocked right now, but I was wondering if there's any possibility she could be pregnant."

"No, of course not. You know me better than that, Willow."

"Well, it's just that she felt faint in the store today, and she said she'd been battling the stomach flu lately. Then, when I stopped at Books 'n' Brew, Shirlee mentioned Libby had taken a sick day today, yet was well enough to stop in for hot chocolate, which, apparently, is not her usual choice of beverage."

Connor frowned in concentration, then jumped from his chair, saying, "That little shit!" and slammed out of Willow's door. *Oops,* thought Willow, *my good intentions may have stirred up a hornet's nest.*

Connor headed for the Officers' Mess, where he knew Matt would probably be having an after-dinner drink with his buddies. Sure enough, Matt's car was in the parking lot. Storming into the Mess, Connor tried to get his temper under control, but it was barely down to a simmer when he approached Matt and demanded, "Lieutenant, I need a word with you—outside."

Matt frowned, but he followed Connor outside, where Connor turned on him and said, "I thought I told you to treat Libby right."

"Of course I'm treating her right. What's up, man?"

"What's up? Apparently, a certain part of your anatomy. You'd better come clean and do the right thing if you're going to be a daddy," Connor declared, storming away to his car.

Matt couldn't remember the last time he could have even been with a woman since being stuck in this semi-isolation. He called out to Connor, "A daddy? What are you talking about? I can't be a daddy to anyone."

*He's right about that,* Connor thought. *He's too irresponsible to be a real daddy. Any immature idiot can father a child, but it doesn't make him a daddy.* Still fuming, he roared out of the lot and headed toward the Parkers' PMQ. Aimée would know something, and Stephen, who was always level-headed and often the counterpoint to Connor's sometimes-short fuse, would help him understand and work through things.

When he arrived, he knocked on their door and walked right in just like he often did, being accepted like family in the Parkers' home. When he saw them on the couch, watching television, he immediately demanded, "Aimée, why didn't you tell Libby that

Willow is my sister? Did you know she's probably pregnant? And that little so-and-so Matt denies he could be the daddy!"

"Hey, cool it Connor," Stephen said, rising to defend his wife against this tirade. "What are you talking about?"

Aimée gulped, wondering how she was going to diffuse their friend's understandable anger and frustration while keeping Libby's confidence. "Well, Connor, *mon cher ami*, did it occur to you that maybe you should have told her about your sister?" She paused, and taking a breath, continued. "We naturally assumed you had."

Connor sank onto the nearby loveseat that he and Libby had cozily shared at the Parkers' Christmas Eve party. He sighed, and recognizing what a jerk he was being, apologized. "I'm sorry, Aimée. I'm frustrated with such needlessly lost time with Libby over a silly misunderstanding, and I shouldn't take it out on you. But could she be pregnant? I can't bear to think of her with Matt."

Aimée knew she could reassure him somewhat without betraying Libby, so she proceeded cautiously. "Well, I do know, Connor, that if she were pregnant, Matt would not be the father. Libby did tell me that they were nothing but friends, and she had told Matt right from the beginning that they could be nothing more."

At this juncture, Stephen stepped in. "If she is pregnant, Connor, couldn't you be the father?"

"Oh, come on. Libby was on the pill, and I almost always used protection."

"What do you mean 'almost always'?" Stephen continued questioning while Aimée prayed that Stephen would help Connor figure out the truth without her having to say anything. She knew, for both his and Libby's sake, she would break her promise if the need arose.

"Well, I guess there was the one time when it was kind of spontaneous after I came back from the symposium in Queen Charlotte City. She was recuperating from that cold, and I didn't have protection, but since she was on the pill and we're both healthy, we didn't worry about it."

"You idiot," Stephen exclaimed. "She might have been feeling better, but I'd put her on an antibiotic for her ear infection. You bloody well know that antibiotics can counteract the effectiveness of birth control pills!"

Connor blanched. "Damn! I didn't know she had an ear infection and was on an antibiotic. Um…shall we say…there wasn't much talking that evening. Libby probably wouldn't realize the implications of the drug interactions, so didn't say anything." Realization hit him like a brick. "If she's pregnant, that baby is mine." Both he and Stephen looked at Aimée expectantly.

"Connor," she said, acknowledging without acknowledging, "Libby is leaving the day after school is finished. You have to fix things, and you don't have much time."

After Connor left, Stephen was a bit chagrined. "I didn't mean to break patient-doctor confidentiality. I figured Connor would have known about the ear infection from Libby."

"It was an innocent assumption, my dear husband. And, in this case, a very happy accident. And you are my hero!" She kissed him sweetly, and continued coyly, "And I think you deserve a reward."

# CHAPTER
# SEVENTEEN

*M*att drove Libby to the Trans Provincial Airport after they had dropped her car off at the wharf to be loaded on a barge later that day and taken to the mainland. From there, it would be shipped home with some of her other belongings. She could have met the car in Prince Rupert and driven across the Canadian West, but she just wanted to escape and get home as quickly as possible. So she was taking the Goose to Prince Rupert on the mainland and flying a major airline home from there.

She could have asked Aimée to bring her to the airport, but they had said good-bye the previous evening, and another good-bye at the airport would have been just too difficult. Besides, Aimée had continued to implore her to stay and work things out with Connor. It was better to have someone neutral and lighthearted like Matt to see her off. She hadn't told him of her pregnancy, and he had never mentioned his encounter with Connor to her. Some things were best left alone.

They walked into the small terminal, Matt carrying her bags. "Well, hey there," a friendly voice greeted her. She looked up and, of course, there was Gus. She'd forgotten there was one friend she couldn't avoid with her departure.

"Oh, hi, Gus. How are wee Sadie and her mummy doing?" she asked, attempting small talk.

"They're doing just great. Poppa, not so much! I've been trying to help with the night feedings, so I'm a little bleary-eyed by morning."

"That's really great of you, Gus. I'm sure Maggie appreciates it. Please give my love to her and squeeze all the little ones for me, if the boys will let you." She managed a weak smile. "You have a wonderful family, Gus, and I'll really miss you all."

"We've all enjoyed having you a part of our lives, too, Libby. And who knows? You may be back someday."

"Yeah, maybe," she replied, knowing it would never happen. She was running away again—away from this place. And this time, she knew it was for forever.

"Well, we'd better get these bags loaded and you boarded. Not too many passengers today. I'll take it from here, Lieutenant," Gus stated, nodding pointedly at Matt.

"Hmmm," Matt said. "I think I just got dismissed."

Libby turned to him. "Yes, Matt. You need to get back to the base, and I don't want any long farewells. Thank you for being a friend, and I wish you all the best. I know just the right girl will come along for you." With that, she kissed him on the cheek and walked toward the doors leading to the landing.

It was a sunny day, and Libby kept her head down against the glare as she walked toward the Goose. When she glanced up, she froze in her footsteps. Leaning so very casually with his arms folded against the bright golden-yellow amphibious plane was the pilot. Dark brown hair curled at the nape of his neck; wraparound sunglasses concealed what she knew to be very bright blue eyes; and the corners of his mouth quirked in a gently amused smile. Her heart had stopped along with her feet. This was a very familiar figure, and unfortunately, one that was very dear to her, for there stood Connor. *Why now? I can't do this*, she thought, starting to move hesitantly closer.

"Hello, Prairie Rose," Connor said, using the old endearment.

Libby remembered how she had fumed when he had called her that the first day she arrived on the Charlottes, but she'd grown to love it along with him. Her voice quavered as she asked, "What are you doing here?"

"I brought you to the islands, Libby. It seemed fitting that I take you from them. I'm your pilot today."

Her heart sank along with her shoulders. There was so much water under the bridge that could never be dammed up. She felt like such a fool, and she couldn't let him know or see all the rubble floating under that bridge. "I can't do this, Connor. You shouldn't be here."

"I can't be anywhere else, Libby. I have been such a fool, and I can't let you leave from my life forever without trying to make amends and convince you to stay." Libby was shaking her head, but Connor went on. "First, I need to apologize for not explaining that Willow is my sister. I can try to make excuses by saying everyone knew and you should have picked up on that. But I've realized that would be blaming the victim, and there wasn't any way you could have known unless someone told you. That someone should have been me. What I can't accept though, Libby, is how you could have thought I would be involved with anyone else. Why didn't you ask me?"

Libby's eyes were filling with tears, and she bit her lip. "I don't know, Connor. I had been so afraid of losing you, and I've had enough loss. I should have believed in you and asked, but time slipped by, and then I felt silly when I found out. By then there were other complications, and it was too late."

"Other complications, like the fact that you're carrying my baby?" Connor smiled down at her.

Libby's eyes grew wide with disbelief when what he had said registered. "You know," she stated flatly. "How did you find out? Did Aimée tell you?"

"Not exactly. I said I was a fool, but with a little help from Willow and Stephen, I figured it out. Aimée didn't tell me, but she didn't deny it, and she emphatically told me to fix things. Why wouldn't you tell me? You know I'd want to care for you."

"That's just it, Connor. I knew you'd want to do the honorable thing, but how could I tie you down when I'd been so stupid and had lost your affection, and maybe even your love?" she asked, eyes downcast.

"Lost my love? How could you ever have thought you'd lost my affection? Libby, I'm standing right here, loving you right now, just as I have ever since you got off this plane last fall with your armor of independence protecting that delicate Prairie Rose inner sweetness."

"But I botched it all when I made you believe I could never forget Ben, and you said you wouldn't or couldn't compete with a ghost." She paused. "You love me?" she asked, incredulous but hopeful.

"Of course I love you," he said, and he drew her into his arms as he had done so many times before. "That was just my male pride talking. I understand about Ben. I don't expect you to forget him. I should have been patient and willing to wait for you to be ready to love me. You are worth waiting for, you know, Libby. But I want you to stop running from your past and from me. I want you to stay."

"Oh, Connor, I love you, too. Maybe that's why I put up my defenses right away. I was afraid of falling in love again, and I recognized that it could happen again—with you. I do want to stay. But the arrangements have all been made. My car and things are being shipped as we speak, and the Jordans will be returning for the summer soon. I have no place to stay."

"Don't worry about your car being shipped. We'll need one in Manitoba, and we can drive it back here on our return with the rest of your things."

"What do you mean, we'll need it in Manitoba?"

"Well, my little Prairie Rose. I'm coming with you. I'm booked on the same flight out of Prince Rupert with you. I have connections, you know." Grinning, he waved to Gus, who was watching the proceedings unabashedly from the waiting room window. "I think the little pumpkin needs a mummy *and* a daddy," he said, patting her tummy, "and I knew you would want to be with your family for a wedding, even if it's just a small one. We will also visit Ben's grave together and ask him for his blessing. I'm asking you to marry me, Libby. Will you?"

How had she found this wonderful man? "Oh, Connor, I love you so much. I can't believe this is happening. Of course I'll marry you. But what about Willow? She's your only family. Don't you want her to be with you on such an important day?"

"Well, yes, I would, and since she was instrumental in getting us together, along with the Parkers, they will all fly out to the prairies once the arrangements have been made. And a place to stay? I do believe, Libby, we will be making a home together with the pumpkin at my place—I mean *our* place—when we return."

Stunned, Libby said, "You've thought of everything."

"You once called me a Boy Scout, always prepared for everything. Well, I may have slipped up once," he smiled, patting her tummy again. "Now, Libby, will you stop running?"

"I'll never stop running, Connor, but now I'll be running to forever—forever with you."

# PART II

# PLAY UNDER REVIEW

# CHAPTER ONE

"*H*e thoots, he thcores!" lisped three-year-old Zach Ferguson sitting on his father, Connor's, shoulders, his tiny hands clutching his daddy's dark, curly hair. Connor laughed, turning to his friend Stephen Parker, whose three-year-old son's chubby legs also straddled his neck.

"I envy you, Steph," said Connor, "growing up on the prairies and getting to play hockey. Best we could do on the islands was street hockey. The climate's too temperate here for outdoor ice."

"You wouldn't have loved freezing your ass off in those twenty-below temperatures. Uh, I mean freezing your *behind* off," Stephen corrected himself, suddenly remembering his young son, Jonathan, on his shoulders.

"Maybe our boys will have a better opportunity than I did," Connor replied as he edged closer to the front of the line, waiting to get the cherished autographs of the National Hockey League players.

"By the looks of this crowd, we're lucky the team made a quick stop on their way out to Old Massett for the main celebration at the Longhouse. It's going to be a great ceremony with the Haida traditional dancing, drumming and all, but with the crowd out there, we might not get this close for autographs," Stephen observed.

"You're right. I think both villages have pretty much shut down for this event," Connor agreed.

A small crowd had gathered on the former military parade square at Masset, British Columbia. The Vancouver Canucks players were signing autographs for starstruck young boys who dreamed of playing hockey—not in the NHL like most Canadian and American boys dreamed, but just on a rink of their own. The people of the Queen Charlotte Islands were avid hockey fans like the rest of Canada, but with the temperate climate of the archipelago and few resources, there was no possibility of making ice for prospective young skaters. A committee had formed to look into rink possibilities, such as synthetic ice. Coming north for some team building at a fishing retreat before preseason training, the Vancouver Canucks had offered their services for a Goodwill Day to promote the game of hockey and the prospects of an ice arena for the islands.

As the line inched forward, Connor noticed a handsome, physically fit, greying man, probably in his late fifties or maybe early sixties, talking with some Old Massett village council officials. Shuffling through papers, they had their heads together in consultation.

Though no longer a kid, Connor was starstruck, and he nudged Stephen. "Look over there! That's Deacon Cross! I didn't expect to see *him* here."

Looking in the direction Connor indicated, Stephen responded, "Hey, you're right. I think I read somewhere that he had taken over marketing for the Canucks, so I guess it does make sense he'd be here. Man, he was really something in his day!"

"You're not kidding. When I was an undergrad at UBC in Vancouver, I got tickets to the Canuck home games whenever I could just to see him play. He carried the all-time record for number of goals for years, but his skating and puck-handling, they were beautiful—there's no other word for it. They used to call him 'Dekin' Deacon.'"

"That's right!" Stephen laughed. "I think he picked up that moniker when he played college hockey for the University of North Dakota Fighting Sioux. He was a Saskatchewan boy. Didn't he get his start at Notre Dame, that private high school in Wilcox, Saskatchewan, before he got a scholarship to UND?"

"Yeah, he did. It was when he was at UND that he got drafted by the Canucks. After we get these autographs, we have to see if we can talk to Cross. That's an autograph I'd like to have!" exclaimed Connor.

While Stephen was nodding in agreement, a smiling, softly rounded woman somewhere around sixty with silvery-blond hair approached and greeted them. "Well, here are my four favorite hockey fans!"

Looking down from his perch on his father's shoulders, young Zach Ferguson held out his chubby hand to her and said, "Hi, Doctor Thirlee!"

"Hi there, sweeties," she replied taking his hand, then reached for Jonathan's hand to give it a squeeze, too.

"Are you playing hooky from the coffee shop today?" asked Stephen.

"Oh, no," she replied. "I got Carla, my new assistant, to open today while I took care of some business. I'm heading back there now."

"You already have a couple of customers," said Connor. "Libby and Aimée are getting their morning java fix and enjoying this time to be on their own without all us guys around. They're probably dissing us right now."

"Oh, right," she laughed. "I'd better get over there then right away so I can give them some real dirt on you two! Enjoy your day with the wee fellows."

She hustled off, waving cheerily, not noticing the handsome man striding purposefully toward the group. To Connor and

Stephen's surprise, their hero, Deacon Cross, was standing before them. "Excuse me, fellows. I'm sorry to interrupt, but can you tell me who that woman is who was just talking to you?" Reaching out his hand, he continued. "Sorry for butting in—I'm Deacon Cross."

Somewhat stunned, Connor shook Deacon's hand, saying, "No need to introduce yourself to us, Mr. Cross. We're longtime fans of yours. In fact, we were going to ask for your autograph when we were finished here."

"I'm flattered and happy to oblige, but who was that woman who just left?"

Stephen filled him in. "Oh, that's Shirlee. She runs Dr. Shirlee's Books 'n' Brew, a coffee shop and used bookstore. Our wives are chillin' there right now."

Deacon, looking somewhat confounded, replied, "Oh, I see. Why 'Dr.'?"

"Uh, she named the shop after an old Dolly Parton movie character, but Shirlee also has a PhD," Stephen supplied.

Connor added, "Her place is a town favorite, and so is she. She's just a great gal. Why do you ask?"

Frowning, Deacon replied, "Oh, she just reminded me of someone. Well, I'll let you guys get on with things, and I'd be happy to talk with you later." With that, he headed quickly back to his assistant.

Connor and Stephen looked at one another and simultaneously wondered aloud, "What was that all about?"

Approaching his assistant, Deacon asked, "Can you hold the fort for a while, Bob? I'm going to grab a cup of coffee." Without waiting for a response, Deacon strode off, heading for downtown.

Bob looked at the trainer and commented, "That's odd. Deacon doesn't drink coffee."

# CHAPTER TWO

Sipping their lattes, Libby Ferguson and Aimée Parker sat chatting in their favorite corner of Dr. Shirlee's Books 'n' Brew. When Shirlee had first come in, she visited with the young women for a few moments, telling them for the hundredth time what little charmers their Zach and Jonathan were. She was now back at her post as head barista while her part-time employee, Carla, sorted through a new carton of books that had arrived that morning, preparing them for shelving.

"I love my two guys, big one and little one, but I have to say, this is nice. We haven't had a gabfest in forever," Libby commented.

"I know," agreed Aimée. "It's cool the guys took the boys to the hockey event. They'll have a great time, too. Stephen and Connor are so busy in their practices, but I know they wish they had more time with the boys."

"Yep, and boys need their dads. Hockey is a great bonding activity. It's just too bad they can only enjoy it on television. Connor is really hoping they can get ice in Masset so Zach can learn to skate and maybe play hockey—at least for fun."

"Connor and Stephen are hockey nuts," Aimée added. "I can't believe we let them name our sons after NHL players! I have to admit, though, I do like the name Jonathan. It's a good, solid name for when my Jon Jon grows up."

"Yes, can't say I mind Zach either—it suits my little guy. I do get tired of explaining why he's not named after family instead of an alternate captain of the Minnesota Wild."

"Oh, I know. Folks are forever making jokes that with my French background, I could have at least named Jon Jon after some famous French Canadian hockey players like Maurice as in 'Rocket' Richard, or his younger brother, Henri, the 'Pocket Rocket.' Instead we named him after the captain of the Chicago Blackhawks."

Laughing, Libby asked, "Didn't both Zach Parise and Jonathan Toews play college hockey for the University of North Dakota?"

"I think so," agreed Aimée. "You know, when we first came here and met Shirlee, she talked a bit about UND. She said it was a good school. Can't remember what her connection to it was—or if she ever said."

Libby pondered that information for a moment. "Hmmm. I didn't know that, but then again, I haven't lived here all that long."

"That's true," said Aimée with a smile, "but isn't it great the way it all turned out?"

The young women reminisced for a bit about how Libby had come to teach English and fell in love with Connor. The Parkers had already been on the islands, having been posted to the CFS Masset base. When Stephen had retired as medical officer from the Canadian Armed Forces after they'd closed the base, he and Connor had gone into practice together in Masset and Old Massett.

"And here we are, raising our families together," concluded Libby, smiling at her friend. "Do you ever think about going back to teach French at the high school?"

"Maybe when Jon Jon is in kindergarten—unless there's another *bébé* by that time. What about you?"

"I'm doing a bit of subbing and think about it now and then. I am lucky that Connor's sister, Willow, will look after Zach in her store on days I sub. Time will tell," Libby mused as she sipped her latte.

The bell over the coffee shop door jingled as a striking, silver-haired gentleman walked in. After scanning the shop, he approached the counter.

"Oh, wow!" exclaimed Aimée. "You should see the Richard Gere look-alike who just walked in. If only I were twenty years older!"

Laughing, Libby turned to look in the same direction. "Aimée, you're incorrigible!"

"Hey, *ma cherie*, just because I'm on a diet doesn't mean I can't look at the menu!"

"I think you're pretty content with your diet," Libby commented, but she added, "He is handsome though. Distinguished but oh so masculine, too. Oh my God. Shirlee looks like she's seen a ghost—and she's turned as white as one!"

Upon entering the coffee shop, Deacon had approached the counter tentatively. The woman he had seen earlier on the square had her back to him. Clearing his throat, he inquired hesitantly, "Uh, Sheryl? Sheryl Leigh?"

Thinking he'd said, "Shirlee," she turned around slowly, smiling to greet the customer. She froze. Her smile faded immediately as she looked into those hooded, grey bedroom eyes—the ones she saw frequently in her dreams.

Just as Libby had witnessed, Shirlee paled, sucked in her breath, put her hand on her chest, and thought, *You don't have to be dying to see your life pass before your eyes!*

# CHAPTER THREE

Sheryl stood behind the serving counter in the dining hall used by the students from the dorms that bordered three sides of the quad. She had a scholarship to the University of North Dakota in Grand Forks, but it didn't cover any extras, so working in the residence dining hall helped to offset her expenses. She was a senior majoring in English and minoring in music while taking teacher preparation classes. She hoped one day to teach high school English, and her love of singing might help her land a job after graduation if she could direct a high school choir, too.

It was Friday, and that night was the big hockey game against the Minnesota Gophers. *And here he comes now, Mr. Big Man on Campus himself, Deacon Cross,* she thought smugly. Though she didn't really care about impressing a popular athlete, she kind of wished that she didn't smell like the onions she'd peeled, and that she didn't have to wear the hairnet, covering her long honey-blond hair like an old-fashioned snood.

Deacon approached her station with that confident swagger athletes tend to have, carrying his used plate. "I thought I'd have some more of that stew," he stated, smiling and holding out his plate.

Looking at him in disgust, though unable to avoid those grey, sexy, hooded eyes, Sheryl scolded, "Come on, Deacon. You're a big boy; you know better than that."

Stunned, Deacon stammered, "What? What do you mean? And how do you know my name?"

"If you want a second helping, you have to take a clean plate. Health Department rules," she explained impatiently as she grabbed a clean plate and started ladling stew onto it. "You really aren't that naïve, are you? Everyone knows who the BMOC is."

Taking his heaping plate, but still looking confused, he asked cautiously, "BMOC? I don't get what you mean."

"Really? Where have you been hiding? It means 'big man on campus.' Hockey is a big deal here, and you are the star. So, Deacon, you are a big deal, too, and everyone knows your name."

Perplexed, Deacon replied humbly, "Oh, I don't think so. Hockey's a team sport. We all just do our part."

As he walked away, Sheryl replied with a tinge of sarcasm, "Right. Well, get used to the spotlight." Taken aback by his humility, Sheryl questioned her automatic assumptions about him and regretted being so acerbic. What had caused that little nastiness? She also regretted her unattractive work getup. *Now, why do I care about that?*

Watching him walk away to join his fellow teammates at their table, she had to admit that he was one good-looking dude. Longish, thick chestnut hair that fell across his brow, a strong jawline, full, kissable lips, a straight, well-shaped nose, and those bedroom eyes! *Oh stop it,* Sheryl said to herself. *You're starting to sound like Tiffany. I can't believe I ended up with such a puck-bunny for my dorm roommate.*

Opening her dorm room door after her shift was over, Sheryl was greeted by said puck-bunny, sitting on her single bed and taking her hair out of rollers. Seeing Sheryl, Tiffany bounded off her bed and grabbed Sheryl, demanding, "I saw you talking to Deacon Cross in the dining hall. What did he say? Isn't he dreamy? I want to have his children!"

Shaking off her roommate, Sheryl said, "Uh, Tiff. I work in the dining hall. We were talking about food."

"Oh." Tiffany backed off. "Is that all?"

"Yes, that's all," replied Sheryl, not quite sure why she was avoiding mention of their barbed little exchange about hockey. "I'm going to grab a shower. I smell like Irish stew."

"OK," Tiffany replied, fluffing her brown curls around her face. "You're coming to the game tonight, aren't you?"

"Yes, I'm singing the national anthem." Sheryl grabbed her toiletries and robe, then headed for the door.

"Are you sure a Canuck like you knows the words?" Tiffany teased.

"Yes, Tiff. We're trainable!" Sheryl replied, shutting the door a little more firmly than necessary, and made her way to the second-floor bathroom.

*You're a little sensitive today*, Sheryl mused. *Tiffany's not a bad kid, and she was just teasing.* Sometimes being a Canadian at a university in the United States had its challenges, but she'd been offered a great opportunity to study with a renowned voice teacher while still working on her English major, and being offered a scholarship as an international student helped. She was also fairly close to her hometown in Manitoba, so she could visit her folks easily. Her dad had had a slight heart attack. He seemed great, but what if a major coronary would occur? She worried because her dad didn't always take care of himself.

Dressed in their parkas and mukluks, the girls trudged through the snow to the Winter Sports Center, laughing with the other students headed the same way. They were in high spirits and getting primed for the big game. It was obvious some of them had been getting "primed" and "spirited" with a little pregame partying!

"I'll meet you in the stands," Sheryl said to Tiffany, breaking off from the group as they entered the arena. "I have to get in place for singing the anthem, but I'll join you as soon as I'm done. Save me a spot."

"OK," Tiffany replied. "Break a leg, or whatever it is you say. I'll try to get a good spot by the penalty box. Then we can scope out some of the Gophers and our guys, too, if they're naughty boys!"

"Whatever," Sheryl said, shaking her head as she trudged toward the timekeeper's box from where she would sing the anthem. Once there, she took off her parka, smoothed her hair, and straightened the cowl collar on her turquoise angora sweater, which accented the brilliant blue of her eyes. She took out her notecard with the words to "The Star Spangled Banner" to use as a prompt in case nerves overcame her during the performance. She asked the gentleman getting things ready in the box where she should stand so she could discreetly lay her notes down by the microphone.

"Well, Missy," said the older man a little gruffly, "you won't be standing in here and getting in my way."

"What do you mean? I was told to come to the timekeeper's box."

"Right you are. But you'll be singing out there." He pointed to the ice surface outside the box. "When the lights go down after the players are introduced, you'll step out into the spotlight. Your name will be announced, and you'll take it from there." He studied her face. "You're looking a little pale, girlie."

"Guess I never paid any attention to the singer before," Sheryl admitted. "I was always facing the flag during the anthem." Sighing and realizing this situation had just become a real performance, one where notecards wouldn't be admissible, Sheryl began to pace in the little box, getting herself revved up and shaking off the nerves. She was totally oblivious to the fact that the players were warming up on the ice.

Deacon Cross glided smoothly around the rink, handling the puck with finesse and occasionally impressing the fans with bouncing and flipping the puck in the air and catching it back on his stick. Though many viewed this as "hot-dogging," to Deacon it was just his routine in prepping for the big game. As he glided past the timekeeper's box, he caught a flash of honey-blond hair and did a double take. The girl pacing in the box seemed familiar in some way, but he was sure he'd never seen this blond beauty before.

After the ice had been resurfaced by the Zamboni, the players were introduced and the lights went down except for the spotlight, into which Sheryl stepped confidently. She looked up toward the flag, and as she did so, Deacon, who was standing on the blue line with his teammates, and just slightly inside the circle of light, looked up and saw the most beautiful angel with sparkling blue eyes he'd ever seen. *I must have died and gone to heaven.* Realizing she was about to sing, he stepped outside the spotlight, giving her the limelight.

*Interesting,* thought Sheryl, seeing his move out of the corner of her eye.

The announcer introduced Sheryl and asked the crowd to join her in singing the national anthem. As usual, she had been able to turn her nervousness into energy, and she performed the song a cappella beautifully. Meanwhile, Deacon slid side to side nervously on his skates, in part getting pumped in anticipation of the game, but also attempting to shake off the angelic vision in his head. *Come on, Cross, focus, dammit,* he berated himself.

Finishing to thunderous applause, Sheryl grabbed her parka and clambered up the bleachers to join Tiffany. As the players lined up for the face-off, the crowd started chanting, "Let's go, Sioux!" Tiffany high-fived Sheryl, saying, "Good job, roomie!"

"Thanks. Wasn't really expecting a spotlight and all."

"Yeah. What was Cross doing getting out of the spotlight? Thought the stars all liked to hog the limelight."

"Hmmm," Sheryl mused noncommittally, wondering that herself. "Oh well, let's watch. They're going to drop the puck."

The five players on each side lined up, jockeying for position against their opponents. They appeared to be jawing at one another. "What are they talking about?" asked Tiffany.

"Oh, they're just talking smack." At Tiffany's quizzical look, Sheryl continued. "They are saying unspeakable things they're going to do to one another's mother or sister. Just trying to get under one another's skin to get each other off his game."

"I thought maybe they were planning where the party was after the game," Tiffany suggested. Sheryl just shook her head in disbelief.

The referee made motions to drop the puck, seemingly toying with the centers, who clashed sticks trying to be the first to knock the puck back to one of their players. The crowd started shouting, "Drop the damn puck!" Finally, the ref did, and Deacon Cross got to it first and scooped it back to his wingman, Rob Black. Rob took off for the opponent's goal. Gliding at top speed, Deacon cruised ahead, and Rob made a perfect pass to Deacon just as he reached the blue line. Skirting the Gophers' defense and crossing the blue line, Deacon was headed for a breakaway. A goal was in sight just as the linesman blew his whistle, stopping play.

Tiffany jumped up, yelling, "You idiot, ref! What are you doing?!"

Tugging on Tiffany's coat, Sheryl pulled her onto the bleacher and hissed, "Sit down, Tiff! You're embarrassing yourself. It was an offside. He had to blow the whistle and stop the play."

"What do you mean, an 'offside'? It wasn't *on* or *off* a side. He was going right down the middle."

Sighing, Sheryl explained, "The puck must cross the blue line before any of the players on the team trying to score. Deacon mustn't have realized his other winger was ahead of him and crossed the line before Deacon and the puck did. Really Tiff, why do you come to the games when you haven't a clue about the sport?"

Grinning, Tiffany looked at the players' box across the rink. "If you haven't noticed, there are twenty good hunky reasons sitting on the bench right over there! How do you know so much about the game, anyway?"

Shaking her head, Sheryl explained, "My brother played hockey. Being dragged all over the province to his games, I grew up learning the game."

The teams were evenly matched, and by the third period, the game was all tied up. The guys were getting a little testy, and the game had become chippy. When a penalty was called, the referee had to drag the offending Gopher player away from his UND opponent, but they continued to jaw at one another. As the Gopher player entered the penalty box, Tiffany wondered aloud, "What was the penalty for?" Just then, the announcer called the penalty for spearing, and Tiffany continued. "Oooooh. He's kind of cute. He can spear me any day."

"Really, Tiff? I can't believe you! Just watch the game." Sheryl couldn't help but smile inwardly at her friend's suggestive pun.

There was a minute left in the third period, the score was tied, and it looked like they'd be going into overtime. Once again at the face-off, Deacon won the draw, pulling the puck back to Rob, who started toward the opponent's end but was checked by one of the Gopher players. Before going down, he was able to push the puck forward to Deacon, who took off at full speed, demonstrating his smooth puck handling as he deked around the opposing defenseman. Once again on a breakaway, he charged unimpeded toward the goalie, who, reading the play, got into position to stop the oncoming charge. As Deacon moved left, the goalie moved to block his shot. At the last minute, Deacon deked right and buried the puck in the net over the goalie's shoulder just as the buzzer sounded the end of the game.

The arena erupted into boisterous cheering, as the Fighting Sioux had won the game. The announcer's expressive voice boomed, "Here's your University of North Dakota Fighting Sioux sco-r-ing!" After stating the details of the final goal and outcome of the game, he quipped, "Dekin' Deacon strikes again." Latching onto this play on words, the excited crowd erupted again, chanting, "Dekin' Deacon! Dekin' Deacon!"

"Oh brother!" Sheryl commented. "Another big-headed jock is born!"

Tiffany, on the other hand, had joined the crowd and admonished her friend. "You're such a killjoy, Sheryl! You don't have a life. It's time you got your nose out of your books and lived a little. And I know just how to do it! There's a party tonight, and we are going. Most of the players will be there. Maybe you can get down off your high horse long enough to get to know them. Or," she continued, smirking, "maybe you can climb on a different horse, if you get my drift."

"Good grief! You can't be serious! Is your mind always in the gutter? How did we ever get to be roommates? I have a paper due next week, and I'm working in the dining hall, too. I really don't have time to waste at a party, especially one full of drunken jocks. I've heard about those parties."

Crestfallen, Tiffany pleaded, "Please, Sheryl? I really, really want to go, but I don't want to go alone. I know I seem brazen, but I really don't feel comfortable barging in by myself. Just for a little while? Pretty please, with sugar on it?"

Reluctantly, Sheryl acquiesced. Once again, she considered that Tiffany really wasn't a bad kid, and if she was going to go anyway, Sheryl should probably go along and keep an eye on her.

Maybe she could escape after Tiff was safely settled in with some of the other girls who'd be there. "OK, just for a little while!"

"Oh, thank you, thank you!" Tiffany squealed, grabbing her coat. "It will be a blast! I promise!"

"Yeah right," Sheryl sighed, knowing she'd probably live to regret this. Picking up her mittens and hat, she didn't notice that as the teams lined up to give their traditional handshake to their opponents, Deacon Cross looked up into the stands, hoping to catch another glimpse of the blond singer.

# CHAPTER
# FOUR

*How did I get myself talked into this?* Sheryl was having second thoughts after agreeing to accompany Tiffany to the after-game party at the apartment of one of the older players. Many of the younger players shared rooms all in the same dorm, but most of the juniors and seniors opted to share apartments off campus, though close to the arena. One of these seniors opened the door to the girls' timid knock. "Come on in, girls. The party's ready to start now you're here! Look guys. Fresh meat!" he leered.

"Knock it off, Zeke!" Deacon called across the room, then, looking up, he spied the beautiful blond with the angelic voice.

"Oooooh," giggled Tiffany, "there's Deacon. Let's go say hello." Dragging Sheryl with her, Tiffany rushed across the room and sidled up to Deacon. Caressing his arm, she cooed, "Thanks, Deacon, for protecting our virtue. You're my hero."

Catching Sheryl's embarrassed eye roll, he grinned and looked straight into her crystal blue eyes. "Any time, ladies. May I get you something?"

"Anything you've got to offer," Tiffany replied suggestively.

Still ignoring her and looking at Sheryl, he continued. "There are snacks on the table by the wall over there, but what would you like to drink?"

Before Tiff could embarrass her further, Sheryl asked, "Do you have a Coke?"

Deacon smiled directly at her and said, "Absolutely! My choice of beverage every time."

Finally, noting that Deacon's attention was not on her, Tiffany flounced off, saying, "Guess I'll look for something a little more spirited."

"Sorry about that. My roomie is a little over the top at times, but she's harmless. I didn't really want to come, but I sort of feel like I have to look out for her."

"I'm glad something brought you here tonight. I didn't know how I was going to get to meet you."

"You noticed me? I thought you guys were so focused on the start of the game, you didn't notice anything else."

"That's usually true," Deacon replied sheepishly. "But tonight I was a little distracted when I saw you pacing in the timekeeper's box before the game. Were you nervous?"

"I was a little, after I found out I had to sing out on the ice. Like you guys, I was just revving myself up. By the way, why did you step out of the spotlight?"

"It was your time to shine. It was just the right thing to do. You have a great voice." He passed her the bottle of Coke he'd retrieved from the cooler and opened one for himself.

"Thanks," Sheryl replied, taking a sip. "I thought all you star-athlete types wanted to hog the limelight."

Deacon's eyebrows knotted together. "Have we met before? You look a little familiar, and that comment . . ."

"Don't recognize me, eh, without the hairnet?"

"The dining hall. You seemed a little snarky with me, like I'd treated you badly or something. Don't you like hockey players?"

"I owe you an apology, Deacon. I grew up loving the sport. I don't know what got into me. Maybe it was just that the first time I was getting to meet you, I was wearing a hairnet and smelling like onions!" She smiled up at him shyly. "Guess I made some assumptions about you, too. I'm learning that maybe I was wrong. Could we start over? Hi, my name's Sheryl Leigh."

"You got it, kiddo! Guess you already know my name, as you so rudely pointed out in the dining hall," he chuckled. "Do you want to get out of here? You mentioned you hadn't really wanted to come," he said, looking around at the couples pairing off. "Do you live in the dorms? I could walk you home, and we could get acquainted."

Sheryl looked around for Tiffany, who was ensconced in the corner, pawing Rob Black, Deacon's winger. Following her gaze and seeing the frown that appeared on her face, Deacon assured her, "Don't worry about Tiffany. Rob is one of the good guys. He won't take advantage of her, and he'll see she gets home OK."

After telling Tiffany and Rob they were leaving, Deacon and Sheryl donned their heavy outer gear, ready to face the North Dakota cold. It was, however, a surprisingly beautiful and mild night, so they strolled slowly while sharing their backgrounds. Hearing about Sheryl's scholarship and her concerns about her father's health, Deacon was surprised to discover she was a Canadian, too.

"OK. It's your turn now. What brings a Canadian prairie boy to North Dakota?"

"Like every boy growing up in Canada, I wanted to play hockey and had the dream of playing in the NHL. UND has a great tradition in the sport, and many have gone on to make careers of it from here."

"Why didn't you play Major Junior hockey? That's a route many take to professional hockey, and you could have stayed in Canada."

Deacon smiled. "You really do understand the sport. I had some talent, and I could have played for the Swift Current Broncos. My dad wanted me to go the Juniors route, but my mum, a teacher like you're going to be, wanted me to get an education, too. The NCAA rules won't allow guys to play hockey in US colleges if they've played in the Major Juniors. They consider the Juniors pros. I could have gone to a college in Canada, but that wouldn't have led as directly to the NHL as the American universities do, like UND. So instead of that route, I went to the Father Murray private high school in Wilcox, Saskatchewan. It has produced many good athletes who have also gone on to play professional hockey.

"I did well in school," he continued, "as well as hockey, and got an athletic scholarship to UND. I still hope to reach my goal of playing in the NHL, but I'm also working on my business degree in marketing. That keeps my mum happy, too." Sheryl could tell by his smile that making his Mum happy pleased Deacon, too, and that pleased Sheryl.

They were in the quad now. Snow had begun to waft down in big flakes. As they faced one another under a streetlight, Deacon gently brushed a flake from Sheryl's cheek, and leaning down, brushed her lips gently with his own. Fearing he had overstepped a boundary too soon, he asked, "I'm sorry, was that OK?"

"No," replied Sheryl, an impish grin on her lips. "I think we'll have to try it again."

# CHAPTER
# FIVE

"So, where are you lovebirds off to tonight?" Tiffany asked through pursed lips and narrowed eyes.

"We're just going to study in Deacon's dorm room."

"Yeah right. How convenient that the men's dorm allows female visitors. And what are you going to study—anatomy?"

Noting the sardonic tone in Tiff's voice, Sheryl asked, "What's the matter, Tiffany?"

"Oh, you're just spending a lot of time together. You have no time for your friends anymore. Besides, you're getting exclusive and hogging Deacon's time. Maybe others would like to get to know the captain of the hockey team." Had the green-eyed monster bitten Tiffany?

Not quite sure how to respond, Sheryl said tentatively, "We enjoy one another's company and have great discussions about our hopes and dreams. You're spending just as much time with Rob."

"Yeah, well, that's not the same. Don't give me that discussion routine. No star like him is going to dilly dally around with anyone who's not putting out. He could have anyone on campus."

"Deacon's not like that. He respects me, and besides, he . . ." Sheryl's voice trailed off as she wondered if Tiffany's last comment included herself.

"Besides he what? L-o-o-ves me?" Sarcasm dripped from Tiffany's voice.

"This conversation is over. I have to go. Don't you have to get ready to meet Rob?"

"Yeah, we'll probably hit the bar in East Grand Forks." Tiff sighed. "When's North Dakota going to get with the times and change the drinking age to eighteen or nineteen? We can vote and go to war, so why can't we drink?"

They'd been round and round this topic before. Minnesota was just across the Red River from Grand Forks, and many of the UND students took advantage of the lower drinking age in the 1960s and 70s. Sheryl worried about them, and especially Tiff, coming back to the North Dakota side drunk. Not only was it illegal, it was dangerous.

"Be careful, Tiffany. I worry about you." And she did. As much as Tiffany frustrated her at times, Sheryl did care about her.

"Don't worry about me little Miss Goody-Two-Shoes. You live your life, and I'll live mine." With that, she stomped out to go down the hall to the showers.

Not knowing what else to do, Sheryl grabbed her books and headed across the quad to Deacon's dorm.

She found him in the hallway, arguing with some of his younger teammates. "Look, fellows. Is it really smart to go drinking tonight? If you want to keep your head in the game tomorrow, you're not going to want a hangover."

"Ah, we can take those guys with our eyes closed." That came from a cocksure freshman.

"And that attitude is a surefire way to get defeated. We can never rest on our laurels."

"The Deacon doesn't want us to have any fun. It's 'hockey, hockey, hockey' with him," a sophomore weighed in.

"That's right. I know you need to unwind, but if you get caught coming over the bridge under the influence, you could get arrested and suspended from the team. If we're going to make a run for the Frozen Four, we need everyone on board."

"OK. The Deacon speaks." The small group moved away, resigned to his words of admonishment, muttering under their breaths about his choosing to stay in the dorm to watch over them rather than renting a house or apartment with the other upperclassmen.

Sheryl had waited around the corner in the common area during the discussion. She came up to Deacon now. "That was quite a speech. Will they listen?"

"Oh, they'll listen," he sighed, "but it might not stop them from sneaking out when I'm otherwise occupied." He grinned and cocked an eyebrow at her as he opened the door to his room and ushered her in.

"Why do they call you 'the Deacon' instead of just Deacon?"

"Guess it's my paternal attitude toward them, as if their care is in my hands. And I do care about them. It's not just their value to the team, but their own development as strong, ethical young men that's important to me."

She looked up at him with shining eyes and a sweet smile. By this time, they had moved into his room. "And that's why I—" She stopped abruptly.

He looked down at her, a slow grin spreading across his face. "And that's why you what?"

She bit her lip. Was she ready to wade into deep waters? More importantly, was he? "Maybe you don't want to hear this, Deacon, but I guess I love you."

He cupped her face in his strong but gentle hands. "Not want to hear it? I've been longing to tell you that I'm head over heels in love with you, but I didn't want to scare you off."

Leaning down, he brushed her lips gently with his, then, taking his hands from her face, he wrapped his arms around her and drew her to him. Clinging to one another, they made their way to his couch, which also converted into a bed.

Leaving it in its couch formation, they sat on it, still snuggled together. Deacon ran his fingers through her hair while nibbling her neck and collarbone gently with his soft lips. She sighed with pleasure as he slid his hand under her sweater and stroked the silky-smooth skin of her back. It almost tickled. Noticing the bulge forming in the front of his pants, Sheryl reached out tentatively to touch it, making Deacon moan. He pulled her closer then with one arm around her shoulders while sliding his other hand from her back around to her torso. His touch and nipping lips sent shivers through Sheryl's body, making her squeeze her inner thighs together and wonder at the sensations.

Her breath quickened as Deacon's hand trailed down her torso and slipped under the waistband of her jeans. He raised his mouth from her neck to her lips, and kissing her deeply, he moved his hand further down her abdomen until his fingers probed her womanhood. Sheryl gasped and cried out. Feeling an uncontrollable spasm between her legs, her femaleness squeezed around Deacon's fingers. *Can this be what an orgasm feels like? How can this be happening?*

Realizing what had just happened, Sheryl pulled away, stood up, and, hanging her head, felt the heat rush to her cheeks as she tried to pull her clothes back in order.

"I'm so sorry, Sheryl. I went too far. I got caught up in the moment. I should have asked if it was OK."

Unable to look at him, Sheryl whispered, "No, Deacon. It was obvious I was OK with it. I'm so embarrassed. What must you think of me? I responded like a slut. Honest, this has never happened before."

Deacon stood up, placing his hands gently on her shoulders. "Sheryl, I don't think anything other than I love you with all my heart." Taking her chin in one hand and tipping her face up so that her eyes had to meet his, he continued. "You are no slut. You just responded in a natural way to lovemaking. I won't ever force you to do anything you don't want to do. We can take it slow. This is no casual romance. I intend us to be together a long time."

"Oh, Deacon. I love you with all my heart, too. I shocked myself with such a physical reaction. I know this is the 1970s and it's the era of 'make love, not war,' but I've never been in a serious relationship before. I wasn't prepared for my reaction. I didn't want to lose your respect."

"Never, Sheryl. And you'll never lose me, either."

"Thank you, Deacon." She reached up and caressed his cheek. Planting a chaste kiss on his lips, she whispered, "I think I'd better go back to my room and think about all of this."

Deacon watched her walk away—hoping she would turn and look back at him.

# CHAPTER
## SIX

*A* few days later, Sheryl sat cross-legged on her dorm bed, surrounded by a pile of books. Hunched over with her elbow poised on her knee and her hand cupping her chin, Sheryl paged through the book in front of her on the bed, a pensive frown furrowing her brow.

The door crashed open and Tiffany charged in, stomping her snow boots on the floor and brushing wet snow from her hair. Seeing Sheryl absorbed in her reading, Tiffany demanded, "My God, do you always have to have your nose in a book? Aren't straight As enough for you, Keener, as you Canucks would say?"

As Tiffany moved toward the bed, Sheryl unsuccessfully tried to cover up the books. "What's this?" Tiffany asked as she picked up one and turned it over. "Masters and Johnson's *Human Sexual Response*?" Laughing, she picked up another. "*The Kinsey Report*? What is this, a crash course in sex?"

Heaving a big sigh, Sheryl relented. "OK, Tiff. I admit it: I'm kind of naïve in certain areas."

"No kidding!" Tiff retorted.

"It was something Mum avoided talking about, and I didn't have a big sister to ask. I used to delve into her 1950s Harlequin romance novels and *True Confessions* magazines, hoping to get some insight, but they weren't very helpful in specifics."

Tiff's laughter became gentler and more sympathetic. Patting Sheryl on her shoulder, she concurred, saying, "I can see your problem." Reasserting herself, she continued. "But really, Sheryl! This isn't the 1950s! You need to get up to speed. They've invented the pill, and Deacon's not going to wait around forever when there are plenty of other girls who would step into your place."

Wondering once again if Tiff meant herself, Sheryl sighed. "I'm from a small town, Tiff, and our family doctor delivered me. I just can't approach him for a prescription. He'd be disappointed in me."

"Suit yourself. Good luck with those books." Tiffany laughed again, this time with a sardonic twist to her grin. "Gotta get ready for the game. Are you coming tonight, or are you too engrossed in your education for after the game?"

"Just drop it, Tiff. Yes, I'm going to the game. Isn't tonight a big game for Rob?"

"Yes, there's going to be a scout here from the Vancouver Canucks. Deacon's lucky he's already been drafted."

"Yes, he is, but I know he'd love to be teammates with Rob in the NHL." She closed the book she was holding and said, "I'll get ready and come with you."

Ninety minutes later, the girls were sitting in their usual spots next to the opposing team's penalty box. Tiffany claimed she liked to size up the competition, not as players, but as potential conquests. Sheryl also liked the spot, mainly because she could see the UND players' box across the ice, allowing her a perfect view of Deacon when he wasn't on the ice—a rare occurrence.

After the singing of the national anthem by one of Sheryl's fellow choir members, the starting lineup from both teams took their positions for the face-off. With Deacon at center and Rob on his right wing, the guys faced their opponents on the Wisconsin

Badgers team. It wasn't quite as intense a rivalry as the Gophers, but a rivalry all the same.

By the third period, the game was all tied up, 3–3. Emotions and adrenaline were running high. Deacon swiped the puck from a Badger forward and broke for their blue line. He had a perfect shot at the Badger net, but he could see Rob to his right, crossing the blue line right behind him. Knowing it was an important night for Rob, Deacon, an unselfish player, made a perfect pass to Rob so he could take the shot at goal. Rob deftly picked up the puck and skated toward the goal. Out of nowhere, a Badger defenseman caught up to Rob and tripped him with his stick, a penalty definitely in order.

Such a penalty would have put UND on a power play, but Rob, steamed at having his chance thwarted, bounded to his feet, grabbed the Badger player, and began pummeling him. The referees eventually pulled the two apart, but Rob's ferocity flowed from his fists to his mouth as he spewed a stream of obscenities at the refs. The result was that he not only got a five-minute penalty for fighting, but also a game misconduct and, therefore, was tossed from the game.

Still seething underneath, he skated dejectedly to the bench and stumbled down to the locker room. He knew he'd probably lost his shot at the big time. He had not only lost his team's chance at a power play in a tied game, but his team was also now short one of their better players for the rest of the game.

"What does it all mean?" asked Tiffany. "How can the scout assess him if he's not playing? It's just not fair!"

Once again surprised at Tiff's incomprehension of the game, Sheryl tried to soften things even though she knew it didn't look good for Rob. "Well, it's not a promising situation, but you never know; some of the NHL teams want goons. Oh, not that Rob's a goon," she added quickly, "but sometimes they like guys who aren't afraid to go a round for their team."

"Guess I might have to console him after the game." Tiffany smiled smugly at Sheryl, who smiled in return, thinking, *I'm sure you will!*

During the last five minutes of the game, neither team gave an inch, players dogging one another up and down the ice. The horn sounded that regulation time had ended, and they were headed into overtime.

Sheryl sat with fingers crossed, biting her lower lip as the team regrouped for the opening face-off in overtime. Deacon grabbed the puck before the Badger center had a chance and knocked it back to Zeke, who had taken Rob's place as Deacon's winger. Zeke headed straight for the Wisconsin blue line. Deacon skated to his left, slowing just enough to straddle the blue line to let Zeke get the puck across before him so they wouldn't get called for an offside. Once Zeke crossed, Deacon streaked ahead to catch his pass to the left of the Badger goalie. Just as Deacon was about to shoot, an opposing defenseman caught up and nudged him toward the corner.

Deacon momentarily lost his balance, but not his handling of the puck. He shot it down the goal line, even with and toward the goalie, who in anticipation of the move had done the splits to cover the entire opening of the net.

The crowd couldn't believe their eyes at what happened next. The puck slid across the goal line, hit the inside of the goalie's stretched legs and deflected off the inside of his pad and into the net. The crowd erupted, but the referee held up his hand and gathered with the linesmen around the goal judge for a consultation.

"What's going on?" Tiffany asked.

"It looks like the play is under review. They're not sure the goal went in, I guess. The ref probably couldn't see it from his angle, but the goal judge flashed the light that it was in." Sheryl frowned. It would be years before technology would make it easier to review the tapes to see a play from all angles.

The consultation over, the referee skated to center ice and signaled that it was indeed a goal, and the temporarily deflated crowd erupted again, chanting Deacon's name as the announcer boomed, "Dekin' Deacon strikes again!"

The game was over, and the Fighting Sioux had won. The teams lined up to shake hands before acknowledging the crowd's cheers of appreciation for their UND home team. It was with mixed emotions that Deacon skated toward the bench, where his buddy Rob stood fully dressed in street clothes. Deacon patted him on the shoulder, but Rob, head down, just nodded and headed back to the locker room.

Later, as they walked across campus, Deacon and Sheryl discussed Rob's fate. "Does Rob have a chance with the Canucks?" Sheryl asked.

"I'm afraid not. The scout talked to him after the game and told him they couldn't afford to have players who were so hot-headed that they would jeopardize their team's chances at a win just because they were pissed off. Uh, sorry. I was just quoting him. The thing is, Rob's not a hot head. It's just that so much rode on this game for him, and he let his emotions get the best of him. There's something about hockey that changes our personalities on the ice."

Sheryl smiled, recalling Deacon's own intensity and aggressiveness. "Yes, so I've noticed! At least you pulled out the win for them. Dekin' Deacon strikes again! I'm afraid that moniker has stuck."

"Yeah, guess that's my cross to bear!" Deacon laughed at his own little joke.

"Very *punny*, Mr. Deacon Cross," Sheryl quipped, joining in his laughter.

By now, they were in the Memorial Union, having a Coke and fries. "Speaking of names, Deacon, don't you think it's strange that most of the teams have animal names like Badgers, Gophers, Bulldogs, and Huskies, and we have the name of a people?"

"Why would that be strange? The Sioux are a proud people, and they fought their rivals and their environment for their survival. We're proud to carry their name."

"I know, but to have a people as a name and logo that is a caricature of an Indian head somehow seems disrespectful. Some folks are starting to think the name should be changed."

"Yeah, but I don't see it happening. We have a long tradition here, and we use the name and logo with respect."

"Perhaps," Sheryl acknowledged, "but not everyone does, especially the fans of our rival teams. I try to personalize it by thinking if I were watching the Vancouver Canucks, and the fans of say, the Boston Bruins, started to yell, 'Canucks suck!' over and over, I just think it would get to me after a while. You know, we are Canadians in a foreign land right now, and occasionally that nickname Canuck is used in a derogatory way. Sometimes it hurts, so I think maybe it hurts the Sioux people, too."

Deacon's eyebrows knit together in a frown. "Well, I haven't thought about it that way. You may have a point, but I think if they ever tried to change it, there'd be a helluva battle over it." He stood up, gathering their used paper cups and plates to put in the garbage. "Since we're getting into such deep subjects, maybe we should discuss them further in my room."

"Oh, I have lots of ideas to try out on you." Sheryl looked innocently up at him, thinking about her earlier reading. Looking at her quizzically, Deacon took her hand as they left the warmth of the student union and trudged across the crunchy frozen snow to the dorms.

# CHAPTER
# SEVEN

*I*t was March. Mother Nature was making sure North Dakotans hadn't forgotten they lived on the northern plains, and winter wasn't over yet. Blizzards of horizontal blowing snow created whiteouts that swept across the flat, open spaces. Even in town, one couldn't see buildings across the street, but the university never shut down, and students, bending into the wind, fought their way to classes.

The cold and snow didn't bother Sheryl. She had grown up in the same environment in Canada, but more than that, the tune to an old song kept running through her head: "I've Got My Love to Keep Me Warm." She smiled as she thought about Deacon and how close they had become, mentally, emotionally, and physically. She thought of him as her soul mate.

Although they had explored one another's bodies with tenderness and passion, they hadn't consummated their love completely. It was an era before AIDS, and the only concern for them was an unexpected pregnancy that could derail their plans. *Guess I'm what the books would call a technical virgin,* thought Sheryl. *There's not much we don't know about one another. Wish I could get my courage up to get on the pill. As Tiff says, this is the 1970s. Deacon never carries any protection. He says he doesn't want it to look like he's expecting anything.* She pulled her hood closer together against the wind and snow, grasping it under her chin. *Maybe we'll have to talk about it tonight.*

After supper that evening and Sheryl's shift in the dining room, Deacon met her outside the dining hall. "Hi, Sheryl. Do you have anything planned tonight? I was wondering if we could go for a walk. The weather has settled down, and I have something important I want to talk to you about in private."

"Sure, Deacon. I have something I want to talk to you about, too. Let me get out of this uniform and into some warm clothes. I'll meet you outside my dorm in about twenty minutes." *Hmmm. I wonder if he wants to talk about the same thing I do.*

True to her word, Sheryl came out the dormitory door and into the frosty air to greet Deacon. Bundled into her parka and toque, she smiled happily at the prospect of talking seriously about their love and where it was going.

"Hi, Sweet Pea!" Deacon reached down and pecked her on the cheek.

Sheryl laughed. "Where'd that come from? You've never called me sweet pea before."

"Just heard that old Tommy Roe song 'Sweet Pea' from back in high school on the radio. Like the singer, I'm just wanting you to be my girl." He grinned at her.

"I think I'm already your girl, Deacon. Always."

"Glad you said that, 'cause I've got something important to talk to you about. Let's walk." He grabbed her hand, and they began a slow stroll through the quiet residential area bordering the university.

"Me, too," said Sheryl, but hesitated, biting her lip. "You go first."

"OK." Deacon took a big breath. "Here goes. You know the Canuck scout that was here the other night assessing Rob? And you know they already have my rights. Well, this is their second year in the NHL, and they haven't got a great record. They think I can help them, and they want me to go immediately to their farm team, the Americans, in Rochester, New York, to play out the rest of the season and get some experience in professional hockey so I'd be ready to move up to the Canucks next season." He paused to catch his breath, then asked, "What do you think?"

Sheryl was stunned. Stopping in her tracks, she looked up at him with wide eyes, speechless. Silence engulfed them. Stars twinkled. Sheryl shoved her hands in her pockets.

"Say something, please!" Deacon pleaded.

"It's a bit of a shock. Do you want to go? What about school?" She wanted to say, *What about me?*

"Well, I think it's my big chance for the big time. As the scout said, I'm not developing as much here as I might in Rochester." He thought for a moment. "Guess I'm a little afraid I might lose some of my skill, and then they might not want me later."

"But doesn't your mum want you to get an education, too?"

"Yeah, she does. But I figure I at least got started, and I can always finish later if the NHL doesn't work out for me, or I get too old to play. It may be 'an offer I can't refuse.'" Deacon grinned as he quoted the blockbuster movie they'd just seen.

"Sounds like you've made up your mind. It is a fantastic opportunity, Deacon, and you have to do it. I really am thrilled for you." Putting on a brave face, she tried to joke with a half laugh, "Maybe not for me, however."

"Now, that's the big thing I wanted to talk to you about. You have become so important to me, and I can't imagine going on without you. I want to share all this excitement with you," he said, taking her hand. "And frankly, I don't think I can do it without you. After you graduate, I want you to join me. I want us to be together forever."

"Are you saying what I think you're saying, Deacon?"

"Yes, I am. We don't have time to make long-term plans now. I have to leave by the weekend, and I've got a lot of loose ends to tie up beforehand. But I want you to know that our future is together. I can't imagine a future without you in it. What do you say?"

"I say we need to seal it with a kiss." She reached up and drew his head down to her, putting aside the fact that she, too, had something she'd wanted to discuss.

# CHAPTER EIGHT

*D*eacon left for Rochester, and Sheryl settled into final projects and exams for the spring semester and graduation in May. She had written a couple of letters to Deacon's boarding house, and he'd responded once. These were days long before email and cell phones. A long distance call was only made in the event of an emergency, so with Sheryl in the dorm and Deacon living in a boarding house, neither were in a position to make a long-distance call just to chat. Sheryl knew Deacon would be busy trying to make his way with the Americans, doing his best to make a good impression of his skill and work ethic; in fact, he'd probably be on the ice even after hours to practice his signature moves and shots on goal. *Oh well,* she thought, smiling to herself, *we'll have some time this summer, and we'll make our plans to be together forever.*

Sheryl had just returned to her dorm room after her last final, and throwing her bag on the bed, she heaved a sigh of relief that exams were over. *Hope my analysis of transcendentalism as it is evident in Emerson's and Thoreau's works hit the mark.* A quick rap on the door broke into her reverie. One of the girls from across the hall poked her head in and said, "There's a long distance call for you. You can take it on line two at the end of the hall."

*Oh no, who is it? What's happened? No one calls unless it's bad news.* Running down the hall, she changed her tune. *Maybe it's Deacon and he's coming back for my graduation and to make plans.*

Smiling hopefully, she picked up the phone and answered cheerfully, "Hello, this is Sheryl."

"Hi, kiddo. It's J.D." Her brother's somber tone told Sheryl that all was not right with her world.

"J.D.? What's the matter? Why are you calling? I thought I was going to see you next week at grad."

"Sorry, little sister, but I have some bad news. Dad's had a heart attack, and he is in intensive care. It's worse than last time. I think you'd better come home. I can drive down to get you. Can you be ready in the morning? I don't want to leave Mum alone for long. She's not doing well with this."

"Wha—How? Where?" Sheryl stammered in shock. She drew in her breath and continued. "Yes, of course I'll be ready. I can maybe get a bus if you need to stay with Mum."

"No, Aunt Nora is here to be with her, and it's probably quicker for me to come than your having to change buses in Winnipeg. I can fill you in on the drive, too."

"OK," Sheryl agreed. "Give my love to Mum and Dad for me, and I'll see you soon."

Sheryl slowly dragged her feet back to her room. Tiffany was there when she entered. Grabbing Sheryl's two hands, Tiffany tried dancing her around the room. "Hey, gloomy Gus! It's all over. Time to celebrate. Let's party hearty, girl!"

Sheryl pulled her hands away and burst into tears. "My brother just called. Dad's had a heart attack, and I have to go home."

Chastened, Tiffany hugged Sheryl. "Oh, I'm so sorry. I didn't know. Is he all right?" When Sheryl shrugged her shoulder, Tiff continued. "Will you be back for graduation?"

"He's in the ICU, and I don't know the details. J.D. is coming to get me tomorrow. I don't know about grad." She sank on the bed. "My whole world is up in the air right now. Guess I'd better pack a few things, but I have so much to do. I'll have to come back to move out anyway, I guess, so I'll finish up then."

Tiffany watched her go through the motions of packing, and sensing Sheryl didn't want to talk, sat on her own bed and, for once, kept her own counsel.

Leaving North Dakota on their way to Crocus Plains, Manitoba, J.D. explained that their dad, John Leigh, had been filling prescriptions in his drugstore when he suddenly keeled over, pestle dropping to the floor as he collapsed. Alice, his clerk, had called for an ambulance and then his wife, Alma. J.D. happened to be home on leave for his little sister's graduation.

Having been christened with his father's first name, John, J.D. was called by his initials for John Daniel to avoid confusion between father and son. He was a major in the Canadian Armed Forces, stationed on the Queen Charlotte Islands as the Commanding Officer. He'd left his family on the islands for this supposed quick trip home for Sheryl's graduation. It would have been too long of a trip for the little ones. It was now uncertain as to when he could return.

On the drive north, Sheryl told her brother about Deacon and her hopes for the future.

"Seriously, Sheryl? A hockey player? Those goons have probably had too many knocks on the head to have any sense left. Case in point—he left school before he finished to chase a dream."

"Need I remind you, big brother, you played hockey. I was dragged all over the province to your games!" Sheryl retorted.

"Yeah, I did, and I love the sport. But I never played it at that level. I never would have given up school for it. And I've heard the stories of their parties and what those bevy of beauties that follow them around are willing to do for their attention. Don't know many guys who can resist that!"

"Deacon's not like that!" Sheryl proclaimed. "He's smart and kind. This is his shot. He can always finish school later."

J.D. shook his head. "He's got you hoodwinked, anyway. Be careful, little sister. If he makes it in the big time, you can kiss him good-bye."

"I already did," Sheryl exclaimed, a twinkle in her eye. "But it wasn't forever."

Sighing, J.D. cautioned, "I just don't want to see you hurt, Sheryl. I've seen these big egos before. So, as I said, just be careful."

Agreeing to disagree, they changed the subject, though the air in the car was charged. Sheryl watched the passing scenery, while J.D. concentrated on driving.

# CHAPTER
# NINE

*J*ohn Leigh improved steadily, so that six days after Sheryl arrived in her hometown, Dr. Jones declared the prognosis was good for his recovery, but he'd need a few more days in the hospital. When he was allowed to go home, he'd have to follow a rigid regimen of healthy eating, rest, and slow implementation of exercise, beginning with walking.

J.D. and Sheryl worried about their mother's ability to cope. "I'm afraid, kiddo, none of us will be able to go to your graduation, and I really have to get back to the base."

"And don't forget back to your family, big brother!" Sheryl chastised. "It's OK. I'll take the folks' car and go down for grad, pack my things, and check out of the dorm. Then I'll get right back to relieve you so you can get back to the Charlottes."

*I hope Deacon and I can talk so we can make plans, but maybe postpone them for a bit. I know he'll understand. Maybe I'll risk it and see Doc Jones about getting on the pill while I'm here.*

Graduation was nice but bittersweet. It was great to be finished after four years of hard work, but no one had been there to share her accomplishment with her—not her parents, not her brother, and—not Deacon. In fact, Sheryl hadn't heard from him at all. She'd written him about her dad, but there'd been no word.

"Are you sure Deacon never tried to get in touch with me?" Sheryl asked Tiffany.

"Ummm." Tiff hesitated. "This came for you today."

Sheryl grabbed the envelope eagerly, but her face fell when she realized that it was her last letter to Deacon, stamped with "Unable to deliver. No forwarding address."

"I don't get it. He wouldn't leave without telling me. Where could he have gone?" Sheryl paused as she looked again at the returned letter in her hand. "Hasn't Rob heard from him? In fact, where is Rob? I haven't seen him since I came back."

"Oh, he's busy getting ready for the hockey camp the Sioux run for kids in the summer."

Realizing Tiffany hadn't really answered her question, Sheryl tried again. "But where could Deacon be? He wouldn't leave without a word."

"Oh, face it, little girl. He's probably forgotten all about you. Deacon could have anyone, and he's not going to save himself for someone who doesn't put out. If he is moving on in hockey, you can bet there'll be lots of more willing female opportunities, and he'll be moving on there, too."

Turning to her boxes so Tiffany couldn't see the hurt and tears stinging her eyes, Sheryl thought that it just couldn't be true. Not the Deacon she knew.

Returning to Crocus Plains to care for her father and support her mother, Sheryl finally resigned herself to the fact that Deacon wasn't going to be in touch. The weeks passed, and her father's health improved so much that he was working part time. Sheryl realized she had to find a job to give herself something else to think about other than her disappointment in the man she'd thought was her one true love. Besides, she needed to support herself. Fortunately, a position opened for an English teacher at the Crocus Plains Collegiate Institute due to a maternity leave for one of the teachers. It was perfect. She could use her education but still be close at hand to help her parents if needed.

School didn't start until after Labor Day, and with her parents' encouragement to take a break, she decided to see her brother and his family on the Queen Charlotte Islands. He probably wouldn't be posted there beyond the year, and she'd always wanted to explore that unique area. O*h, but it means I have to fly over the Hecate Strait in that crazy little plane they call "the Goose."*

She survived the splash landing on the plane's belly and was greeted warmly by her brother. As he hugged her, Sheryl, chagrin in her voice, mumbled into his shoulder, "It's OK. You can say it."

J.D. pulled back to look at her. "Say what?"

"'I told you so'—about the hockey player."

"Aw, Sheryl, I wasn't thinking that, and I really wanted to be all wrong about the guy."

"Guess it's water under the bridge now. So-o-o let's go greet that great little family of yours. And I want to see everything on the islands!"

And that she did. She got reacquainted with her sister-in-law, Stella, and was charmed by her little nieces, Abbey and Lucy, who loved their auntie wholeheartedly. The family took her on picnics on the Tlell River, beach combing at Agate Beach, hiking up Tow Hill, and out to Old Massett to see the Haida village and some of the artists at work carving in argillite, a black slate found on the islands. She bought a couple of small pieces to take back with her. A few of the young lieutenants at the Officers' Mess showed her some interest, but she wasn't ready to reciprocate. Once one had found true love and lost it, she wondered if it could ever be found again.

She returned to Crocus Plains somewhat refreshed and ready to focus on her classes and planning for them. Both became her salvation in surviving her desolation at losing her true love.

In October, she heard from Tiffany. She had finally snagged her hockey player. Tiffany had chased and dated several hockey players besides Rob, but she had finally settled on him. He at least had the potential for a substantial paycheck. She and Rob were getting married over the Christmas holidays, and she wanted Sheryl to be her maid of honor.

Sheryl had mixed feelings about the situation. She didn't want to return to Grand Forks, where the wedding would take place. She feared difficult memories would haunt her. On the other hand, maybe Deacon would be there. After all, he had been Rob's closest buddy not all that long ago.

Wondering if she were doing the right thing, she arrived in Grand Forks a few days before New Year's Eve, the date the wedding was scheduled. The ceremony would be at St. Michael's Catholic Church, with the reception at the ballroom of the Memorial Student Union. She toured her old haunts, facing the ghosts she found there, and fought the nostalgia of lost dreams.

She ran into Rob first at the Union, where she had stopped for some coffee. She asked him straight off, "Is Deacon going to be here?"

Rob tensed, visibly uncomfortable. "Uh, no, Sheryl. He's busy now that he's being moved up from the minors to start with the Vancouver Canucks in January. Haven't you been in touch with him?"

"No. I haven't heard from him since he left Rochester. Where did he go?"

"They moved him out to the Seattle Totems, another farm team for the Canucks. He trained with them over the summer, and played some games with the Totems this fall. Apparently, he developed enough to move up to the Canucks."

"I don't understand, Rob. Why has he never gotten in touch with me?"

Rob shrugged and moving away said, "Gotta go, Sheryl. I'm supposed to check the ballroom for the setup for the dinner. You know Tiff. Everything has to be perfect. See ya at the rehearsal."

Left alone to ponder the strange conversation, Sheryl wondered how she'd get through the wedding. There were bound to be several of Deacon's former teammates asking difficult questions, and several former puck bunnies gloating that she hadn't won the big prize after all. *Like that matters.* What really mattered was losing her true love.

Tiffany was a beautiful bride, and she seemed genuinely happy to be marrying Rob. Sheryl put on her stoic persona and muddled through, but she was relieved to return to her hometown, her parents, her work, and her students. Sheryl always put her students' best interests first, and her work with them helped her to cope with her own disappointments.

# CHAPTER
# TEN

The years passed, and Sheryl developed the reputation of being a favorite teacher. She was tough but fair, and above all, she cared about students, and they thrived under her guidance. Soon after Rob and Tiff were married—in fact, awfully soon after they were married—they had twin girls. Sheryl was their godmother. *Trust Tiff to call her girls Bambi and Candi. I'm surprised Rob went along with it, but then, Rob goes along with whatever Tiff says or wants.*

Over the years, Sheryl followed Deacon's career in the NHL religiously. She knew his stats, watched any game in which he played when it was televised in her area, and clipped articles in the news about his hockey career and, sadly, his personal life. She had started to keep a scrapbook, but it became more difficult to do when so many photographs featured him and a different starlet on his arm every few months. *I wonder why he doesn't settle down? His relationships seem very short.* Indeed, the headlines on both the sports and the society pages were beginning to read "Dekin' Deacon Dekes Another Trip to the Altar."

Sheryl was overwhelmed with melancholy. She'd experienced so much loss. Her parents were both gone now. Her father had had several episodes with his heart, and unable to change his lifestyle, he eventually succumbed to a massive coronary. A few short years later, her mother, Alma, passed on. Sheryl and her brother, J.D., felt she'd died of a broken heart.

Had Sheryl ever really gotten over her own broken heart? Perhaps it was time to assess her life and move on, too—not to the great beyond, but to a new challenge. She no longer had a reason or an obligation to stay in Crocus Plains. She'd always thought about furthering her education, and perhaps teaching college students rather than hormone-driven adolescents would be more rewarding. *I think it's time to visit my old alma mater—the University of North Dakota.*

She soon found herself enrolled in a Master of Arts program in English, and teaching composition as a graduate teaching assistant to freshmen. *Why did I think they would be more mature than high school students or less hormonal? Ah well, I guess their frontal lobes don't mature until they're twenty-five.*

She enjoyed working with the young people, however, as they kept her young. Finishing her master's didn't seem enough, so she went on for her doctorate in Education at the Center for Teaching and Learning. She was able to obtain a teaching assistantship there as well. Her classes were paid for, and the accompanying minimal stipend helped to cover some of her expenses. Her savings filled in any gaps in her funds, but she occasionally took on tutoring jobs on weekends to supplement her income.

Sheryl loved teaching and the academic atmosphere of the university. When she graduated, it was serendipitous that an opening for a faculty position in her department became available, and she was offered the position after an exhaustive process to prove she was a more qualified candidate than any outside applicant. Her background was advantageous for teaching future secondary teachers because her own experience in the high school classroom gave her credibility with her college students.

Life was good. She loved her work, enjoyed her colleagues, had good friends, and even engaged in the occasional romantic involvement. An avid reader, she always had a good book to sink her teeth into, and one of her favorite places to read or grade papers was the new coffee shop on campus. There were also many cultural and athletic events to enrich her life, but the one she would normally fully embrace brought Sheryl the most anguish— the Fighting Sioux hockey games. They brought back so many tender memories and a longing for a love that was gone forever, a love that prevented her from fully engaging in any meaningful relationship. *Will I never be free? Can I never forget Deacon and what we had? It was brief, but it was real—at least, I thought it was.*

Returning from one of those games on a Friday evening, the phone rang as she entered her town house. Tossing off her parka, Sheryl picked up the receiver and said, "Good evening."

"Sheryl?" a shaky male voice asked. "Is this Sheryl Leigh? Is that you, Sheryl?

Recognizing Rob Black's anxious voice, she responded, "Yes, Rob. What's the matter?"

"She's gone, Sheryl. Tiff is gone." His voice broke.

Thinking, *She's done it this time. Tiff's finally flown the coop,* Sheryl asked, "What do you mean, Rob, 'Tiff's gone'? Where did she go?"

"To heaven, I hope. She passed away earlier today."

"No. I can't believe it! What happened?" Sheryl asked, gasping with the shock.

Sheryl could tell Rob was crying, but he managed to continue. "She was diagnosed with ovarian cancer six months ago. She had surgery and chemotherapy, but it couldn't do the trick. It took her, and it took her fast."

"Oh, Rob! I had no idea. Why didn't she tell me?"

"She knew you were busy with your work and research, and she thought she'd beat it. So did I. Tiff could tackle anything. She was only forty-two," he choked out.

"Oh my God!" Reeling from the shock, she grabbed the back of a chair. Regaining her composure, she continued. "How are the girls? I'm coming right out. I'll book a flight for Denver tomorrow."

"Would you really, Sheryl? We'd all like that. I think the girls need you. We have family, but you've always been special to them, like a second mother or a favorite aunt."

"Give them a squeeze for me, and tell them I'll be there soon. And, Rob, you try to take care of yourself. The girls will need you."

Stunned, Sheryl hung up the phone and sank into a nearby recliner. *How can this be? Tiff was always so full of life. Yes, she could sometimes be a pill, but she had a good heart. I think. No time to fret or ponder. Got to pack, get a flight, notify my GTA to look after my classes. Time to move.*

Rob and his twin girls met Sheryl at the Denver airport the next day. She had visited the family in the Mile-High City a few times over the years. They had hopped around some with Rob coaching in the Junior leagues, but they'd finally settled in Denver when he'd landed an assistant coaching job with the University of Denver Pioneers. He hoped someday to be head coach.

Bambi and Candi rushed Sheryl, both trying to hug her at once, crushing her in the process. Through tears, they exclaimed in unison, "Oh, Auntie Sheryl. Thank heavens you're here. Why did this have to happen to our mom?"

Sheryl was touched, and patting their backs, she tried to comfort them. "There, there, everything will be all right," she said, knowing full well this wasn't true. Through tears, she couldn't help but smile a bit to herself. *Who would believe my girls are now young women in college? How many times did I comfort them just like this when they were small children? But this is more than skinned knees.*

# CHAPTER
# ELEVEN

Somehow they got through the next few days. Sheryl took the lead in planning and executing all the final arrangements. After all the well-wishers had left Rob's home following the funeral, he and Sheryl sat at the kitchen table, sharing a glass of wine and reminiscing about Tiffany and their shared memories of happier times together.

"Auntie Sheryl?" Bambi asked as she and Candi entered the kitchen.

"Yes, girls, what is it?"

There was a pause and an intake of breath before Candi took up the conversation. "Bambi and I have been going through Mom's things the last few days, and we found this. We thought you should have it." She handed an envelope to Sheryl.

Sheryl looked at the sealed envelope and stopped cold; then her world started spinning out of control. It was addressed to her, with the return address of Deacon's Rochester, New York, boarding house. The postmark was smeared, but the year looked like 1970-something.

Noting her pale face and the flurry of expressions crossing it, Rob asked, "What's the matter, Sheryl?" The girls stepped back, looking frightened and wondering if they'd done the right thing.

"It's from Deacon," Sheryl stammered, "when he was with the Americans in Rochester. I think I'll go up to the guest room to open it." With so many emotions tumbling through her, she knew she had to be alone to read whatever was inside. As she stumbled from the room and up the stairs, she felt the thickness of the large envelope, and noted the extra postage on it. *What can it be? Why now?*

Closing the guest room door behind her, she sank into the cushioned rocking chair by the window. Holding the envelope and staring at it for a long while, she wondered, *Do I want to open it? Can I open it? What will it do to me? How will my world change? How can I not open it?*

Finally, sucking in her breath, she slit the envelope open. She pulled out one sheet of folded paper. Folded inside was an Air Canada round-trip ticket in her name to Vancouver from Winnipeg, dated for use on June 2-4, 1972. *I don't understand. What is this? What was Deacon thinking?* Realizing the only way to find out was to read the note that came with it, Sheryl opened the one sheet of paper and began reading. *Short and to the point. Just like Deacon—a man of few words, but, oh, the action!*

*Dear Sheryl,*

*So sorry I haven't been in contact much. They are working us pretty hard, and I really want to make a go of it. Just because I haven't called or written, it doesn't mean I don't miss you with all my heart.*

*I had hoped to get back for your graduation so we could make our plans, but the Canucks are sending me out within the week to their other farm team, the Seattle Totems. They think if I train over the summer with them and play a few games in the fall that I'll be ready to move up to the Canucks in Vancouver at some point next season. I may be able to go back and forth a bit when the Canucks start training later in the summer. It's all happening so fast.*

*Anyway, I still want us to be together and to start planning for our future, whatever it may bring. I know you'll want to use your education, but I make enough for us to survive while you look for a job after we're married.*

*We apparently get a long weekend off training this summer at the beginning of each month. I've enclosed a ticket for you to come out to Vancouver the first weekend in June so we can make some plans. I scheduled the flight from Winnipeg, as I thought you'd want time to move back home and maybe talk things over with your folks. I really wish I'd been able to meet them, and you mine.*

*The way things are happening, I'm afraid it may have to be a simple, quick wedding. I hope you're OK with that. In case you didn't get the message here, I'm asking you to marry me. I really want you with me. At any rate, please come to Vancouver so we can talk it all out. Can't wait for your response.*

*Sorry I can't send you my Seattle address, but I don't know where I'll be staying yet. I'll try to call, but you can always reach me in care of the team.*

*Love, forever and always,*

*Deacon*

Tears running down her face, Sheryl couldn't believe what she had just read. *He did love me. He asked me to marry him.* Questions soared through her mind. *Why didn't I get this letter? Why did Tiff have it and not give it to me? No wonder my letter about Dad came back. He'd left Rochester, and I didn't know where he was. He never knew I'd been called home or that I hadn't received his letter. Why didn't he call? Did he change his mind after all?*

A light tap on the door roused her from her reverie, and she heard Rob's concerned voice. "Sheryl, are you OK? Can I come in?"

Reaching for some tissues, Sheryl invited him to come in. "Did you know about this?" she inquired, handing him the ticket and the letter.

Rob frowned at the ticket and then, glancing at the closing and signature, asked tentatively, "Is it OK if I read this? Looks kinda personal."

"Yes, please. So much time has passed, and I don't understand."

After perusing the letter, he commented, "I always thought you and Deacon were meant to be together. I wasn't sure why it didn't work out."

"I never got this letter, for one thing. Did you know anything about it? Did you know Tiff had it? It must have come while I was in Crocus Plains when my dad was sick. Why didn't she give it to me?"

"Once when we were talking on the phone, Deke mentioned something about a ticket and wanting you to come out, but I never knew he'd actually sent it. I didn't know Tiff had it, either. She probably knew better than to tell me. I'd have tried to get her to hand it over."

"Why would she hide it? Did she not want me to have any happiness? I always thought she had an interest in Deacon, and she acted a little jealous at times." Catching herself, she looked apologetically at Rob. "Oh, I'm sorry, Rob. I shouldn't have said that."

"It's OK. I kind of knew Tiff had ambitions to get a rising star, but in the end, she settled for me."

"And she was lucky to have you. She seemed happy with her life with you and the girls all these years. Do you know if Deacon ever called?"

"I was visiting at your dorm while you were still up north before graduation, and she got a call. I think it was Deacon. I heard her say you'd moved back to Manitoba and were going to make a life for yourself there. When she got off the phone, I told her she knew that wasn't the truth. She made up some story about wanting to protect you from the big bad jock who'd eventually forget about the little prairie girl. Her motives seemed right, but I always sensed the green-eyed monster had a little to do with it."

"Why did you never say anything to me about the call or what Deacon had said to you about the ticket?"

Chastised, Rob hung his head and confessed. "I'm sorry, Sheryl. I was head over heels in love with Tiff. I'd have done anything to keep in her good graces. But by not saying anything, I guess I destroyed my best friend and his best girl's lives."

Sheryl got up from her chair and hugged Rob. "It's OK, buddy. I know what it's like to be so in love you'd do anything for the object of your dreams." *I remember a certain embarrassing trip to my family doctor to get on the pill.* "It's water under the bridge now, and Deacon certainly moved on easily enough. He never lacked for female companions."

"Yeah," Rob agreed, "but did you ever wonder why he never settled down with one? I always thought Deke was the marrying type."

Sheryl shrugged. "Maybe we never really do know another person."

"Maybe," Rob once again agreed, wondering if he had ever really known Tiffany.

On the trip back to North Dakota the next day, Sheryl mulled over all that had been revealed. *What do I do now? Maybe Alfred, Lord Tennyson was right. "'Tis better to have loved and lost than never to have loved at all." Hmmm. And then again, maybe not.*

# CHAPTER
# TWELVE

*B*ack at the University of North Dakota in Grand Forks, Sheryl began to assess her life, where she'd been, where she was now, and where she wanted to go from there. *I don't think I can stay here at UND now that I know what could have been. It has too many memories rolled up with Deacon. I'm at a crossroads, but where will I go? What will I do?*

It was the end of the spring semester. While she went through the motions of all that the end of the semester and school year brought, she continued to reflect on her future and what was next for her. She had tenure at UND, so it was tempting to just stay on, where she was comfortable and secure. *What good is comfort and security when life could have been so much more?*

She had always wanted to write fiction, but somehow she'd never gotten around to getting started. Maybe she could take some time to do that. She had some savings and good investments, but being in midlife, she was probably too young to just focus on writing with the blind faith that she would get published and be able to support herself from writing alone.

During one of her life-analyzing sessions, Sheryl remembered her time at Masset on the Queen Charlotte Islands when she'd visited J.D. and his family there after Deacon seemed to be out of the picture for her. She'd loved those remote islands with the towering spruce and cedar, rugged ocean beaches, the culture of the Haida

First Nation, and the variety of transplanted people. She had felt at peace there. With limited shopping and entertainment, it had seemed a fertile ground for a bookstore and coffee shop—two of her favorite things! She had wondered why no one had opened one.

*Well now, there's a thought. Could I really do it? I'm not a business major. But what a great place for solitude and some serious writing, too. There's nothing holding me here. I haven't committed to any major projects or committees for the next year at the university. I never really see my brother anymore. His kids are grown, and after moving so often around Canada and for overseas deployments with the Canadian Armed Forces, he and Stella spend their winters in Arizona and summers at their cabin at Clear Lake in Manitoba. The folks have been gone a long time, too. There's nothing stopping me except my own chicken heart. That does it.* Sheryl resolved to investigate the prospect over the summer, and to make her move in the fall if it seemed feasible.

And it was. Throughout the fall, she worked out all the details of leasing an empty building, furnishing it with tables and chairs, hiring some high school boys from the shop classes to build bookshelves, and contacting new and used book distributers and barista suppliers. By spring, she was ready to open Dr. Shirlee's Books 'n' Brew, taking the name Dr. Shirlee from *Straight Talk*, an old Dolly Parton movie.

Through all the arrangements over the fall and winter, she'd gotten acquainted with some of the locals, like Gus Davis, who operated the airport, and his young wife, Maggie. In fact, she had boarded with his parents temporarily when she'd first come to the islands. Two of her favorites were Connor Ferguson and Willow Shaw, half brother and sister. In their late teens, they'd lost their parents in a plane crash, and Sheryl became sort of a surrogate parent to them, often acting as a sounding board. The name Dr. Shirlee fit, as the character from the movie gave advice over the radio, and soon that's what they began calling her just for fun. It wasn't long before everyone in Masset used her nickname, and soon no one remembered her real name.

Over the years, newcomers to the island like those doing their tour at the base soon found and fell in love with the shop and Dr. Shirlee. Dr. Stephen and Aimée Parker were two, as well as the young English schoolteacher, Libby Campbell, whom she'd mentored when Libby first came to the islands. Libby had fallen in love with Connor Ferguson and married him. The four young folks had settled into life on the Charlottes, and had started their families there. They were regulars at Dr. Shirlee's Books 'n' Brew.

Sheryl had continued to follow Deacon's career as he moved from the Vancouver Canucks to other NHL teams, the highlight being his time with teams who had won the Stanley Cup. He, however, returned to the Canucks, where his national career had begun for his final couple of years, and Sheryl knew Deacon had retired from the NHL. Even though he was still a skilled player, he had reached an age where he was getting too old for such a physical sport, and it was time to move over for the younger players. She wasn't sure where he had gone after retirement nor what he was doing, but she knew he wasn't in British Columbia when she made her move to the Charlottes to begin her own new venture. She hadn't needed to worry about running into him.

Now, years later, here in her own little shop, Sheryl was looking into those grey bedroom eyes of the man she'd loved and lost. "Deacon?" she whispered. "What are you doing here?"

"I'm here on the goodwill tour with the Canucks," he replied.

"With the Canucks! How can that be? You're too old to play hockey."

"Thanks a lot," he laughed and beamed that old familiar smile. "I think we have a lot of catching up to do. Is there someplace we can go to talk?"

Still stunned, she replied, "Yes, my cottage isn't far from here. We can walk. I just have to let my assistant know."

Deacon followed her every move as she stuck her head in the doorway of the storeroom and asked Carla to cover the shop for her for an hour…or two.

Meanwhile, Libby and Aimée's coffees were getting cold as they watched, fascinated by the developing scenario. As Sheryl and Deacon left the shop, the two women looked at one another in wonder. Aimée broke their stunned silence. "Who was that? Why did Shirlee look so shocked to see him? Did you see how he watched her while she talked to Carla?"

Shaking her head, Libby agreed. "As usual, you are full of curiosity and questions that I certainly can't answer. I think our Shirlee has a life we don't know about."

"I think she's got some 'splainin' to do, Lucy!" Aimée quipped, giving her best Desi Arnaz imitation. She smiled at the prospect of Shirlee having a secret life.

# CHAPTER
# THIRTEEN

"This way," Sheryl directed Deacon. "We can walk to my place. It's just down the road and over in a bay off the harbor. In fact, it truly just became my place this morning when I signed the papers for its purchase." *How ironic that I signed my real full name this morning for the first time in years, and here is Deacon who knows me by no other.*

"So you've settled here permanently? How long have you been here? What were you doing before? Why did you come here?"

"That's a lot of questions," Sheryl said aloud, then thought, *I could ask the same ones about you.* She gave him a quick synopsis. "I've been here about twenty years. I taught high school English in Manitoba for a few years, then I went back to the University of North Dakota, got my master's and PhD, and taught for a while there." Sheryl hesitated before responding further. "Guess I came here for a change. I'd visited my brother when he was posted here."

"That's quite a change, going into semi-isolation." Deacon frowned.

"What about you? What have you been doing since retirement?" Sheryl asked, quickly diverting the focus away from herself and her reasons for needing a change.

"Perhaps you remember my telling you when I left UND early for the Rochester Americans that I could always finish my business degree later. And that's what I did. I returned to the university"—he sucked in his breath and licked his bottom lip—"about twenty years ago. I then got my master's in Marketing and came back to the Canucks as their marketing manager. So that's what I've been doing since I'm 'too old to play,' as you so nicely reminded me," he teased.

*Twenty years ago. I just missed him. Again,* Sheryl thought.

"Well, we're here," she announced, walking up a pathway to a lovely little cedar cottage. "I had boarded with a family for a while when I first came, then rented a PMQ—er, Private Married Quarters—after the station stood down and greatly downsized its personnel, but I didn't really need a two-story house and full basement for just me. A young friend of mine who taught at the high school rented this cottage from a retired captain during the school year. She fell in love with a young doctor on the island, and after they married, she moved into his log home on the Tlell River. I took over renting the place, as the owners were spending fewer and fewer summers here. When they decided to sell, I decided to buy. It suits my purposes very well."

Stepping inside, Deacon surveyed the open, cozy space that encompassed the kitchen and a combination den/sitting area, centered by a stone fireplace. He smiled. "It looks just like you."

"Oh, old, round, and dumpy?" Sheryl, the master of self-deprecation, laughed.

"No. Warm and comfortable," he suggested, looking deep into her eyes.

*Oh my God, those eyes. How can he still do this to me?* Sheryl quickly looked away and moved around him to the kitchen. "Can I offer you coffee? It's sort of my specialty."

"I'm afraid I don't drink coffee. Water would be fine."

"Still looking after that bod of yours, eh?" She coughed. "I mean, you still eat healthily. Good for you. I do have lemonade. It might be more refreshing on such a warm day," Sheryl continued, her cheeks flushing pink.

Amused at her discomfort, Deacon grinned as he responded, "Yeah, I try to look after this old self. Lemonade would be fine."

After pouring two cold glasses of lemonade over ice, she moved toward the back door. "Let's sit on the porch and continue to catch up." Turning to him, Sheryl asked, "Won't you be missed at the Haida ceremony out at Old Massett?"

"I think they'll be fine without me for a while," he said, holding the door open for Sheryl, but just enough that she had to turn to face him and squeeze through, brushing ever so slightly against him. Places she thought she'd long forgotten tightened. He too sucked in his breath before he continued. "I have to be back by five, though, when we have to meet the charter flight to Vancouver tonight."

Trying to distract herself from the physical awkwardness, she laughed, "Oh, the big hockey player's afraid to take a floatplane to Prince Rupert to catch a jet? You're lucky they're not still using the Goose. Now there's an experience for you!"

"No smarty, there's too many of us for the pontoon planes. Our charter can get us right into Vancouver from Sandspit. Hey, I understand they're building a new airport with an asphalt runway that can accommodate a 737. Soon you'll be able to take a direct flight in and out of Masset to Vancouver." Deacon's face brightened at the thought.

Their hands brushed as he took his lemonade from her and sat in one of the willow rocking chairs. Still feeling the touch of his fingers upon hers, Sheryl sat in the other one and avoided looking at him.

Gazing at the rippling water of the bay and breathing in the scent of cedar, Deacon commented, "It's so calm and peaceful here. A person could lose himself here."

"And many have," Sheryl replied. "When I first saw you today, my whole past life passed in front of my eyes. It was like a hockey play under review, being replayed on a huge Jumbotron. But instead of hockey, it was my life."

Deacon turned sharply toward her. "OK, Sheryl, enough tiptoeing around here. Why did you really come to this remote place? Why didn't you come to me when I sent you the ticket? Why didn't you call me back?"

He paused a moment and took a sip of lemonade, then went on. "I waited for you. I thought we were going to get married. What happened? Tiff said you had gone home to Manitoba and weren't interested in a hockey life. I just couldn't believe her."

"Again with all the questions." Sheryl sighed, took a breath, and said, "And you shouldn't have believed her. Have you talked to Rob Black at all over the years?"

"Not often, I'm sorry to say. We kind of lost touch. I tried, but he always seemed reluctant to carry on our friendship. I was kind of surprised he married Tiff."

"Don't think he had much of a chance. She had her sights set on snagging a hockey player. She didn't quite get the prize, but Rob was the next best thing."

Deacon looked at her quizzically, eyebrows drawn together. "What do you mean?"

"Never mind. Anyway, *twenty* years ago," she emphasized, "Tiffany died of ovarian cancer. I went to her funeral and helped Rob and the girls. The twins were going through her things and ran across a letter addressed to me, and they thought I should have it." She took a breath and looked directly at him. "It was your letter, Deacon. The one with the plane ticket to Vancouver. I never got it."

Deacon looked at her, dumbstruck, then managed to say, "What? I don't understand."

"My dad had a heart attack after I finished exams, and I went home for a while. Your letter came while I was gone, and Tiff chose not to give it to me when I returned for graduation. Meanwhile, a letter I had written to you at Rochester was returned to me because there was no forwarding address, so I knew nothing about your move out to Seattle. Until I read the letter, I didn't know you were going to call me." She looked away for a moment, then continued. "I never got that call."

"Oh my God, Sheryl. I can't believe this! When I called, that's when Tiffany said you'd gone home and weren't coming back, and that you weren't interested in me anymore. Why would she do that?"

"Rob and I discussed that after her funeral. He said Tiffany always insisted she was trying to protect me from a hard life in the spotlight and all the attention you would get from the many women chasing you. She had also told me that probably the reason I hadn't heard from you was that you were being swamped by attractive females wanting to give you everything I wasn't. I always felt Tiff really had her sights set on you for herself, and when that wasn't going to happen, well, she didn't want me to have you, either. Although he didn't want to believe it, Rob eventually agreed with me."

"Sheryl, I can hardly absorb all of this. You said you found out twenty years ago. Is that when you came here?"

Nodding her head in the affirmative, she continued. "I lost you once, Deacon, thinking you no longer wanted me. When I read your letter and realized what had happened, I felt like I had lost you all over again. I was back at UND by then, where in our youth we had loved and lost the first time. I just couldn't stay there. So, I guess you could say I did escape to lose myself somewhere so remote I could forget the past. Now I'm finding out that I just missed you again when you came back for your degree. Fate has played some nasty tricks on us."

"Yes, along with a little help from Tiffany. Sorry, guess I shouldn't speak ill of the dead."

"And here you are again." *Why must this man continually interrupt my equilibrium? Yes, he literally makes me dizzy.*

"Yes, I am here." He turned in his chair to face her, and taking her hand, he confessed, "And those old feelings are stirring again. They haven't gone away. Don't deny it, Sheryl. I know you're feeling it, too. It's not too late. We can be together again."

It was nearing five o'clock, and they rose from their comfortable chairs on the porch and moved indoors, where they faced one another. Looking up into those grey hooded eyes, Sheryl admitted, "Yes, Deacon, I do feel it. But a lot of years have passed, and we are both different people now. We can't jump into anything too quickly."

"Yeah," Deacon agreed, "but we're not getting any younger! We've gotta make hay while the sun still shines," he laughed. "No, I'm just teasing. I know what you're saying. We can take our time getting to know one another all over again. Is that a deal?"

"Yes, that's a deal," Sheryl replied, holding out her right hand to shake his.

Deacon moved a little closer to her. "Shall we seal it with a kiss?"

Sheryl dropped her hand and replied, skepticism tinging her tone, "I think I said that once to you, and look what happened."

"Sheryl, that was in the Dark Ages. We can't lose track of one another so easily these days. We have email, texting, and cell phones, so we can be in constant contact. I have to go now, but I intend to return to the Charlottes for visits, and I want you to come to Vancouver. Please tell me you want to try," Deacon pleaded.

"I'd be lying if I tried to deny it. Now, where's that kiss?!"

Deacon drew her into his arms, and his mouth sought hers. Their bodies were older, but there was a comfortableness about them along with the sensations of long-ago young love.

# CHAPTER
# FOURTEEN

*I*t was Sunday afternoon. Having returned home from church services in the morning, Libby and Aimée left their guys at home and made a beeline for Dr. Shirlee's Books 'n' Brew. As Aimée had said the day before when the young women witnessed the interaction between their friend and the handsome man and then their leaving the shop together, Shirlee had some 'splainin' to do.

Bursting into the shop, Aimée demanded with her typical enthusiasm, "Who was that gorgeous man in here yesterday? Why did you look so shell-shocked? Why did you leave with him?"

Expecting this interrogation from her young friends, Shirlee smiled and replied, "And good afternoon to you, too, ladies."

Libby interjected, "Sorry, Shirlee. You know Aimée's like a whirlwind. Forgive us, but we really are curious about yesterday. We were a little concerned about you, too."

"You're forgiven, and don't call me Shirlee."

It was the girls' turn to look shocked at her reference to the old line from *Airplane.*

Shirlee chuckled at their reaction. "Yes, I will explain. It looks like it's going to be a typically quiet Sunday afternoon, so why don't I make us all our favorite beverages, and we'll sit down while I tell you my story."

After they settled comfortably at a table, Shirlee began by first telling them her name was really Sheryl Leigh, and how by default everyone had adopted the name Shirlee for her. After explaining who Deacon was and describing their young lost love, Sheryl surveyed the faces of her young friends absorbing all this information. *Once again, my life has become a play under review.*

Looking at Sheryl from a whole new perspective, tears rolled down their cheeks at her sad lost love story. Wiping away tears, Libby reached for Sheryl's hand and choked out, "Connor mentioned that his hockey hero, Deacon Cross, was here, and he was disappointed that he left before Connor could get his autograph. But you, Shirlee…er…Sheryl, have lost so much more."

"I don't think I'll ever get used to calling you 'Sheryl,'" Aimée stated. "But you're getting together again, aren't you? You have a second chance. He's so hot! Did you . . .you know, get it on?"

"Aimée!" Libby retorted, and frowning, gave her friend a stern sidelong look and kick under the table. "You don't have to answer that, Sheryl!"

Sheryl smiled and said, "It's OK. But it's been quite a shock, and I'm not quite sure what to think yet. We are much older, and we've lived different lives for many years. We straightened out a lot of the misconceptions from the past, but there is a lot more territory and years of experiences to cover. So we're going to take it slow and get to know the people we are now."

"But neither of you married!" Aimée insisted. "It's destiny that you're meant to be together!"

Sheryl again smiled at her young friend's enthusiasm. "If it's meant to be, it will be." Looking at Libby, she continued, "And tell Connor he will get his autograph. Deacon is coming back to Masset for a few days before the hockey season starts in earnest. I'd like you all to meet him. It will help him understand the life I live now and the people in it who are important to me."

Libby had been quietly thinking during this last exchange, then suddenly inspiration dawned on her. "Wait a minute, Sheryl. You said you went home to Crocus Plains. How could we not have realized we were from the same hometown in Manitoba?"

Sheryl looked at Libby in astonishment. "You're right. We never discussed it. Let's see, your last name was Campbell. Were your parents from there?"

"No. We actually moved there when I was just a baby, and my brother Corbin started kindergarten there. Dad had been transferred to Crocus Plains as the bank manager."

"That explains it. I was probably teaching there at the time, but after the folks had both passed on, I went back to UND for graduate school. I never really came back often, as J.D. was never there anymore either, moving around with the military."

"Your dad was a druggist? The new owners must have kept the name for a while. I used to like to go into Leigh's Drug Store with my mum to look at the stationery. And I loved it if she would let me get a bag of cashews from the nut warming trays there."

Leaning over to give Libby a hug, Sheryl smiled. "No wonder we have such a connection, Libby. We're both prairie roses."

# CHAPTER
# FIFTEEN

True to his word, Deacon did return to Masset a month later, and in the meantime, he had called Sheryl every night. During the past few days, Sheryl had shown him the island, exploring Agate Beach, Tow Hill, and the village of Old Massett—the typical tourist tour. To understand some of the Haida culture and art, Sheryl took Deacon into Willow Shaw's shop, Raven's Nook.

Introducing the raven-haired Haida beauty, Sheryl said, "Willow is our local expert on Haida culture and art. She has studied down in Victoria and Vancouver, and she spends a few months each winter there learning more from the museums, but also teaching the curators what she has learned from the stories of the elders and the local artists." Turning to Willow, she said, "I took Deacon out to give him the tour of totem poles at the village."

"Hello, Deacon. We've all been so anxious to meet you. I'd be happy to show you around the shop and explain some of the many pieces carved in argillite, gold, silver or copper, and to interpret the Haida symbols for you. I can also give you some of the background of the artists, and perhaps introduce you to them. Will you be here often?" Willow smiled with a knowing look at Sheryl.

"I would like that very much, Willow," replied Deacon and, grinning down at Sheryl, continued, "and I do hope to be here as often as I can—or as often as Sheryl will let me."

"Oh, you," Sheryl punched his bicep playfully. "Will you be at the Fergusons' tonight, Willow?"

"Yes, I plan on it," Willow responded. "Libby and Aimée are planning quite a spread!"

"I'm sure they are. Willow is Connor's sister. She helped to clear up some misunderstandings between him and Libby to bring them together. Aimée and Stephen Parker are their good friends. They came here when Stephen was posted at the Canadian Forces Station, and when he got out of the service, he and Connor went into practice together, building up the local clinic and hospital after the station closed down along with most of its operation."

"I look forward to meeting them all. It was nice meeting you, Miss Shaw, and I really am interested in some of the pieces you have here in your beautiful shop. I will look forward to seeing you this evening as well."

"Me, too, as always, Willow," Sheryl said, giving her a quick hug.

Willow watched the couple leave her shop, smiling to herself as Deacon's hand at first brushed Sheryl's and then firmly clasped it in his own.

Driving down the one paved highway on the island to the Fergusons' place, Deacon admired the natural, pristine beauty of the area, while Sheryl explained that Connor had built his log home on the Tlell River, and that he and Libby had made their home there when they'd married and soon added little Zach.

Opening the door to his hero, Connor grasped Deacon's hand, saying, "Welcome, Mr. Cross and Shir—Sheryl."

"Call me Deacon, and thank you for the invitation. It smells great in here!"

"Yes," agreed Sheryl. "It smells like the girls have outdone themselves!"

"Oh, you know those two when they get their heads together. And, of course, they wanted to make things special for you, Sheryl. I think they've been hatching plans ever since they heard your story."

Deacon looked at Sheryl, cocking one eyebrow. "Story? Plans?"

"Oh, ignore that. They are a pair of romantics, that's all," Sheryl replied, trying to shrug it off.

Gus and Maggie Davis arrived soon after, along with Willow. Sheryl had explained to Deacon that Gus, a local boy, ran the old airport and occasionally helped his family with commercial fishing. His wife, Maggie, like Libby, had come to Masset as a school-teacher, married the local boy, and stayed, raising their three children. Connor, a licensed and exceptional pilot, had occasionally helped Gus out with transporting passengers when the need arose. Everyone having arrived, the group of friends soon delved into the delicious buffet Libby and Aimée had prepared.

Full to the brim with good food, Connor, Stephen, and Gus soon cornered Deacon, plying him with questions about the NHL and the Vancouver Canucks in particular, wanting to know why they just couldn't bring the Stanley Cup home.

Meanwhile, the women circled Sheryl and pumped her for information on her and Deacon's relationship, past and present. *Once again,* thought Sheryl, *this is just like a hockey play under review, analyzing if it's a goal or not.*

She assured them that all was going well, but cautioned them not to jump to any conclusions. At that moment, they overheard Connor mentioning to Deacon that a committee was looking into getting a rink with synthetic ice, and he hoped that his son, Zach, would be able to learn to skate and maybe play hockey as he himself hadn't been able to do in his youth. Stephen, having played hockey on the prairies as a kid, expressed the same wish for his son, Jonathan. Amused that these fellows had named their sons after

NHL players, Deacon wished them well and offered any resources and contacts he had to help them in this pursuit.

Picking up on this opportunity, Aimée immediately interjected, "Oh, and Deacon, maybe you could help with setting up lessons and coaching here. We'd love to have you as a part of our community!" She grinned at Sheryl, who closed her eyes, and shaking her head, bowed it in embarrassment. Stephen meanwhile gave his wife a warning look.

Good-naturedly, Deacon laughed it off and said, "Well, Aimée, I can't make any snap decisions about my future. My contract as Marketing Manager for the Canucks lasts until the end of this season, but I have been toying with the idea of retiring." Aimée gave her husband a "so there" look.

Seeing Sheryl's discomfort, Connor broke in with the suggestion that he and Stephen take Deacon fishing on the Tlell River the next day. "Best steelheads you'll find anywhere."

"That does sound enticing, but I'm not sure if Sheryl has any plans for tomorrow," Deacon responded, looking at Sheryl.

Trying to emphasize the casualness of their relationship to her friends, she replied, "Go ahead. It would be great for you to get to know more about our world up here. I've been leaving the shop too much in Carla's hands the last few days, so that would give me a few hours to check up on things at Books 'n' Brew."

Plans for the fishing excursion made, the party broke up with Sheryl and Deacon expressing their appreciation to the group of young people for a wonderful evening. In return, the young folks bid them adieu with affection and hopes in their hearts for this couple's second chance at happiness.

# CHAPTER
# SIXTEEN

On their way back to Sheryl's place, Deacon commented on the high esteem Sheryl's young friends obviously held her in. "Oh, they're a great bunch of young folks. It gives me hope and faith for the future when it is held in the hands of such responsible representatives of the next generation," Sheryl affirmed.

"I think they have some hope and plans for your future," Deacon said, grinning at her.

"Oh, sorry about that," Sheryl replied, embarrassed.

Enjoying her discomfort, he said, "I'm not. I think I share their hopes."

Keeping her eyes averted, Sheryl sucked in her breath. *He can still make my heart flutter. Damn him anyway!* Then she smiled to herself.

"So you said Connor and Willow are brother and sister. They don't look that much alike, and they have different last names." A question was implied in Deacon's statement.

"They are half brother and sister. Willow was just a toddler when her widowed mother married Sean Ferguson. Subsequently, they had Connor. Unfortunately, the two lost both parents in a plane accident when they were just teenagers. Did you notice the photo on the mantle? That was their mother and Connor's father. If you look closely, you can see the resemblances."

Sheryl continued, "I've always had a special place in my heart for those two young folks. I was so glad when Libby came along to be in Connor's life. She's special to me, too, because I mentored her as a fairly new teacher when she first came to Masset. She was the one who rented the cottage before I did. I do wish Willow could find someone to be in her life to make her as happy as Connor is."

"And you explained the Parkers' arrival here and their friendship with the Fergusons, but what about Gus and Maggie Davis?"

"I think I explained their connection to Connor, and thus their friendship with Libby and the Parkers. Remember when I said I had boarded for a while when I first came? Well, that was with Gus's parents. Their boys had all grown up and were out of the nest and starting families of their own, so they had the space. So now you know the background of all my young friends who've become my adopted family. I think they think of me as another mother. I'm very lucky."

"No," Deacon objected. "I think they think of you as a beloved big sister. You are lucky, and so are they."

By this time, they'd arrived at Sheryl's cottage. "Would you like to come in for a while, Deacon, or do you want to get back to the hotel to sleep? I really am sorry you can't stay here, but I'm afraid there's only the one bedroom." Her voice trailed off a bit at this last word.

"Sure, I'll come in for a while if *you're* up for it," he declared with a twinkle in his eye.

*Now, what does he mean by that?* Sheryl wondered as she said, "OK," and hopped out of his rental car.

As they entered the cottage, Sheryl steered the conversation in another direction. "I noticed the guys ogling your Stanley Cup ring. I'm sure they were impressed, but what I wanted to tell them was I was most proud of your winning the Lady Byng Trophy several years for gentlemanly conduct on the ice."

"How did you know that?" Deacon asked, startled.

"Silly, I followed your career. In fact," she added sheepishly, "I kept a scrapbook. By the newspaper reports, it sounds like you were a gentleman on and off the ice. It didn't surprise me. I always knew you were."

"You're kidding! A scrapbook? Seriously?"

"Yes, seriously," Sheryl laughed as she pulled the book of memories out of a drawer.

Flipping through it, Deacon was both pleased and embarrassed, the latter especially when his name was linked with some female. He also noted that she had been clipping items about the University of North Dakota and its controversy over the Fighting Sioux nickname and logo. "I remember our discussion years ago, Sheryl, about the concern for the name and perhaps some reasons why it might be changed. I think you were right, and I think they are headed in that direction. Guess I'm still a little conflicted about it, but I do understand."

"Time changes things, and we gain different perspectives on a lot of things as we age," Sheryl commented while pouring them each a glass of red wine. *Not the least of which is where are we going with our relationship, and do I want to go there?*

Sheryl then led Deacon to the porch, where they gazed at the full moon glistening across the calm bay water. Sipping from her goblet, she sighed, "It's a beautiful night, and that moon! What a beautiful sight!"

"A sight for sore eyes, I'd say," Deacon stated, looking directly at Sheryl rather than the moon. Startled, she looked up at him. Gazing into her eyes, he continued. "You were a knockout, Sheryl, when we were in college, with your long honey-blond hair and crystal-blue eyes. You are even more beautiful to me now. Those eyes are still a sparkling blue, and full of life along with its wisdom. And in the moonlight, your hair still glistens." As he said the latter, he ran his fingers up her temple and through the hair that fell across her brow.

Sheryl shivered at his touch, and trying to regain her composure, laughed off his comment. "I'm afraid it's the silver running through my once golden locks that makes it glisten now."

Taking her wine goblet and his own, Deacon set them on the small wooden table between the willow rocking chairs. Turning back to her, he stroked her cheek and slipped his hand around the back of her neck, pulling her upturned face towards his own as he wrapped his other hand and arm around her waist and pulled her to him. "You're sidestepping the obvious, Sheryl, and avoiding the inevitable. We may have just found one another again, but we both know our love for one another has been there in our lives all these years." Not giving her a chance to reply, he leaned into her and brushed her lips with his, then searched her mouth more deeply.

Sheryl did not pull away and gave in to her own longing. "Can we really do this, Deacon? Can we make it work?"

"I'm sure we can. We both want it, and we bring maturity to it, not just passion."

"Passion, hmmm . . ." Deacon kissed her again before she could go further. Sheryl felt the longing. "Yes, passion." She grinned. "Speaking of which, do you want to stay tonight?"

"Really? Are you sure? Will we remember how?"

"Yes, I'm sure. I don't know if we'll remember how. It'll be like starting over. If you recall, we barely got to third base." She laughed.

"Third base? What's with the baseball metaphors? You know I don't understand that boring sport," he retorted, also laughing. "Were we really so innocent?"

"Well, it was the times. We were barely out of the sixties. I know it was the time of love, sex, and rock 'n' roll, but that wasn't for you and me. Well, maybe the rock 'n' roll. You were respectful, and though I wanted you, I found it too embarrassing to seek out going on the pill. As you know, in those days, the big fear was getting pregnant. When I went home after Dad had his heart attack,

I did actually pluck up my nerve and got the prescription from my family doc, but when I got back to UND, well, you know the rest of the story."

"Another missed opportunity. Are you still on the pill?" he asked eagerly.

"Really, Deacon? That ship sailed a long time ago. No worries there!" Sheryl laughed. "How about you? As you asked me earlier, are you *up* to it, so to speak?"

"Again with the *old* insinuations. Like Toby Keith's song, I'm 'As Good As I Once Was.' Well, you know the rest of the song."

They both laughed. "This is why we're going to make it, Sheryl. We're older and wiser, and we can laugh together at ourselves and at life. We bring our longtime love that never died, but we're also bringing experience and maturity this time. We can look at the past and learn from it to make this great."

"A play under review, in other words."

"Yes," Deacon agreed. "And we're going to get the goal and make this a win!"

Taking his hand and leading him to her bedroom, Sheryl invited him in with, "Then let's get this play underway."

# PART III

# RAVEN'S SONG

# CHAPTER
# ONE

"Shirlee, I mean, Sheryl! What's the matter?" Willow Shaw asked, entering the bedroom. An attractive older woman with silvery-blond hair was sitting in a rocking chair, hands clamped tightly around a rumpled piece of paper and tears quietly rolling down her cheeks from troubled blue eyes. Kneeling before her, Willow gently encompassed the clasped hands in her own. "You're not getting cold feet, are you?"

"Humph." Sheryl attempted a weak smile at her beautiful young friend kneeling before her. "Not at my age. Not when I expected to be a lifelong spinster."

Brushing her long, silky raven hair back from her face and over her shoulder, Willow reached for a tissue and gently dabbed the tears from the sixty-plus, still youthful face, of her dear friend. With concern in her dark brown eyes, Willow again asked, "Then what's wrong? This is the day you and Deacon should have shared almost forty years ago. How many true loves get a second chance?"

"That's true, Willow, and you now know our story. In fact, it doesn't seem so long ago that I found out the whole story myself. It was the reason I came to the Charlottes. The betrayal of my college roommate prevented what should have been our lifetime together. I only learned the truth when I went to her funeral, and her girls found the letter and airline ticket from Deacon that I should have received when I graduated from university." Sheryl sucked in her breath. "And now, today on my wedding day, I receive this letter from her that her husband, our friend Rob, recently found and forwarded to me. Here, you can read it for yourself. I don't think I can read it to you."

Smoothing out the rumpled paper, Willow began to read the short letter while Sheryl dabbed at the tears that were beginning to squeeze again between her lids.

*Dear Sheryl,*

*If you are reading this, I will have succumbed to the cancer that is destroying my body and my precious family life, a life that you should have had as well. But I destroyed it for you. I'm sure Rob or the girls have found the letter that Deacon sent you just before our graduation while you were visiting your sick dad, and which I kept from you. There is no excuse, so I won't even try. I guess jealousy of the life you would have had with an NHL hockey player overcame my loyalty to you as my very dear friend.*

*As it turned out, marrying Rob and having the girls were the best things that could have happened to me. I truly came to love Rob, and I had the kind of life you should have had with Deacon. You have continued to be there for me and my family throughout the years, and I wanted so many times to tell you what I had done. But it seemed that it was too late. Both you and Deacon had made lives of your own, and telling you might not have changed anything but would have only brought you pain.*

*Now the time has come for me to meet my Maker, and I no longer can hide in my shame and carry the guilt with me. I only hope, my dearest friend, that you can find it in your heart to forgive me.*

*Farewell and lovingly yours,*

*Tiffany*

"Oh, Sheryl. I don't know what to say. There's probably nothing I can say that would ease this new pain."

"I know, Willow. I only wish she could have told me. It would have been painful, but of course I would have forgiven her, just as I do now. But now it makes me sad that she has taken this burden with her to her grave, and will never know that I have forgiven her."

"I think she does know, Sheryl." Willow patted Sheryl's hand. "And I think she's looking down right now, smiling and grateful that her true friend has a chance at that lost love you should have had in your youth. Tiffany has accomplished in death what she couldn't in life. With this letter, she has also allowed you to let go of any bad feelings you may have harbored against her for her betrayal. Now you can move forward happily and freely with your life with Deacon. In a way, it's like a blessing on your second chance."

Sheryl reached up to touch her young friend's cheek. "How did you get so smart, Willow? You certainly have a spiritual nature, and an old soul." She smiled.

"My old soul to match my old age." Willow laughed, happy to see her friend smile. "I'm knocking the door on forty, after all."

"That's still young in my book. I've felt so lucky to be in yours and Connor's lives for so long."

"We were lucky to have you after our parents were killed in the plane accident. You gave us direction and encouraged us to pursue our dreams of an education. Now, let's repair your makeup. There's a very handsome groom waiting for your appearance down on the shore of the river. He's probably getting nervous. And your adoring friends are so excited for this ceremony."

"Thank you, Willow. You are a first-class maid of honor." Sheryl patted Willow's hands clutching hers. "Deacon is lucky to have your brother, Connor, as his best man, too."

"We were thrilled to be asked," Willow responded as she comfortably moved around the room, finding the items she needed, and expertly began giving Sheryl a quick makeover.

Watching her friend moving with so much familiarity in her surroundings, Sheryl asked, "Does it seem strange to you, Willow, to be in the log lodge your brother built for himself and shared with Libby after they were married?"

"Oh, no, I am thrilled that you and Deacon are making it your home. And it worked out so well for Connor and Libby. It seems like you have all been playing musical houses."

Sheryl laughed. "Yes, it does."

They reflected a moment on Sheryl's renting and then buying the little cottage Libby had rented from the Jordans until she married Connor and moved into his lodge on the Tlell. Then they bought the PMQ next to the Parkers after the base closed, and Connor and Stephen went into practice together at the regional clinic. In town, Connor would be closer to work, and Zach would be closer to school when he started.

"And now, Deacon and I are making our life together in this beautiful lodge that Connor built. Oh, Willow. It's a dream come true for me. I do wish you could find a love like I have and like your brother has with Libby."

"Thanks, Shirlee. There I go again. You were just Dr. Shirlee to us for so long. Anyway, love doesn't seem to be in the cards for me, Sheryl. Or maybe what is in the cards is that I'm just unlucky in love. You know my stories, too."

"Don't say that, sweetie. I'm living proof that one must never give up on love." Recovering from the shock of Tiffany's letter, Sheryl was finding it easier to smile again. "By the way, speaking of our musical houses, Libby's brother, Corbin Campbell, is here and renting my cottage. He's starting as the new principal here at the high school. Now there's a good looking young fellow about your age. Some potential there," Sheryl noted, a twinkle in her eye.

"Oh, Sheryl, are you going to be like a reformed smoker? Now that you're getting married, you think everyone needs a happily-ever-after?" There was a bit of an edge to Willow's teasing. "Besides, I gathered from Libby that Mr. Campbell has had many girlfriends. Even Connor jokes with each new one, 'Do we have to remember this one's name?' Don't think he's a very good risk."

Raising an eyebrow, Sheryl cautioned, "Well, never say never."

"Enough about me and my nonexistent love life. It's time for this beautiful bride to make her entrance."

"And you, Willow, would make a stunning bride. I'm just saying . . ." Ignoring her, Willow took Sheryl's elbow and ushered her toward the door and the group that had gathered on the shore of the Tlell River for this special wedding.

# CHAPTER TWO

Sheryl and Willow stepped onto the veranda that surrounded the lodge. Sheryl Leigh and Deacon Cross had chosen to have a small, intimate wedding with their closest friends on the shore of the Tlell River that ran in front of the log lodge, their new lifetime home. Sheryl's brother, J.D., had introduced her to the Charlottes when he was posted at the station in the 1970s. He and his wife, Stella, were unable to attend the wedding. They were in Manitoba, awaiting the arrival of a new grandchild, and wanted to be available to help their daughter and her family after the baby was born.

Pausing, Willow surveyed the small, familiar group of friends, waiting to witness and celebrate this momentous occasion. The tide was out, leaving ample shoreline for the assemblage to gather. At the edge of the water, facing the lodge, Gus Davis stood, *Bible* and notes in hand, ready to officiate the wedding. Gus had become ordained online so that he could perform the ceremony. He had known Sheryl since he was in his early twenties when she'd boarded with his folks until she could find a place to rent.

His wife, Maggie, and their three children, getting a little antsy with the wait, were sitting on folding chairs to his right, facing him and the river. Sitting across from them were Stephen and Aimée Parker and Libby Ferguson, Connor's wife. Both Aimée and Libby were trying to keep their five-year-old boys, Jonathan and Zach, from wiggling out of their chairs to chase one another down the river's shoreline. This task appeared a challenge, as both women were obviously midway through a pregnancy.

Deacon and Connor, Willow's half brother, stood next to Gus, also facing the lodge. At the movement on the veranda, both men looked up. Willow watched the slow grin cross Deacon's face and a sparkle appear in his adoring eyes when he saw his bride, dressed in a flowing calf-length dress in ecru lace with a matching pearl-encrusted crocheted shawl.

When Gus gave the nod to the man sitting on a tree stump to his right, Willow's eyes also shifted in that direction. Perched casually on the stump was a forty-something man holding a guitar in position, ready to play. He was dressed in khaki pants and a blue denim shirt open at the neck, which was topped by a light tan suede leather jacket. *Are those cowboy boots on his feet?* Raising her eyes to his face, Willow was startled to see his hazel ones connecting with hers.

His features were chiseled, much like Connor's, but softened by a lock of sandy hair falling over his brow. His sandy hair was slightly tinged with silver at the temples. He looked like a fellow comfortable in his own skin. *This must be Corbin Campbell, Libby's brother,* Willow mused. *He's changed a little. I heard he was going to sing at the wedding, but I thought maybe it would be some operatic aria sung a cappella.*

"Ahem." Gus cleared his throat to capture Corbin's attention. He immediately pulled his eyes away from the beautiful brown ones regarding him and began the opening chords to "Morning Has Broken." Sheryl and Deacon had chosen this song because Cat Stevens had made it popular in the 70s when they'd first found love. Then, when Sheryl had returned to North Dakota for her higher education degree and a professorship, she discovered it in the Presbyterian hymnal. It just seemed right that it be sung at their wedding. A new morning was breaking for them.

At the opening phrase of the lyrics, Willow tucked Sheryl's arm in hers, and the two walked slowly toward the group waiting at the river's edge to the rich baritone of Corbin's rendition of the song.

There was much sniffling and reaching for tissues as the small group watched this mature couple gazing into each other's eyes as they made their promises and took their vows. They had lost so much time through no fault of their own. Now they had a second chance at the love they had never lost for one another during the years apart. At the end of the ceremony, Corbin began his version of Alan Jackson's "Remember When," changing the lyrics slightly to fit the couple's history. Then, to much cheering and hoopla as Sheryl and Deacon kissed, the friends surrounded the couple, while the children hopped around in excitement for the party to begin.

The group moved toward the veranda, where tables and chairs had been set up. Libby and Aimée put their husbands to work carrying the food they'd prepared from the kitchen to the serving tables. The other guests gathered around the small table holding champagne and unspirited punch for the children and the pregnant friends hosting the bridal luncheon.

After grabbing a fluted glass of champagne, Corbin sidled up to Willow, who was leaning against the railing. Her long raven hair flowed over her shoulders and shone sleek and silky in the sunlight. The crimson wraparound bodice of her dress with diagonal ruching was tied in a knot at her waist, from which a crimson, black, and white skirt with an authentic Haida Raven design flowed. The ruched draping of the dress accentuated her shapely body. A silver pendant, engraved with a killer whale in the Haida tradition, hung around her neck, the whale teasing the top of her slightly revealed cleavage.

"Hi! I'm Corbin Campbell, Libby's big brother. You must be Willow Ferguson, Connor's sister," Corbin stated with a grin as he leaned on the railing next to Willow—maybe a little too closely.

*Here we go again,* Willow thought, her eyebrows drawing slightly together. "It's Willow Shaw, actually. I'm Connor's half sister." *He doesn't remember meeting me before.*

"Oh, that's right." Corbin laughed. "Libby told me about her jumping to the wrong conclusion about your and Connor's relationship. She said when she first saw you, she just knew you were a gorgeous Haida princess, and wondered how she could compete with that."

"I'm afraid Libby's idea of a princess is somewhat influenced by Disney. There were princesses of chiefs in my family, generations back, but that lineage kind of weakened and died out over time."

"Well, she was right about the gorgeous part, anyway."

Eyebrows furrowing again, Willow straightened and said, "I think they're getting ready for the toasts."

Noticing she had a punch cup in her hand rather than a champagne flute, Corbin offered, "Say, let me get you some champagne for the toasts. I think you're old enough for an adult beverage."

"Thank you, but no. I don't drink."

It was Corbin's turn to frown quizzically. "Oh, OK. No problem."

After the toasts and a delicious luncheon of fresh coho salmon caught in the Tlell River, potato salad, pickled beets, and other homegrown delicacies, it was time for the bride and groom to cut the wedding cake. Willow had managed to avoid Corbin's proximity during the luncheon by sitting at a table for six with Gus and Maggie Davis and their three kids. But when the group arose for the cake cutting and photographs, Willow once again found Corbin by her side.

"Libby tells me you are an expert on the Haida culture, and were a wonderful resource for her in reaching her students from the Haida village."

"Libby did a fantastic job with her students. She really was interested in each one of them, and she tried various techniques to reach and include them all. They loved her. She will be missed, but with another little one on the way and Connor so busy in his medical practice, I can understand why she wants to focus on family right now."

"I think Libby and I have the same educational philosophy and approach to teaching. I would like to foster that pedagogy in all the teachers at the high school. With the base having closed a while back, the majority of the students now are Haida and some locals, so I really want to understand the culture. I need to figure out how to enhance the teachers' preparation through in-services and workshops. I wondered if you could help me like you did Libby."

Looking into his hazel eyes, Willow determined Corbin was sincere and that this wasn't just another line. "OK. Maybe a good place to begin would be for you to come to my gift shop, Raven's Nook, and I can give you some background through Haida art. When would you like to start?"

"How about tomorrow? Oh, tomorrow is Sunday, and your shop won't be open. But wait, maybe that's best. Then we can focus on the lesson without interruption."

*Do I really want to be alone with this guy?* Sighing, Willow relented. "OK, meet me at one o'clock at the shop. I like to attend church out at the village in the morning."

"Great, it's a date!" Corbin grinned with enthusiasm.

*No it's not,* Willow thought, eyebrows furrowing for the third time that day. *Why do I think this is a bad idea and the beginning of something out of my control?*

Driving back to the cottage he'd rented from Sheryl, Corbin reviewed the events of the day. It had been really a simple but touching ceremony, and it renewed one's faith in true love that can overcome obstacles and last a lifetime. The small group of friends were really close, too, in spite of differences in cultures, age, and backgrounds.

*Libby has been very lucky to find a family of sorts in this remote place. I hope I can fit in as well.* His thoughts then turned to Willow. *Man, that sister of Connor's is stunning. She looks vaguely familiar. She seemed a little chilly toward me. Your boyish charm hasn't worked on her, ol' boy. Oh well, I'll get another chance tomorrow.* He drove on, smiling at the prospect.

# CHAPTER
# THREE

Promptly at one o'clock, Willow heard a light tap on the window in the door of her shop. Seeing Corbin through the glass, she opened the door. "Welcome to Raven's Nook."

"Good morning to you. Oh, I guess it's afternoon already." He drank in her jean-clad body appreciatively.

Ignoring his gaze, Willow stated firmly, "Well, let's get down to business. As you can see, there is a wide variety of Haida art represented here: argillite carvings of small totems, masks, and canoes, as well as pendants for jewelry. The jewelry case also holds silver, gold, and copper pendants and bracelets engraved with art in the Haida style with symbols of the culture, especially animals, such as the killer whale, bear, eagle, and raven. You'll notice that the ovoid shape is prominent in Haida designs. It's kind of a combination of an oval and a rectangle. I think of it as an oval with flattened ends."

"Yes, I see that now. The patterns are kind of geometric in design." He paused a moment, looking at the items. "Now wait a minute. What is argillite?"

"It's a black or grey slate-like material formed millions of years ago. The only place in the world it is found is at Slatechuck Mountain down by Skidegate at the lower end of Graham Island. Only Haida are allowed to harvest it from the quarry, and carvers or their representatives usually do this gathering once a year. The argillite in its raw form is dull, but many of the artisans polish it to the shine you see here."

"How did your people get into carving?"

"Well, it kind of evolved throughout our history. It is believed that Haida have inhabited the islands for thousands of years, and were hunters, fishermen, and gatherers, living off what nature could provide them. When the European fur traders discovered the islands, the Haida found it lucrative to provide sea otter pelts in trade for goods such as blankets, fabric, tools, and, unfortunately, guns. Trade became competitive between the tribes on the islands and those on the mainland and Alaska, resulting in violence among them and one of the causes of the reduction in the number of Haida on the islands."

Having Corbin's rapt attention, Willow continued. "Eventually, the sea otters were depleted, and the people had to find other means of trade. Learning that the Europeans and Americans had an interest in their carvings, represented by the tall totem poles and their large seafaring dugout canoes, the Haida men developed their craft for trade with smaller, more portable items representing the culture."

"Did the women carve, too?"

"Not at that time, but there are women carvers and artists today. In the past, however, they did weave baskets and hats, like the ones hanging on the walls, out of spruce roots and cedar bark. It was believed, however, that the men were the artists, so the painted decorations on these items were done by them. But that, too, fortunately has changed. There are many women today who are artists and artisans in their own right."

"What about these blankets? They have cool patterns on them. Are they typically decorated with shells or buttons like these?"

"Exactly." Willow smiled up at him. "They are called button blankets. Again, the male artists painted the designs on the blankets, then the women would adorn them with shells in the early days, but then later with buttons they had received in trade from the fur traders. Now, of course, you can see some of the buttons are made from the beautiful abalone shell. It has an iridescent mother-of-pearl sheen to it. Some of the artists working in silver, gold, or copper will accent their jewelry with the abalone shell as well."

"Wow! What a long history of craftsmanship," Corbin commented, picking up a miniature totem pole of argillite. Admiring it, he ran his fingers over the smooth, slate-like surface.

"Well, yes and no. As I mentioned, Haida numbers were greatly reduced, not only by tribal competition and guns, but also by the diseases the white man brought to the islands, like small pox and tuberculosis, or consumption as it was known back in the day. And, of course, the introduction of alcohol." Willow's eyes momentarily dropped along with her chin to her chest. Recovering, she continued. "The numbers were so depleted that the many small villages on the islands no longer existed, and most of the people lived in two villages, Old Massett, or 'Haida' as it was known back then, and Skidegate on the lower part of Graham Island."

"How could that affect the continuation of the art and craft?"

"Of course, many of the artisans had died, so there were fewer who could train the younger generation, but that wasn't all. The white traders were replaced by white missionaries, whose goal was to Christianize Haida, and that meant taking away our symbols, such as the totem poles, which were considered 'graven images.' The symbolic figures on them and the smaller carvings, such as the Raven and the Eagle, represented the legends and mythology of our early beliefs, which the missionaries sought to replace with Christian beliefs."

"The Raven. Connor told Libby that represented your family."

Willow chuckled lightly in the back of her throat. "Well, although Connor is half Haida, he hasn't exactly kept up on his cultural heritage as I have. In actuality, the Haida First Nations are divided into two clans, or more accurately, two equal halves or moieties: Raven and Eagle. There are several families within those halves, each with their own lineage, descending through the maternal line. Many of the animals in the carvings on totems represent the crests of families. These carved animals often bore human characteristics. Some legendary animals were considered supernatural with human qualities, like the Raven. So, you can see the objections of the do-gooder missionaries. In fairness, I guess their intentions were well-meaning."

"How do you know so much about your heritage and culture?" Corbin appeared to be more and more intrigued with his lesson, and especially the teacher.

"My grandmothers on both sides of my family taught me a lot about Haida art and culture. My mum's mother, of course, was familiar with the Raven moiety, and my dad's mother, my Grandma Shaw, taught me about the Eagle lineage. Then when I went to university, I studied art history and anthropology."

"Libby said you spend a couple of months in the winter in Vancouver and Victoria. Is that where you went to school?"

"Yes, I got my undergraduate degree at UVic in Victoria. Later on, I worked on my master's degree periodically through UBC in Vancouver. I had opened my shop, so it took a few years to complete that degree. When I go down now, I work on marketing the work of the artists from Haida Gwaii, and I volunteer at the museums that host Haida work. It's a reciprocal arrangement, because I can educate tourists and the docents of the museums while I get contacts for Haida art."

She paused and added with a grin, "I also take advantage of a different cultural exposure to the theatre and restaurants. It's also a chance to catch up with old friends from university days."

"You mentioned the artists from Haida Gwaii. Where is that?"

Willow shook her head and laughed. "You're standing on it right now. My people have always referred to the Queen Charlotte Islands as Haida Gwaii, which in our language means 'islands of the people.' We hope someday the islands will once again officially be known as Haida Gwaii. In fact, it looks like it may be happening soon."

Corbin hung his head, embarrassed, and sighed. "Guess I have a lot to learn. Libby sent me the book *Raven's Cry* by Christie Harris. That did give me some of the background, but you've brought it to life and made it real. Would you help me run some workshops for the teachers?"

Softening toward Corbin and his good intentions, Willow patted his arm and encouraged him. "You are willing to learn, Corbin, and more important, you *want* to. I can see that you are like Libby, and have your students' best interests in mind."

The surprised look on his face at her touch and the much too enticing warmth of his skin through his shirt sleeve made Willow quickly withdraw her hand. "I can maybe get some of the artists themselves and elders of the band to speak to your teachers. In fact, the communities of Old and New Masset worked together to get a community college going in association with Northwest Community College. Perhaps we could work on putting a class together for the teachers to get credit for continuing education. I know Deacon and Sheryl have been enlisted to offer classes, Deacon in marketing and Sheryl in English or teacher education."

"You remind me of my little sister. Libby was always full of ideas. That's an excellent one! I'm counting on you to help me make it happen."

"Of course. Now, Mr. Campbell, I think you've absorbed quite enough for one day."

"As long as you promise me it won't be the last lesson. I expect this to be a long partnership." Corbin looked down into Willow's warm brown eyes.

Not sure what kind of partnership he might mean, Willow pulled her eyes away. "OK, I'll lock up now. Maybe I'll take you out to see some of the totem poles next time."

"Maybe we can explore some of the area at the same time. I haven't had a chance even to see North Beach and Tow Hill. It's a date!" He smiled confidently and reached for the door handle. "Thanks again for all your help. I really enjoyed it."

Willow nodded, then closed and locked the door behind him. *There he goes again with "It's a date!" Now, what did he mean by that? Oh, Willow. You're reading too much into this. Probably didn't mean anything by it, but why are you intrigued at the prospect?* She admitted to herself that seeing him again had unsettled her.

Walking back to his rented cottage, Corbin reflected on all he'd learned, and on Willow. *She's not only a knockout, she's smart, too.* Remembering her hand on his arm, he also remembered the warmth, both in her touch and the emotion that had spread over him. *Whoa, Campbell. Not so fast. Don't think this one is interested, nor will she be easily won over. Be grateful for her willingness to help you, and be satisfied with nurturing at least a friendship.*

*Campbell & Willow*

# CHAPTER
# FOUR

It was the long Labor Day weekend. Corbin had held orientation with his teachers on Friday, and the students would begin classes on Tuesday. It was Saturday, and Willow had promised to take him to see some of the totem poles and to visit some of the artists' studios out at Old Massett. Afterward, they were going to go beach combing on Agate Beach, and Corbin had promised to bring a picnic.

He dashed into Dr. Shirlee's Books 'n' Brew to get the thermos of hot chocolate Sheryl had said she'd prepare for him. He'd have preferred a flask of wine to go with the fruit, cheese, and crackers he'd packed, but Willow had said she didn't drink.

Deacon was behind the counter, helping out, while Sheryl was actually across the room, chatting with Aimée and Corbin's sister, Libby. Corbin called out to him, "Hey, Deacon. How's married life going?"

"It's great." Deacon grinned and winked. "A long time coming, but worth the wait. Here's your hot chocolate. All set for the school year? It'll be a little different than on the prairies, won't it?"

"Yeah, it will be. But kids are kids, no matter where you are. We seem to have a good bunch of teachers who are open to my ideas for reaching the students through their backgrounds. Thanks for this." Corbin lifted the large thermos. "Guess I'd better go say hi to my little sis before I leave."

Libby and Aimée were seated at a small table in a corner, lattes in hand, while Sheryl stood chatting with them. Walking up to the close-knit little group, Corbin greeted them warmly. "Hello, ladies. How are my favorite island women this morning?"

Aimée giggled and, looking up at him, said, "Oh, you smooth-talking devil. *Je ne comprends pas!* What's a handsome catch like you doing unattached?"

"Don't mind her, Brother. She flirts with everyone even though she's totally devoted to Stephen. Just her romantic French nature, I guess!" Libby shook her head in amusement at her ever-effervescent friend.

Corbin put his arm around Sheryl and pulled her close. "I'm waiting like Deacon did for a gem like Dr. Shirlee here," he said, using Sheryl's local nickname from her coffee shop and used bookstore. "He says she was worth the wait, so I can wait for mine."

"Where are you off to with that thermos?" Libby asked. After he explained his and Willow's plan for the day, she looked at him quizzically and asked, "You're spending a lot of time with Willow, aren't you? I'm not so sure we are your favorite women on the islands!"

Feeling the heat rise up his neck, Corbin cut her off before it reached his cheeks. "Oh, it's nothing like that. We're just friends. Hope we become good ones. I don't think Willow's interested in anything more than that."

Patting his cheek like the big sister she was to everyone, Sheryl said, "Don't dismiss the idea completely. I think Willow is capable of great love. Like I cautioned Connor about Libby, don't rush her. Willow's had some challenges, but she's worth your patience and friendship, even if that's all it ever is."

"Thanks for the advice. I'd better get going or she'll dismiss me as irresponsible if I'm late!"

The women watched as Corbin quickly exited, then Aimée broke the silence. "Man! I don't get it. Why isn't Willow all over him? She's not getting any younger, and he'd be a great catch for her. Bet one of those young teachers will soon snatch him up."

Libby frowned at Aimée. "That's my brother and sister-in-law you're talking about. It does worry me sometimes why Corbin hasn't settled down by now. He's had several chances. I've asked Connor what it is that holds Willow back from finding someone. I'm sure she's had plenty of opportunity. Just look at her. She's gorgeous and such a great person, too!"

Both Aimée and Sheryl turned to look askance at Libby. "I know, I know," she quickly interjected. "I didn't always think that, but that's when I was still under the impression that she was Connor's sweetheart, not his sister." She paused and smiled, reflecting back. "It's funny. In the end, she was one of the ones helpful in bringing us back together. I asked Connor once why she avoided romance, and he said it wasn't his story to tell." Addressing Sheryl, she asked, "But what is her story, Sheryl? Do you know?"

"I guess I'd have to agree with Connor. It's not my story to tell either. I do hope she can overcome the obstacles holding her back. Just like you did, Libby, and your memories of Ben." Sheryl patted Libby's hand, as she had her brother's cheek. "I'd better get back to help that wonderful hunk of a husband of mine. We're truly a mom-and-pop business now. Enjoy your lattes and visit, girls."

Libby and Aimée watched their friend go back to the counter, both smiling at her happiness.

"They are so happy. You'd think Deacon would be a little bored here after the big-city life and NHL career," Aimée commented.

"He's actually well suited to the coffee shop. When he helps out, it brings in a lot of business to the shop. His former fans love to come in and talk hockey with him, and he's so outgoing that I think he enjoys it. His background in marketing is helpful for the shop, too. Anyway, I think he just likes to be wherever Sheryl is. They lost so much time," Libby added a little wistfully.

"True. I understand he's working on trying to bring ice to the islands. What a great coach he'd be for our little guys if it all comes to fruition. Right now, there's just the outdoor roller rink." Being realistic, Aimée added resignedly, "Maybe we'll have to be satisfied with the boys pretending to play hockey on ice."

"Corbin also mentioned that both Sheryl and Deacon have been asked to offer courses occasionally at the community college for the residents if the need arises. Deacon could certainly give pointers on marketing and entrepreneurial topics to help the Haida artists and the people starting up new tourist businesses since the base closed. Sheryl also has firsthand experience in starting a business."

"Yeah. Not only that," added Aimée, "she could teach composition and literature classes, either for transfer credit or just self-improvement and personal interest. In fact, with her teacher education background, she could probably assist the instructors at the college in teaching techniques and lesson planning for their trades classes. Isn't she helping with a workshop Corbin's putting together for his teachers in drawing on students' backgrounds for understanding them and choosing the best teaching methods to reach them all?"

"Yes, she is," Libby concurred. "She was a wonderful teaching mentor for me when I first came to Masset. She has this cool activity called 'Butterflies in Our Classrooms' that demonstrates the diversity of students. She used it when she taught teacher education courses at the University of North Dakota."

"Isn't Willow helping Corbin with that workshop, too?" Aimée asked. "I suppose that's what they're doing today. Not sure what strolling Agate Beach and having a cozy little picnic have to do with it. What do you suppose her story is anyway?"

Libby sighed and shook her head. "I don't know, but if this so-called friendship keeps developing, I'm going to have to pump Connor for more information. I know Corbin is a lot older and supposedly wiser than I am, but he hasn't always been smart about women."

"You may have to start fishing for the scoop soon. From the look on Corbin's face, I think it's more than friendship he's fishing for. Wonder how they're making out on Agate Beach . . ." Aimée winked and tipped her cup for the last sip of her latte.

Libby pursed her lips and tilted her head in amused disgust with her friend's innuendo. "You really are incorrigible, Aimée!"

# CHAPTER
# FIVE

*W*illow and Corbin stood before the forty-foot carved and painted totem pole rising near the Anglican Church in Old Massett. They hadn't yet gotten to the beach.

Corbin's eyes slowly scanned the totem upward, appreciating the skill of the carver and the colorful painted details. "Impressive. I don't get it, Willow. You said that a lot of Haida artistry had died out, but the carvers' studios we visited today, and the totem tour we took, and now, this," he paused, his eyes again sweeping the massive totem before him. "This…I'm speechless. The work is phenomenal. How can you say it's dead?"

"I didn't say it was dead, Corbin. I said it had been lost for a while, but after the first carvings replaced the sea otter trade, there have been two other main artistic eras of note. There was the golden age of Haida art, its most notable carver being Charles Edenshaw, during the turn of the twentieth century. The cusp of the nineteenth and twentieth centuries, that is. He was also a Haida chief. You read about him in *Raven's Cry*."

Corbin nodded his head in acknowledgement. Willow continued. "When the missionaries tried to take away the culture of our people, there was another lull in the art. Then, in the latter part of the twentieth century, there was a renaissance of Haida art led by the great-grandson of Edenshaw, Robert Davidson, who in 1969 raised this totem pole. There hadn't been a pole raised on the islands in almost a hundred years or so at that time. Many of the old ones had been left to weather and deteriorated, or were maybe even stolen from the islands."

She paused to gaze again at the totem. Reflecting on the Davidsons, she then added, "Robert and his many forms of art have become world renown, as have those of his younger brother, Reg. We visited his studio today. They began learning to carve at a young age from their father and grandfather Davidson. Their grandmother Florence Edenshaw Davidson, Charles Edenshaw's daughter, was an artist in her own right and a respected Haida elder."

Impressed, Corbin stated, "The country needs to know of this work. It's beautiful, and as you've also explained, it's so tied to the history and culture."

Smiling at his naïveté, Willow continued, "But the country does know, Corbin. And not only this country, but also the world. Totems, large dugout canoes, and other artworks are in museums, outside embassies, and even in airports in major cities in Canada, the United States, Europe, Japan, and Russia. Smaller works and jewelry are available in shops and online, and not just the Davidsons' work. Haida art has become renown worldwide. By the way, didn't you see all the Haida art in the Vancouver airport on your way here?"

"Oh, that's right," he replied sheepishly. "Guess the prairies are more isolated in some aspects than these islands. I was totally unaware of all this."

Willow laughed. "Did you notice *The Spirit of Haida Gwaii: The Jade Canoe* by Bill Reid? It's a very prominent piece. There is another one just like it, only black, outside the Canadian embassy in DC. It, of course, is called *The Spirit of Haida Gwaii: The Black Canoe*. Reid was another descendant of Charles Edenshaw on his mother's side. He's like Connor, with parents from mixed cultures.

"Reid also contributed a lot to the restoration of totem poles and the renaissance of Haida art. He took on Robert Davidson as an apprentice. Haida art has evolved over the years, alternating between traditional styles to more modern interpretations and back again. By the way, Robert and his brother, Reg, began the Rainbow Creek Dancers. Dancing and singing in the Haida tradition were a part of potlatches."

Seeing his quizzical frown, Willow elaborated. "Potlatches were ceremonies where important occasions such as naming, adoption, and memorials were celebrated with dancing, feasting, and gift-giving by the host chief to the guests. These celebrations represented wealth and status. They were outlawed by the Canadian government, but have been brought back. With the Davidsons' art and music, along with the work of other Haida, there has really been a lot done to revitalize Haida art and culture, too."

Corbin, nodding his head in agreement, noted, "I've heard and read that it is the study of artifacts of the art and crafts of past cultures that helps to know and understand them. Even the drawings on cave walls of early homo sapiens has helped to speculate on the life of the caveman. It is definitely important to preserve the art and culture of any group. When the art lagged and no longer a source of income, how did the Haida survive?"

"They were commercial fishermen, and some worked in the canneries here and on the mainland. Some worked for the logging companies as well. I think I explained the other day that, in early times, they lived with and off the land and nature, and continue to do so along with their jobs and their art. Because of their respect for the environment and its link to Haida beliefs, they have tried to protect it and have sometimes protested the over-extraction of natural resources by the fisheries and loggers. There's been some success in preserving some lands by the establishment of parks and wildlife preserves. A group of concerned Haida are also working to reclaim our title to lands and our heritage."

Looking at Willow with admiration of her knowledge, Corbin reflected, "You are giving me quite an education, Ms. Shaw, and lots to reflect upon. How can I ever thank you? I think I need some time to absorb all of this. You need some time to relax after, I'm sure, your exasperating time trying to educate this dunce about your heritage."

"You're not a bad student," Willow laughed up at him, and patting his arm, added, "but let's go to the beach. You did remember the picnic, right?"

Taking her hand from his arm and enfolding it in his own hand, he agreed. "Yes, I remembered it, so let's go to the beach!"

Surprising herself by allowing Corbin to hold her hand as they walked to the car, Willow was quiet on the ride to Agate Beach. In this unfamiliar territory, Corbin kept his attention on his driving along the narrow gravel Tow Hill Road, which wound through thick underbrush and towering spruce and cedar trees. Occasionally, a raven or an eagle would distract him as it broke through the trees and soared above them.

Finally tuning in to Willow's reticence, Corbin broke the silence and asked, "Why do the people here refer to the villages as Old Massett and New Masset?"

"You've probably gathered that Old Massett is the original Haida Village of our people. New Masset arose when the Europeans arrived, including the missionaries, traders, and, eventually, the fishermen and loggers. Then the military base, CFS Masset, became quite a presence on the island until it reduced its personnel to become operated remotely."

Looking out the side window at the thick forest she never grew tired of seeing, Willow expounded on the relationship of the villages. "Actually, compared to many First Nation and white communities, Old and New Masset[t] residents have had a fairly cooperative relationship and coexistence. Many Haida, like myself, also live in Masset. The infrastructure is connected, so both village councils work together on those issues."

Turning again to look at Corbin, she proffered, "Perhaps their relationship is even stronger now with having to work together to bring businesses and other entrepreneurial ventures to the communities for income and to replace potential employment opportunities vacated by the military. When the military left, many jobs went with them. As a result, tourism has grown as an important industry to both communities."

"You amaze me," Corbin sighed, turning to gaze into her beautiful brown eyes.

To distract him and herself from the look in his hazel eyes, Willow quickly averted her own. "Better watch where you're going." After a few moments, she announced. "Oh, we're here. Pull over there into the Agate Beach parking lot." *Don't let him get to you, girl. You can't risk it.*

Corbin pondered her change in tone. *Hmmm. I thought she was warming up to me when she let me take her hand. Now she's suddenly withdrawn into herself. I'd sure like to crack that shell. I've never met a woman like her.*

Taking the picnic basket and thermos of hot chocolate from the trunk, Corbin tried to lighten the mood. "Lead the way, my expert guide. I'm in your hands."

Willow gave him a weak smile as she put on her fleece sweater. "The breeze has come up, and it's usually cooler on the beach, especially with fall just around the corner. The dampness in the climate here can chill right through to the bone at times. Hope you brought a jacket."

Reaching into the back seat, Corbin pulled out a red-and-black buffalo plaid wool jacket. "Yeah, I threw in this ol' thing. It served me well for hunting and fishing on the prairies." Seeing her eyes narrow, he added, "I don't do that much goose hunting anymore. One of my buddies used to say, 'You can only call hunting a sport if you give the goose a gun, too.'"

Willow couldn't help but laugh at that one. "OK, let's go beach combing and see if we can find some Japanese glass balls or agates. Put the picnic things by that huge piece of driftwood. We won't stray too far."

"That's good. I'm getting a little hungry after all our wanderings, trying to absorb all this new knowledge. It's been quite a workout for this old head of mine."

"Methinks you protest too much, Mr. Campbell. Didn't you tell me that you have a master's degree in Education Administration? I think your head has been stretched before." She grinned teasingly.

"Got me. But this has all been a new experience." Walking along the beach, Corbin suddenly spotted a greenish-tinted glass ball about the size of a softball. "What's that? Litter from campers, or debris washed up with the tide?"

"You're partly right. It was washed up with the tides, and that's one of the Japanese glass balls I mentioned. They're from Japanese fishing boats, and they're used as floats on their nets. Some, of course, fall off and are lost. They eventually find their way to our beaches. Folks like to gather them and use them as decorations on nets they hang on walls. Sometimes you'll even find them in gift shops for that purpose."

They both reached for the ball at the same time, and with both their hands grasping it, they rose until they were face to face, their mouths inches from one another, so that they could feel their breaths commingle. Their eyes met briefly as Corbin considered, *Normally, I would just lean in and kiss those delicious-looking lips. But I think that would be a mistake. Sheryl said to be patient and take it slow with Willow.*

Placing it in her hand, he stepped back. "Here. Rather than an apple for the teacher, here's a souvenir of today and all your hard work educating me on Haida culture and history. Now, let's get something to eat."

As he strode away, Willow tilted her head in puzzlement, somewhat surprised at his not taking advantage of the situation. Following him to where they'd left their picnic lunch, she perched herself on the pile of driftwood while Corbin unpacked the sparse lunch.

Willow sipped the hot chocolate he handed her. "Mmmm. This hits the spot on a cool, breezy day."

"That's good. I didn't bring much. I wasn't sure how long we'd be out here, so it's really just a snack." Sitting beside her, he asked, "Why do they call this Agate Beach?"

"Well, we didn't spend much time exploring, but often we can find agates. They have such pretty colors and patterns in them. Some folks polish them and even make jewelry from them to sell. You know, that entrepreneurial spirit."

Looking off to the end of the beach where Tow Hill arose, Willow stated, "Someday we will go hiking up to the top of Tow Hill. It was formed by the lava flow from ancient volcanoes. From there, you can see a lot of the island and the sand spit. Even on a clear day, you might catch sight of the mainland and the Alaskan panhandle. We don't have the mountain ranges like the southern parts of the islands, so around here, Tow Hill is one of the highest points. We could also take the hiking trails through Naikoon Provincial Park, which is, in essence, a rainforest. And we must go clam digging on this beach or one of the others, too."

Corbin was liking the sound of "we" in her plans. Playing it safe, he asked, "Are there many clear days? Seems like there's been a lot of fog and rain."

"Oh, yes, there are some beautiful sunny days, but the mist that lingers at times is probably why Haida Gwaii was dubbed the Misty Isles." Looking off toward Tow Hill again, she pointed out North Beach to Corbin.

"Remember when I mentioned that the mythology of Haida beliefs is represented in our art?" At Corbin's nod, she continued. "Well, one of the legends is the creation story. It is believed that supernatural Raven found many small humans in a clamshell on North Beach. After much coaxing, he convinced them to leave the shell, and that's how Haida came to inhabit the islands. Actually, there's more to it than that. I can loan you a book of Haida mythology. In fact, Bill Reid and Robert Bringhurst wrote one in English that's easy to follow. Reid illustrated this book, too, like he did *Raven's Cry*, in traditional Haida art. It's yours if you're interested."

"If I'm interested? This is fascinating." Topping up her cup with the last of the hot chocolate, Corbin hesitantly asked, "Maybe this is too personal of a question, but you mentioned at the wedding that you don't drink. Is that a cultural thing or personal taste? I respect that, and I only ask so I don't inadvertently cross any boundaries."

Willow looked down at the ground. Drawing in her breath, she explained. "My father, Jack Shaw, died of alcohol poisoning. Yes, he was an alcoholic, and since I know that can be hereditary, I've just avoided it."

"Oh, I'm sorry, Willow. I've already overstepped. Introducing alcohol was one more thing the white man did to your people and the other First Nations. I'm sorry for that, too."

Silence enveloped them again as they gathered up their picnic things and walked back to the car. Corbin carried their belongings in one arm, longing to put the other one around Willow. Suddenly, her foot caught on a small piece of driftwood poking out of the sand, and she tumbled forward. Corbin grabbed her with his free arm and pulled her to his side. "Easy there, Beau—uh—Teach." It was instinctive for him to call her "Beautiful," but he knew it wouldn't be appreciated.

"Thanks, 'stu' or 'pupe'—since we're using abbreviations." Willow laughed up at him and allowed him to keep his arm around her, supporting her the rest of the way to the car.

*I'm losing my caution,* Willow reflected on the drive back to town. *He seemed sincerely apologetic for what the white man has done to my people. What is this white man doing to me? I can't let him in. Even if he is Libby's brother, could I ever really trust him? My track record with white guys has taught me not to trust them.*

# CHAPTER
# SIX

Willow Shaw's father Jack had died before she was born, leaving her mother Bella to face a life of raising a child alone. When Willow was a year old, Bella had met Sean Ferguson, and after a whirlwind romance, they were married. A year later they had had her half brother, Connor, whom she adored. Sean had been a good step-father and father figure for her. He had wanted to adopt her as a toddler, but her mother had insisted that she maintain her father's last name Shaw as well as her connection to her heritage and Haida rights. It made no difference to Sean. He had loved Willow and had raised her as his own.

She had just graduated from high school when Sean and Bella were killed in their small airplane when the engines failed over the Hecate Strait. At eighteen, Willow felt responsible for Connor, who had just turned sixteen. There was enough money from their parents' savings and Sean's insurance for their livelihood, and the Haida community rallied around them, but the two young people still felt adrift in the world, alone except for each other. This situation only served to strengthen their bond.

Brother and sister continued to live in the small, white clapboard house in which they'd grown up. Sean Ferguson had built it for his family just off the Tow Hill Road. It had two stories, one and a half really, with the kitchen, two bedrooms, one bath, and a small sitting area on the main floor. The loft that overlooked the main floor served as a small bedroom for Connor when he was getting too big to share a room with Willow. It was situated in a clearing with a few other houses, a short drive from Masset.

Later, after Connor had started his practice in Old Massett and built his log lodge on the Tlell River, Willow maintained the house herself. She'd loved the setting, as there was a worn trail to a beach along the waters of McIntyre Bay. Connor had developed his love of fishing for salmon in the river that ran behind the house. She turned his former bedroom loft into a studio, where she practiced the art of cedar bark weaving that she had started with her Grandma Shaw and was continuing to learn from some of the women elders.

It was during the first year after their parents had died that Willow spent a lot of time with her Grandma Shaw, learning about her Haida heritage and some basic weaving skills. Her other grandmother, Bella's mother, had passed on, and Willow could see that Grandma Shaw was failing, too. She felt like she was losing all of her grounding, except for Connor.

Feeling at loose ends and trying to decide what to do with her life, Willow had taken what she'd hoped would be a temporary job as a waitress in the Seegay Inn's restaurant. She'd been there a year. Folks who frequented the restaurant were locals and hotel guests, often folks who had just been stationed at the base but whose furniture had not yet arrived. It was also a hangout for base personnel, especially the young, single enlisted men. One was waiting in his booth for Willow to give him her attention. He'd been trying to entice her to go out with him for a few weeks.

"Hey, Super Juice! What's the special today?" Blaine Thompson greeted Willow as she approached.

Disgusted, she responded, "That's a lame joke, Blaine, one that I've heard way too often." When waitresses asked guests if they wanted "soup or juice" with their meal, they often slurred the phrase, making it sound like "super juice." As a result, young fellows like Blaine loved to tease them by calling them "Super Juice," sometimes insinuating more than it meant.

"The special is a Nip and Chips with coleslaw on the side for $5.00." Willow realized her mistake as soon as it was out of her mouth. She should have said "a hamburger and fries" rather than using the colloquial Canadian terms for them.

"I thought maybe *you* were the special. I could use a little nip." Blaine winked at her.

"Blaine, I don't have time for this. Do you want the special or not?"

"Yeah, I guess. But what I'd really like is to take you out. They're playing a good movie at the Mess Hall tonight. Willow, won't you just give me a chance?"

Maintaining her cool, she asked, "What's the movie?"

"It's not a new release—they never are—but I think we'd like it. *Grease*," he responded.

*Oh no. How can I say no to that? I've always wanted to see it, and there's no other way on the islands to see movies.* "OK. We'll give it a try. But no funny business."

"Great! I'll pick you up at 7:00. Where do you live? No funny business. My bark is worse than my bite. Or my nip, I should say," he responded, grinning from ear to ear.

"Funny boy. And no, you won't pick me up. I'll meet you here at the Seegay at 7:00." Walking away, she added pointedly, "By the way, have you seen my brother?" Though only seventeen, Connor was physically tall and solidly built. He was also a bit of a hothead and overprotective of his half sister. She knew no one would mess with her as long as he was around.

Thus began a budding romance between the two. Even at nineteen, Willow's beauty was undeniable, and with the year-old, but still fresh, tragedy of her parents' death, she was mature beyond her years, sometimes making her unapproachable. Blaine Thompson, with his outgoing, boyish charm, had broken through her shell and made her laugh again. Though he would have liked to, he never overstepped his bounds. He *had* caught a glimpse of Connor.

Six months later, Willow walked into Dr. Shirlee's Books 'n' Brew, looking as if she'd lost her best friend, and in a sense, she had. She sat at a corner table and put her head in her hands. It was quiet in the shop, so Shirlee immediately went to her. Since their parents' death, Shirlee had become a surrogate big sister of sorts to Willow and Connor. She'd only had the shop in Masset for a couple of years, but she'd met the young people early on and had become very fond of them. Sitting down, she asked, "Willow, dear, what's the matter?"

"Oh, Dr. Shirlee, I've been such a fool." She sniffed. "Blaine is leaving. He's being posted back closer to his home, in Ontario." She pulled a tissue from her pocket and wiped her nose. "I think I was falling for him. Now I'll never see him again."

"Oh, no, Willow. There are trains, and planes, and letters, and phone calls. From what I could see, he seemed very attached to you. It looked like love in his eyes when the two of you came into the coffee shop."

"I thought he loved me, too. In fact, he said so. But now he's leaving, and he said I probably wouldn't like Ontario or his family. I think what he was trying to say was that I wouldn't fit in, and they probably wouldn't like me. That it was over."

"If that's the case, then he's a fool, and so are they."

"He even hinted that there was perhaps a girl back home. I feel so used! How could I have expected more?"

Shirlee leaned over and hugged Willow. "Of course you should be able to expect more. Blaine suffers from a lack of character. I suppose the young guys get lonely here and want companionship, but that's no excuse. Does Connor know?"

"No, and I'm not going to tell him until Blaine's gone. You know Connor; he'll knock the crap out of him. I just don't know what I'm going to do with my life. I'd had a glimmer of happiness, but now I'm lost again."

Patting Willow's hand, Shirlee assured her, "The first thing you're going to do is not let this experience define you. You're not just beautiful, Willow, you are smart and talented. I think you should seriously consider going to university on the mainland. From what you've said, your folks left you with enough finances to get by on, and there is financial support available for First Nation students. You will have to apply for it, but I can help you with the paperwork. What do you think?"

A spark of interest shone in Willow's teary eyes. "Do you really think I could? Can I handle it?"

"I'm sure you can. It won't be without challenges, but all freshmen students are anxious about beginning this new big stage in their lives. But it's exciting, too."

"What would I study? Oh,"—her voice dropped—"and what about Connor?"

"Connor's pretty self-sufficient. He's already working on his pilot's license so he can run some cargo flights like his father used to. And I will definitely keep an eye on him. Between your grandmother and I, we'll make sure he's eating properly and all that. I think there are promising things ahead in his future, too. Connor's bright, and he has ambitions to help the islands and the people."

Returning to Willow's other concerns, Shirlee continued, "Now, as a freshman, you can explore some courses to see where your interests lie, then choose a major. I know you have an interest in Haida art, which is experiencing a renaissance, and you've always wanted to know more about Haida culture and your heritage. You've told me that your grandmother taught you a lot about both. Perhaps you'll find an interest in art history and anthropology, but there's time to make those choices."

Willow knew she would still have moments of regret over Blaine, but Shirlee's encouragement and knowledge was making that fade for the moment, and a glimmer of hope and excitement for the future began to creep into her heart, mind, and soul. She'd always admired Dr. Shirlee, although she sometimes wondered why a university professor would exile herself to isolated islands to run a coffee shop.

*Shirlee really stepped out of her comfort zone by coming here. Regardless of her reasons, she has modeled for me that maybe I can, too.*

# CHAPTER
# SEVEN

Climbing aboard the Grumman Goose, Willow embarked on her adventure. Although her goodbyes to Shirlee and her brother, Connor, were tearful, she was escaping the bitter memories of her brief romance with Blaine and beginning her physical and metaphorical journey with hope and excitement for the future.

She wondered if she would fit in with the other students, but she soon found that many were international students, much further from home than she. She'd become particularly attached to a girl from Seattle. Nikki was actually closer to home than Willow, but being from a different country, she still felt a bit like an outsider, too. The girls were in many of the same introductory classes, and were enjoying the exploration of new ideas. As Shirlee had predicted, by second semester, Willow was leaning toward art history and anthropology.

She was particularly fascinated by Professor Stafford's lectures on aboriginal art, and like most of the other female students, she and Nikki were a little fascinated by the professor himself. Though he was probably close to forty, he was young in appearance. His longish chestnut hair hung over the collar of his tweed jacket, and the pipe he often waved in the air when making a point gave him a debonair aura. Asking the students to call him Greg made him cool in their eyes. Willow and Nikki often left his class, giggling about some slightly "colorful" anecdote he'd told to bring his lectures to life.

ever after
Willow

The rapt attention of Willow in his classes, and especially her long, silky raven hair and soft brown eyes, did not go unnoticed by Professor Stafford. He soon asked her to make an appointment for a conference, under the guise of being interested in her heritage and her acclimation to university life. Nikki naturally teased her about the special attention.

Though she dismissed her friend's insinuations, Willow was, understandably, flattered by his interest in her and his concern for her welfare. Looking forward to an inspiring conversation, she knocked on his office door with eager anticipation.

After inquiring about where she was from, her educational interests, and college life, Professor Stafford then asked, "So, how are all of your other classes going? I'm sure you're getting As in them all."

"Well, I'm a little concerned about my Statistics course, which will fulfill my mathematics requirement," Willow responded honestly.

"Oh, Professor Talbot mustn't like raven-haired beauties."

Willow's eyebrows knit together as red flags rose in her consciousness. *Why would he say that? Is that appropriate? Is that why I'm getting an A in this class? Maybe I'm not as capable nor doing as well as I thought.*

He'd gone too far. Puffing on his pipe, Greg Stafford backpedaled. "Oh, I'm just joking, Willow. You are very bright, and I'm sure you will work hard and do just fine in Stats. I recognize your hard work in my class. I have actually been thinking about hiring a work-study student to help with clerical work, like filing papers, photocopying, mailing letters, a little typing, etcetera. I thought you would be perfect for that. Are you interested?"

Back on an even keel, Willow readily accepted the offer, and she was to begin her duties the following Tuesday. They had a stimulating conversation about art, and she shared with him some of the cultural background of Haida art that her grandmother had taught her. It was later in her dorm room that she reflected again on what he'd said. *I think he negated any confidence I have in my academic ability.* She concluded that he must not have meant it the way it sounded or he wouldn't have asked her to work with him.

Soon, her work for Greg, as he asked her to call him, evolved into a few Saturday mornings, after which he would treat her to lunch off campus. He took her to different restaurants, where there were mainly tourists. Few locals dined at the usual tourist traps. He was very solicitous, and she found herself being attracted to this enthralling older man. At least, to *her* he was older. It thrilled her when he passed her something like the bread basket and stroked her hand as she took it from him.

At the end of the semester, he asked her if she would like to work for him a few days a week while she attended summer classes. She had intended to go home to Masset for the summer, but by staying, she could get ahead on her studies since she hadn't come to university directly out of high school. And she was enjoying Greg's company.

One day shortly after the summer session began, they were both working in Greg's office. Willow was trying to reshelve a book on the top shelf of a bookcase. Greg came up behind her, saying, "Here, Willow, let me help you with that," and ran his hand up her side and along her upstretched arm, brushing her breast along the way. Startled, she dropped the book and whirled around, right into his arms.

"You must know, Willow, that I'm greatly attracted to you, and I think we both feel the tension we've been dancing around." He leaned in and kissed her.

Not knowing what to do, she kissed him back while convincing herself it was OK. *There's nothing wrong with this. I'm no longer his student, and I'm twenty, an adult. He has no pictures of a wife or family. He's never talked about a family, and I've never heard he's married. So why not? He appreciates my intelligence and the cultural background I can give him. We have a lot in common.*

Regardless of this rationalization, she stepped away and leaned down to pick up the dropped book. Suddenly, Greg grabbed her around the waist of her bent-over body and roughly pulled her upright. Slamming her back into the bookshelves, he forcefully pressed his body against hers. Grinding against her, he gripped both her cheeks with one hand, thumb and fingers digging into the flesh on each side of her face. He pulled her head back by grabbing her hair in his other hand, and he forced his mouth on hers. Willow whimpered a protest and tried to pull her face away.

"Come on, bitch, you know you want it. All you native girls do," the professor declared, hostility in his tone. She had to do something. Her hands were free, so she brought up her arms, and even though he was pressing hard against her, she was able to slide her hands between their chests, and she pushed as hard as she could.

At that moment, there was a quick knock on the door, and a miniature Professor Stafford burst into the room. "Hi, Daddy! Mummy and I decided to surprise you with a picnic today. Can we go to the park? Can we? Can we?" Greg quickly stepped away from Willow.

This enthusiastic little boy was followed by a tall, lithe blond dressed in a bright yellow sundress with matching espadrilles and a straw hat. "Hello, dear. Buddy and I thought you needed a break on such a gorgeous day. You've been working far too hard, even on Saturdays."

She turned then to the stunned Willow. "You must be Willow Shaw. I'm Kate Stafford, and you've already met Buddy. Greg has told me so much about you. He's a great admirer of your organizational skills and industriousness as a student. He shouldn't keep a young girl like you from enjoying such a lovely day. I'm sure there must be some young man waiting for you to escape." Kate gave Willow a look that told a whole story.

Taking that as her cue, Willow willed herself to move, mumbling, "Nice to meet you, and have a nice picnic." And escape she did.

While Greg was tossing Buddy in the air, making him giggle, Kate followed Willow into the hall and whispered pointedly, "I was his favorite five years ago. You aren't the first, and you won't be the last."

In her dorm room, Willow sat on her bed, head in her hands as she had done once before, and chastised herself. *I'm so ashamed. Did I ask for it? How could he change so drastically? After Blaine, how can I still be so naïve? I can't go back to that work-study job. Should I tell someone? Who would believe me? He's a professor. Was he so forceful with the "others" his wife referred to? Probably not. They were probably white girls. I'm just—what did he say—"a native." This must be how the kids in the old Indian Residential Schools felt.*

She recalled from her reading how children and teens had been abused and even raped at those schools. Sadly, what the children learned from that environment was then perpetuated in their own lives as adults. *Even today, we First Nations women are just chattel to be possessed and used. I don't think I can even tell Nikki.*

She remembered hearing once that if something doesn't feel right, it isn't. And this didn't feel right. *I am giving up on love. I will never trust a white guy again, and I will never let one get to me.*

# CHAPTER EIGHT

illow's words were coming back to haunt her as she watched Corbin sitting comfortably, strumming his guitar, and singing campfire songs with their nephew Zach, Jonathan Parker, and the Davis children. They looked at him with rapt attention and adoration. *Is he another Pied Piper about to lead me down a dead-end path? Am I letting another white guy get to me?*

It was an unusually warm spring day in Masset, so the usual group of friends had gathered in the backyard between the Ferguson and Parker houses for a barbecue. Libby came out the back door of the Ferguson house, breaking into Willow's thoughts. "Here's Auntie Willow," she said, carrying her five-month-old baby girl while approaching her pensive sister-in-law. "Bella just woke up from her nap. Would you like to hold her?"

"Absolutely," Willow agreed readily, taking the small bundle into her arms. Gazing into the wee infant's cherubic face with big brown eyes and a dusting of dark hair, she commented, "She's just beautiful, Libby. I'm so glad you and Connor called her Bella after our mother. When I look into her face and hold her close, I feel my mother's presence. You know, in the old days, Haida believed in reincarnation, and even today it is sometimes felt that our ancestors are reborn in future generations."

"I didn't know that, but it makes me especially glad we named her Bella."

Gently rocking the contented baby, Willow raised her eyes again to Corbin, who smiled at her as best he could while still singing. Libby hadn't missed this exchange. "You and Corbin have spent a lot of time together this past year. I know you've helped him a lot with learning the culture and educating his teachers to best put that knowledge into good educational practice, but it's more than that, isn't it? Just as you said once to me several years and two babies ago, Willow, *my* brother is crazy about *you.*"

Willow shrugged her shoulders. "Oh, I don't know about that. You and Connor have said he's had quite a few ladies in his past, and I think there are a few on the islands who would appreciate his attention, too. I'm not much interested myself in being his next conquest."

"I really don't think it's like that, Willow. Yes, Corbin has had a lot of girlfriends, and most were just that: friends. I don't think he's ever found the right one. He's just like Deacon, who I'm sure had lots of opportunities with the ladies but never married, because there never was just the right one. And Corbin seems different with you, and how he talks about you. He's certainly attracted to you, but I think he's met his match intellectually, too."

"I do like him, Libby, and what he's doing for the school here, but I just don't know if I can go there again."

"I understand, and I hope you don't mind, Willow, but I pressed Connor to tell me why you are so reluctant to let yourself be open to taking Corbin seriously and being with him. He told me about your experiences in your youth with a couple of white guys. I don't think Corbin is like that. If you were just a conquest, he'd have moved in on you faster than this. I think he's serious." She hesitated a moment before going on. "By the way, has there never been anyone from here who's sparked your interest over the years? Perhaps from your own culture, since the white guys have been such jerks?"

"That's been kind of a dilemma for me, actually. I might have been interested, but I'm not sure that the local guys are willing to take a chance on me. I never felt like I quite fit in the white world at the university, but now I feel like I don't quite fit in here because folks are suspect of my education and trips to the mainland for a different kind of cultural fix. Kind of ironic, isn't it?"

"I get it. I remember Sheryl talking about a Native American student in graduate school with her in North Dakota. He had said something similar, that he didn't feel he fit in at times on the campus, yet back on the reservation he was treated as if he'd sold out to the white man. Guess it's like you've got a foot in both worlds."

"True. I think it's better for the young people now. More have been furthering their education and broadening their experiences, so they're not such an anomaly back home anymore. They are also encouraged more in school to pursue degrees and are given help in doing that. Corbin has actually had a lot to do with that, both personally and by developing his faculty to think the same way. He feels that Haida students can bring their culture to the outside world, and in turn, they can bring back their knowledge and training to benefit their people and all the people on the islands, as well as being good role models for future generations."

"Just like you have, Willow." Patting her on the arm, Libby continued. "Aimée will be over shortly with Sophie, who should soon be up from her nap. Actually, Aimée's probably napping, too, now that she's already pregnant again. They think maybe it's twins this time. I'd be done in!"

"She's quite the gal, your French friend," Willow laughed. "She takes everything in stride. Four kids in six years and still loving life. Or, as she would say, she's never lost her *joie de vivre!*"

"You've got that right! Anyway, I must get back to the kitchen to help Maggie and Sheryl with the salads and relish trays. It will soon be time to get the grill going for the meat and potatoes. The guys get to sit around and drink beer in the meantime. Except for Corbin; he does seem to enjoy entertaining the kids. Just think about what I said, Willow, and give him a chance. We may joke about his paramours, but he really is a good guy. Remember, like Deacon, he never married, because it was never the right one."

As Libby walked away, Willow glanced once again at Corbin, who was smiling at her, but had one eyebrow cocked. *I bet he's wondering what his sister and I were in deep conversation about. Wouldn't you like to know, Mr. Campbell?* Cuddling Bella a little closer, she smiled back.

# CHAPTER
# NINE

*C*onvincing Willow that he was a pretty good cook at the barbecue, Corbin had invited her to dinner a few days later at the small cedar cottage he was renting from Sheryl and Deacon. It was the same cottage his sister, Libby, had rented from the Jordans when she'd arrived on the islands.

A cold, light rain had begun when Corbin let a shivering Willow into the cottage. "Oh, that fireplace looks and feels wonderful," she commented as she immediately went to it, rubbing her hands together. Coming up behind her, Corbin rubbed her upper arms up and down rapidly to help warm her up. "Something smells good, too. Let me get this jacket off." She quickly moved away, out of reach, and taking off her jacket, laid it across the back of the worn recliner facing the fireplace. *No, Willow, you did not enjoy his touch. Keep telling yourself that.*

"Is there anything I can do to help?"

With a sigh, Corbin walked toward the kitchenette, shoulders sagging a bit. "Well, things are almost ready. Maybe you could set the table while I carve the meat and put the finishing touches on things. If you remember, you'll find everything in that cupboard and this drawer," he told her, pointing to both.

"Mmmm. This does look yummy." Willow surveyed the savory pork loin, sweet potatoes, mini cobs of corn, relish tray, and chutney. "What's that?" she asked, somewhat alarmed as she watched Corbin bring two wineglasses to the table and pour a sparkling liquid into them.

He chuckled lightly. "Sorry, Willow. I didn't mean to alarm you. It's just a sparkling, nonalcoholic grape juice. I thought we needed to toast your return from your trip to the mainland this winter. We haven't really had a chance to talk about it. Why were you only gone a month? Libby says you're usually gone two or three."

"Oh, sorry for jumping to conclusions. I should have known you'd remember I don't drink. Well, uh, the trip," she hesitated, choosing her words carefully. "The museums are getting pretty well established with their knowledge on Haida culture and art. They don't really need me anymore. I guess the big city and its attractions have lost some of its fascination for me." *I can't tell him that the islands and home hold a greater attraction and fascination for me now.* "The shop is showing more traffic now in the winter, so I shouldn't really leave it in my assistant's hands for so long."

Corbin's head tilted quizzically, and his eyes narrowed as he raised them from his pouring to look at her. "Well, let's dig in before it gets cold."

Relieved at the change in topic, Willow did just that. "Where did you learn to cook? This is delicious!"

"Our mum is a great cook, and since I lived near the folks for several years, I'd often have Sunday dinner with them, and she made me help in the preparation. Because I was a bachelor, she wanted to make sure I learned some basics to survive."

"I think you learned more than basics." Willow smiled at him appreciatively. "Why did you leave the prairies, Corbin? Your parents must miss both you and Libby."

"Oh, they're busy reinventing themselves. They spend almost six months over the winter in Arizona now, and they have got pretty involved down there with new friends and activities. Left without family close by, I decided there was nothing holding me there. So when the position for principal at George M. Dawson Secondary opened up, I thought I could at least be close to Libby and her family. Like Libby, I can visit the folks during the summer when they're back in Manitoba, or they can visit us here. There you have it, and here I am."

Instead of saying what she was thinking, *And I'm glad you are,* Willow sidestepped his explanation. "How are things going at school? Are those teenagers driving you crazy yet?"

"No," he laughed. "They're really a pretty good bunch of kids, and I've always enjoyed that age group. Guess that's why I do what I do. I have been worried a little about one, though. What can you tell me about Joey Bradshaw?"

"I don't know Joey well, but I grew up with his mother, Lorraine. He kind of has a family story similar to my own. He lost his father when he was a baby, too. But Joey and his mum weren't as lucky as I was. Lorraine never found someone like my stepfather, Sean Ferguson, and she has struggled to raise Joey alone."

She paused to take a bite of the succulent pork. Brows knit together in a frown, she added, "I think she's had some concerns as he's reached adolescence. She's afraid that he'll get into the wrong crowd, start drinking, or get into drugs. Why do you ask?"

"I am kind of worried that he might be getting tangled up with a tough group, and there has been more concern recently about drugs and pushers in the area," Corbin concurred. "He's been a bit of a smartass with some of the teachers, trying to push their buttons. I really like Joey. I've talked to him a few times in the hallway, and I think he's a really smart kid with a great sense of humor, too. He usually greets me with a joke."

Taking a sip of his sparkling juice and shaking his head with concern, Corbin assessed the situation. "I'd just hate to see him waste his talent, or worse, throw it away. Sometimes he seems a bit like a lost soul. Unfortunately, looking for something to fill the void for such kids and trying to fit in lead them to look for a support group that isn't necessarily an appropriate one."

"Oh my," Willow sighed. "What can we do? It must be a terrible worry for his mum, Lorraine."

"I'm sure Lorraine appreciates your friendship, and maybe you can reach out to her a bit to see what she's thinking and maybe what she needs for support—without telling her we've had this conversation, of course."

"Of course not. What about Joey? I don't think there are any uncles in the village anymore to watch out for him."

"That's too bad. Kids who overcome a tough life and succeed in spite of it usually have had an adult in their lives who has taken an interest in them and maybe even mentored them. As I tell my staff, sometimes that adult is a teacher. Hmmm, or maybe a principal. Maybe I should take Joey fishing, with the excuse of his showing me the best spots."

"Sounds like you've already established a kind of rapport with him, so that might be a good way to follow up," Willow encouraged, trying to sound objectively interested. *Oh, Corbin Campbell. It's not just your slightly greying sandy hair and hazel eyes that are attractive. It's your character. Yes, you're attractive, but you have depth, too. God, this is why I love—I mean, like—this man.* Swallowing hard, she added, "Great meal. Now, how about coffee and some of that homemade huckleberry pie I brought?"

"Of course, Ms. Shaw. You have an insatiable appetite tonight." He grinned at her empty plate, which had held two helpings of everything.

*You have no idea, Mr. Campbell,* Willow thought. Tucking in her chin so she wouldn't have to look him in the eye, she quickly started gathering up the dishes to put in the sink.

"By the way, I've been wondering about your name, Shaw. Joey's last name is Bradshaw, and then there is the well-known name Edenshaw. Is there any connection, and if so, why is yours so short?"

"That is an astute observation. It took me some time to track down my father's heritage. As you know, my mother died before I was at an age to be interested enough to ask questions. Even though my Grandma Shaw taught me a lot about Haida art and culture, we somehow never talked about the name. Of course, she and my grandfather passed on several years ago. Many of my other relatives moved to other parts of British Columbia or Canada, so I kind of lost my potential resources.

"Then one of the elders thought he remembered my grandfather mentioning that he had gone to an Indian residential school off the islands. Around that time, I met the anthropologist Margaret Blackman who researched and wrote the life story of Florence Edenshaw Davidson. She had returned to Old Massett for a visit, and she gave me pointers on how to research and contact former Indian schools to see if I could find anything." After this long speech, Willow stopped to catch her breath.

"And did you find out anything?" Corbin was intrigued and gave her his full attention.

"Indeed, I did. It turns out that the missionaries who Christianized the Haida had originally baptized my father's ancestors with the name Crankshaw. Then just like I'd been told, on the recommendation of the missionaries, my grandfather as a young child was sent to an Indian residential school at Alert Bay. I guess someone there didn't like the name or something, and decided to give it an even more Anglicized version, renaming him Shaw, which is a fairly common name in Canada."

Shaking his head at the unfairness of such deprivation, Corbin added, "In trying to assimilate the future generations of First Nation people, the Indian residential schools stripped those poor young children of their cultural heritage by taking away their language and even cutting their hair. I remember Sheryl talking about Native American students in North Dakota saying their elders never seemed to want to talk with their families about their experiences as children in these boarding schools. If it was the same here, it's probably the reason your grandmother never talked about your grandfather's experience. She maybe didn't know the details."

Willow agreed. "I can't imagine children being taken from their families. With no contact, they must have felt so alone. To help me understand what it was like for those children, Libby gave me a novel to read called *The Education of Little Tree*. Reading it, I wept for my very young grandfather."

"Oh, yes. I read that, too. The author is a little controversial, but as historical fiction, the little volume still paints the devastating picture of indigenous children's experience."

"Fortunately, like I've been educating you," Willow smiled, "our culture and heritage is being revitalized. There were few speakers of the Haida language in our recent history, but those who do have the knowledge are working to bring it back and get it written down. There are more Haida also writing our story in books so that our history and culture is described from our perspective rather than a 'white' one."

"You should write a book," Corbin declared.

"Me? Are you kidding?"

"No. Not at all. Look at the knowledge you have. Not just research, but personal experience of your own and other Haida. You have the resources here of the elders to get their stories and perspectives. You certainly have great writing skills. After all, you had to go through writing a master's thesis. I know with her English teaching background, Libby would probably make a good copy editor, and I'd be happy to be a first reader, too."

"Like your sister, you do have a knack for getting me excited about things." *Oops. How's he going to interpret that? Maybe I'm just too self-conscious about potential meanings underlying my words to him.*

Her assumptions weren't too far off the mark. *Oh, how I wish I could get you excited about some things, Ms. Shaw,* Corbin thought to himself.

By this time, Corbin and Willow had finished dessert, cleaned up the dishes, and moved to the worn leather couch by the fireplace to drink their coffee. Corbin picked up his guitar and began tuning it. "You know what? We've been talking about names, and I just found out that the meaning of mine, Corbin, is 'raven' or 'raven-haired.' As you can see, I'm definitely not raven-haired, but I could be a raven and sing you a song."

Willow laughed out loud. "Uh, ravens don't really sing, Corbin. They have many different cries. A lot of them are squawks, and are not very pretty. Now Raven in Haida mythology had superhuman qualities. Besides doing phenomenal things like bringing humans into creation, he was also a bit of a trickster. And that definitely fits you!"

Enjoying the easy banter, Corbin smiled at her and began strumming some opening chords. "Well, this trickster is going to sing you a sweet song. At least, I'll try not to squawk."

After a few ballads, he noticed that Willow had sunk into the corner of the couch, very relaxed, with her eyes half-closed and a gentle smile on her face.

Putting his guitar down, he rose to stoke the fire, then turned back toward Willow. "Looks like I'm putting you to sleep."

She rose to her feet. "No. I was just enjoying your music. You really do have a rich, wonderful voice, Corbin. It's kind of hypnotic, but it is getting on, and I suppose I should be going home."

Stepping forward just as he happened to reach out his arms, she inadvertently walked right into them. He wrapped them around her and drew her closer. Nuzzling the side of her head with his cheek, he gradually slid his cheek down while with one hand he tilted her face up toward his. Still stroking her cheek with his, he slid around slowly until his lips met hers. His gentle caress over her lush lips eventually turned into a deep and passionate kiss. Surprising him, Willow didn't resist, and their bodies molded to one another.

Drawing away slightly, he whispered into her ear, "You must know, Willow, that I'm crazy about you."

His sister's words rang in her ears. *"My brother's crazy about you."* *And now I think I'm crazy about him. But can I trust him, or more important, can I trust my feelings for him?*

Resisting further temptation, she stepped back to arm's length, though not completely out of them. "As I said, I think I'd better be going now."

"Are you sure?" Corbin asked, a wistful tone in his voice.

"No, I'm not. But I think, literally and figuratively, I'd better step back for a bit."

"OK. I will never try to talk you into something you're not ready for. Promise me, though, that you will at least think about us as a possibility."

Donning her jacket and moving toward the door, she smiled and hugged him. "Yes, I will definitely think about it."

Corbin saw her safely to her car, and as she drove off, she mused, *Yes, I'll think about it. And think about it. And think about it. I can't seem to think about anything else.*

# CHAPTER
## TEN

The following Saturday, Willow and Libby sat at the corner table by the window in Dr. Shirlee's Books 'n' Brew. Baby Bella was sleeping soundly in her infant seat on the chair between them.

"What are your guys doing today, Libby?" Willow asked, sipping on her latte.

"Connor took Zach to the beach with Steph and Jonathan. Little Sophie has a cold, and the Parker guys wanted to get out of the house so Aimée could focus on the baby. I think Corbin took one of his students fishing."

Realizing Corbin was as good as his word, and that he was following up on his idea of taking Joey Bradshaw fishing, Willow smiled to herself. "I wondered why Aimée wasn't with us today. You two are inseparable."

"Actually, Willow, I wanted to talk to you alone. I've been wondering what your intentions are with my brother." She looked directly at Willow, but smiled and added, "Honorable, I hope."

Taken aback a little, Willow laughed. "Why don't you get right to the point, Libby?"

Laughing a bit herself, Libby responded, "I'm only half jesting. I think Corbin has really fallen for you, and I'm worried. He moped around here the whole time you were on the mainland after Christmas. Speaking of Christmas, Connor and I were very hopeful for you two at the Parker's Christmas Eve party when we saw you cozily talking on their loveseat in the corner. It brought back another Christmas Eve for us. And that kiss the two of you sneaked under the mistletoe. But then you left for the big city, and now I'm not sure what's up, even though you seem to spend a lot of time together. Connor thinks you feel the same way about Corbin, but that you just keep it bottled up inside."

"I remember Christmas Eve and that kiss. My brother knows me very well. I think I have fallen for yours, but I'm afraid. I don't know if I can trust that it would last and that I wouldn't be hurt in the end." After brief consideration of her next words, Willow explained, "Part of our conversation at the party was about how he hadn't remembered that I was at your wedding. I told him I wasn't surprised with that dazzling brunette draping herself all over him. He was chagrined, but still, you've said yourself that there's always been women after him. That's pretty hard to resist."

Willow paused, then as an afterthought asked, "Did he really mope while I was gone?"

"Yes, he did. And that's what I'm trying to tell you. He can and does resist if there's someone who means the world to him. Connor says the travel nurses who come to work temporarily at the hospital have tried their darnedest to get acquainted with Corbin. And Aimée says the teachers at the school have told her the younger ones have vied for his attention, even inviting him for home-cooked meals and whatever else he might like. Needless to say, Corbin would always be professional, but what I'm trying to tell you is that he wasn't even tempted in the least."

"I have to confess, Libby. He is the reason I came back early. I did miss him, too. I guess real happiness sometimes involves real risk. Have you told him why I've been so resistant to opening up to love?"

"No, Willow. Just like Connor once said to me, it wasn't my story to tell. But I think you should tell him. He would understand, and it would explain so much to him."

"Yes, I will. And thanks, Libby, for 'telling me like it is.' You kind of took a risk, too!" They both laughed and clinked their coffee cups as a toast to taking risks and to the future.

# CHAPTER
# ELEVEN

That evening, both Willow and Corbin were invited to the Fergusons' for supper. They played with their niece and nephew in the front yard while Libby and Connor finished up preparations in the kitchen.

Willow cuddled Bella while they watched Corbin and Zach play a little street hockey in the driveway with a couple of hockey sticks and a rubber ball. "Do you think someday we'll be able to do this on ice with a real puck, Uncle Corbin?" Zach asked.

"I sure hope so, Zach. Deacon is really working hard on it, using some of his contacts. But if it never happens, we can always do it at the roller rink on roller skates rather than blades."

"How was your fishing trip with Joey?" Willow interrupted.

Reaching for his nephew's wild shot at him, he responded enthusiastically, "Great! I think we made a good connection, and he really is a neat kid. He just needs to be pointed in the right direction. Hope I can do it."

"I'm sure you can. You seem to have a knack with young folks," she acknowledged, nodding at her nephew.

"I've always liked kids. Probably too late to have my own now, so at least I can work with other people's kids."

"Yeah. I know what you mean. I'm in the same boat." She looked wistfully down at Bella.

"Well, we can be in that boat together. We can always be the favorite auntie and uncle!" Corbin laughed.

*What does he mean by that? Does he know what I'm going to tell him later? That I want to be in his boat with him?*

Before she could pursue that thought further, Stephen Parker burst out of the house next door. "Corbin! Grab Connor. We've got to go. Gus will be here in a minute to pick us up."

Willow and Corbin both turned to look at him, stunned. "What do you mean? Where do we have to go?"

"Yeah, what's going on?" Hearing the commotion, Connor had come out onto the front doorstep.

"It's Joey Bradshaw. Apparently after you two went fishing, he was so upbeat and in high spirits that he told his mother he was going to take the boat out for a little while in the inlet. He hasn't come back, and they can't find him. The sun's going down, and a gale-force wind is supposed to come up after dark. They are organizing a search party, and Gus is going to take us out on one of his family's fishing boats to help with the search."

At that moment the "boom, boom" of Gus's Ford F-150 announced his arrival in the cul-de-sac. As he pulled up at the end of the driveway, the men grabbed jackets and whatever other gear they had available, and hopped into the truck with barely a wave to the women, who were gathered in the driveway, hugging their kids to them.

Holding Sophie close to her chest above her growing tummy, Aimée began to pace, "*Mon Dieu! Mon Dieu!* Let them find him, and let them be safe."

Recognizing a similar scene from several years earlier, Libby went to her and wrapped her arms around both mother and babe. "I know, Aimée, what you're remembering and thinking. It turned out all right then, and we have to have faith that it will turn out OK this time, too. Our guys are strong and smart. They're older and wiser now, too." She smiled, trying unsuccessfully to lighten the mood a little. "They'll figure out what to do." She turned then to explain to Willow about the time Connor had flown Stephen, Gus, and Maggie, who needed an emergency C-section, to Prince Rupert in the Goose during a thick fog before sunrise.

Even knowing none of them could probably eat a thing, Libby said, "Well, let's go in the house. There's a lot of food that needs to be eaten." They gathered the boys and walked slowly inside, carrying the baby girls. As she had predicted, the women had no appetite, but they fed the children and tried to focus on them to distract themselves from their individual worries.

Wanting to stick together for moral support, Aimée put Sophie to bed in Bella's playpen, then tucked Jonathan into the Fergusons' extra bedroom. Stephen and she could carry the kids next door when he got back. The women willed themselves not to think *if* they get back.

Soon, Sheryl arrived to check on how they were all doing. "As soon as we heard, Deacon and I started making thermoses of coffee for the boats to take with them. We then made more, along with sandwiches, for their return. They'll be cold and hungry. That wind is picking up, and there's a light mist in the air. Hopefully, they'll get back before the wind gets too high or the rain too heavy. Deacon is waiting down by the wharf, and he said he'd let me know as soon as there's any sight of them. I wanted to see how you gals were doing."

"Thanks, Sheryl, but what about Maggie? Where is she?" Libby asked.

"Oh, she's with Gus's mother and other family. She's become more accustomed to having Gus out on the water with his commercial fishing family now that he no longer works at the airport. Joey's mother is also with her, and they are all trying to help Lorraine cope with all of this."

"Oh God, Lorraine!" Willow exclaimed. "She must be frantic. Joey is her whole life."

"Maybe we should clasp hands and say a little prayer," Sheryl suggested, and they did exactly that.

Sensing that Willow seemed especially distraught, Libby asked her to help make some coffee in the kitchen. "Are you worried about Corbin?" Unsure if she should, she asked, "Did you two get a chance to talk?"

"No, we didn't. I had planned to have him take me home after supper tonight so we could talk. I wanted to tell him why I've been so hesitant to begin a serious relationship with him. And I wanted to let him know that for me, it already is a serious relationship." Putting her face in her hands, she fought back tears, choking out, "Oh, Libby, I do love him, and now he's out there in danger not knowing that. What if I never get the chance to tell him?"

"Don't go there, Willow. We have to have faith and hope. And love. Without love, what else is there? I'm glad you've found yours, and that you've opened your heart to it." She hugged her sister-in-law close to her, not letting on that she was extremely worried, too. They each had a brother and a love to lose.

When they re-entered the living room, Sheryl was gone. Deacon had called to say the boats were on their way back. It wasn't clear whether or not Joey was with them. With the weather taking such a bad turn, they would have to postpone the search if he hadn't been found yet.

The news was a mixed blessing. It appeared their menfolk were safe, but what about Joey? "If anything has happened to Joey, Corbin will probably blame himself for getting him so enthused about being on the water," Willow stated, head in hand.

"Oh, knowing my brother, you're probably right," Libby agreed.

Aimée looked from one to the other. "Is there something going on here I don't know about?"

There was a soft tap at the door, and Stephen Parker walked in. Aimée jumped up and ran to meet him. "Oh, thank God you're OK. What about Joey? Where are the others?"

Wrapping his arms around his wife, he explained. "Joey is safe back home, thanks to Corbin. He had strayed a little far out of the inlet into the Dixon Entrance, so that when the wind got up, his little motor wasn't strong enough to work against the waves to bring him back to the inlet. He eventually just shut it off and let the wave action bring him to shore closer down toward Rose Spit. Fortunately, the little boat struck the shore before the wind and waves took him around the spit and into Hecate Strait. He'd have been lost and probably swamped out there in that roiling water in this wind."

"Thank heavens! But how did Corbin fit into this picture?" Willow and Libby asked in unison.

"Well, Joey's little boat was able to drift in, uninhibited by the rocks and the shallow water approaching Tow Hill and the spit. First of all, it was Corbin who saw Joey flashing his flashlight when he caught sight of our fishing boat. Smart kid to have taken that with him. But then we realized we couldn't get close enough with the bigger fishing whaler to get him without hitting rocks or getting stuck on the sandbar. We had gotten as close as we could, and while the rest of us were trying to come up with a plan of action, Corbin just took action. Before we could stop him, he stripped off his shoes, jacket, and pants so they wouldn't weigh him down, and he jumped overboard to swim to shore." The women gasped.

"Yeah, I know. It's freezing-cold water, and we could barely see him in the dark and fog against the growing waves. Hell of a swimmer, that guy. He made it. He got Joey back in the boat, pushed them out as far as he could, hopped, or should I say, *crawled* into the boat, found the oars, and rowed them back out to our boat. Joey was a pretty brave young lad, but I think Corbin is now his hero."

"He built his strength and stamina through hockey when he was younger, but he was also a lifeguard in the summers at Clear Lake in Manitoba throughout college," Libby explained. Noticing that Willow was looking decidedly green around the gills, so to speak, she asked, "Where is Corbin now? And hey, where's my husband, by the way?"

"Connor took both Joey and Corbin to the hospital to check them out. Joey was tired and hungry, but he was quite happy to go home with his mother. It's a wonder he wasn't in shock. Tough kid, that one, as well as smart in using his head out there. Connor was afraid Corbin might suffer from hypothermia. He was cold, but I think he's OK. Connor was going to get him warmed up and into dry clothes, then take him to his cottage to rest. Deacon and Sheryl were sending food and coffee with them. Connor wanted to get a fire going in the fireplace for him and stay for a while to make sure he was going to be all right. We all agreed I should come back here to let you gals know what was going on so you could stop worrying."

Aimée and Libby both started to say, "Oh, thank God . . ." but were interrupted by Willow.

"I'm going to the cottage. He'll need someone to stay all night with him, and Connor will want to come home to you, Libby." With that, she grabbed her sweater and purse, and abruptly left the house without even a good-bye.

Stephen and Aimée looked at Libby. Aimée, not one to hold back, demanded, "OK, *mon amie*. What is going on?"

Libby smiled noncommittally, shrugged her shoulders, and stated, "Not my story to tell."

# CHAPTER
## TWELVE

Responding to the knock on Corbin's cottage door, Connor was surprised to see his sister standing there. "Hey, sis. What are you doing here?"

"I've come to relieve you. You need to go home and rest up yourself. I'll stay with Corbin. Where is he?" She looked around the room, which was empty except for the dying fire in the fireplace and the dirty dishes left on the table where they'd eaten Sheryl and Deacon's offerings.

"I got him to go to bed after we ate. He was, understandably, exhausted, and he fell asleep immediately. Then I realized that with him dead to the world, I couldn't leave him alone with a blaze going in case a spark flew out and caught something on fire. So I'm glad to see you, but I'm not sure *why* I'm seeing you."

"An unfortunate turn of phrase, 'dead to the world,' under the circumstances, Brother. I guess Libby hasn't had a chance to tell you about our talk." With that, she gave him a short synopsis of their discussion and her admission of loving Corbin.

"I do love him, Connor. I know I've resisted, but when I finally admitted it to Libby, I admitted it to myself, too. I think I'm ready to let go of my past trust issues. Who couldn't love that man lying in there, when he's willing to risk his life to rescue a kid? I'm ready to take a risk on him, too. I had planned to tell him that this evening after supper at your place, but I never got the chance. Then I was so scared tonight that I might never get the chance. I just had to be here."

Connor walked over and hugged his sister. "Yes, he's definitely worth the risk, Willow. And I'm really happy for you. You deserve to find a love like I have. Isn't it funny that we both found it in a prairie rose and a prairie dog?"

Willow laughed, hugging him tighter, "Don't let either of them ever hear you say that! Now go home and hug Libby and the kids. I'll call if you're needed here." With that, she pushed Connor out the door and started to clear the dishes off the table to wash.

After she'd tidied the kitchen and checked on the fire, which was now just a few glowing embers, she carefully and quietly opened the door to Corbin's bedroom. Tiptoeing to his bedside, she gazed down on his relaxed face, finding him sound asleep. The down comforter was pulled up to his chin, and it swaddled his body. Willow said a silent prayer, grateful for his safety and hoping for their future.

*Do I dare touch him? I don't want to wake him.* She couldn't resist and brushed a lock of hair from his eyes gently with her fingertips. She was drawn to him and wanted to kiss him. *Those lips are very kissable, but I better not. That can wait until morning.*

Assuring herself he was OK, she grabbed the blanket flung across the end and returned to the couch. She snuggled into the couch, wrapped in the blanket, but knew she probably wouldn't be able to sleep. *I am glad I'm here, though. This is where I belong.*

*Willow & Corbin*

# CHAPTER
# THIRTEEN

*W*illow had the coffee going and was frying bacon the next morning when Corbin stumbled out of his bedroom, still bleary-eyed from a deep sleep. "What's this vision I'm seeing in my kitchen? Is it a ghost? An angel?" he asked.

"Nope," Willow laughed, turning to greet him. "Good morning. You had quite a sleep. Not sure if it was like a baby or a hibernating bear."

"Are you suggesting I snored?"

"Oh, just a low rumbling. It was nice to hear. It reassured me that you were still with me. I was so worried while you were on that rescue mission. I hear you're quite the hero."

Liking the sound of "still with me," he responded humbly, "Oh, probably not so much a hero as a fearless fool." Wondering if he'd heard accurately in his fog, he asked, "Were you really worried about me?"

"I think you're too modest, and yes, I was terrified for you last night. Corbin, we have to talk, but first, let's get some breakfast into you. I'm sure we need to build up your strength."

*"We" again.* "That coffee sure smells good. It's just what I need." *Well, maybe not the only thing I need. Wonder what she wants to talk about.*

They rehashed the night's events over breakfast, with Willow asking questions for more details. When their plates were empty, she pushed back her chair and suggested, "Why don't we have another cup of coffee on the porch. After last night's storm, it's a gorgeous morning. You go get settled, and I'll bring out the coffee."

*Hmmm. Getting a little bossy with me. I think I like it.* Smiling to himself, Corbin settled on the back porch in one of the willow chairs his sister and Connor had sat in several years previously. It was a beautiful day, and he drank in the view of the calm water and the feeling of peacefulness that enveloped him.

After Willow had joined him in the other rocking chair, she sucked in her breath and started in. "I was terribly frightened last night, Corbin, because I had things I wanted—no, *needed*—to tell you after supper last evening. Then I was so terrified I'd never get the chance. You've been very patient with me, and I need to tell you why I've been so resistant to your attention and affection." She then told her story and experiences with Blaine Thompson and Greg Stafford. "I can't believe I was so naïve and stupid!"

Corbin reached for her hand. "No, you weren't stupid, and I wouldn't exactly use the word 'naïve' either. You were very young and innocent. Having gone through the tragic experience of your parents' accidental deaths and your grandmother's passing, you were also vulnerable. Frankly, those jerks took advantage of you when you were fragile and needing love of some kind. Stafford's actions were an abuse of power, and thank God there are policies and procedures in place now to support young women in reporting such victimization."

"I have heard from some of my contacts that other incidents involving the professor were eventually reported, and he was dismissed. I think his wife finally dumped him, too. I still wish I'd been smarter."

Tempering his anger on her behalf, Corbin squeezed her hand gently and assured her. "But I'm so glad the circumstances prevented you from being completely violated. You fought back, and you were strong, Willow. You didn't let the experience define you.

You rose above it, and you became an educated, intelligent woman with goals to educate others about your people. I can understand why you were afraid to trust another white guy, but I wish you'd told me earlier so I could have tried to help erase those memories."

He rose from the chair and stood before Willow. "I know you think I'm some kind of ladies' man, but I'm not really. I've just never found anyone who has touched me in my mind, heart, and soul as you have." He reached for her hands and pulled her out of her chair, toward him. "I think I've been in love with you since Sheryl and Deacon's wedding, when I looked up from my guitar and saw you standing on the porch with the bride."

"And that's what I'm trying to tell you, Corbin." She hesitated, but only for a moment. "I love you, too, and probably from the moment I heard the first chord on your guitar that day. I just couldn't admit it to myself."

Pulling her to him with one arm, he ran his thumb over her lush lips. She slipped the tip of her tongue between her lips to caress him. Encouraged, he enveloped her in both arms at the same time as she reached her arms up and around his neck to enfold him. Their lips came together as she pressed against him, and their bodies molded together.

Pulling back a little, Corbin stated, "You realize, Willow, we belong together. You're from the Raven clan, or as you informed me, the Raven moiety. And as I told you, my name indicates that I'm a raven, too." He grinned at his creative, if silly, rationalization.

"Nice try, trickster," Willow laughed. "I hate to burst your bubble, but in Haida tradition, a person must choose a partner from the other moiety. So for me, that would mean an Eagle."

Stumped for a moment, Corbin then brightened and offered, "I was an Eagle Scout. Does that count?"

Willow laughed out loud. "It works for me!" She leaned in for another kiss. When they came up for air, she added, "And I think from now on, *my* raven's song is a love song."

# AUTHOR'S POSTSCRIPT FOR
# THE READER

*A*s noted in the preface, "To the Reader," I lived on the Queen Charlotte Islands for two years during the mid-1970s, when my husband was posted to the Canadian Forces Station (CFS) Masset. The events of the novel mainly occur in or near the village of Masset, which is situated on Graham Island, the northernmost and largest island of the archipelago, which is made up of approximately 150 islands. Because of their misty rainforest climate, the islands were dubbed the Misty Isles. I have never forgotten our experience living there, so the islands seemed a fertile setting for my trilogy of love stories. Because I have not returned since our time there, I have had to take artistic license with the setting and events in this work of fiction.

Two significant events affecting the setting have occurred since our military tour at CFS Masset. First, in 1997 the Canadian Forces Station downsized its personnel by 90%, and it was then operated remotely from a distant Canadian base. Thus, the PMQs (Private Married Quarters) were sold as private homes or for business investments. Many of the former buildings were taken over by the Village of Masset, and were repurposed for civilian use. Some buildings, such as the base hospital and barracks, have been demolished in recent years. Since 1997, the station no longer holds a prominent position in Masset. The novel begins just prior to the downsizing of the base. Since we were not present during this transition, it has been fictionalized in the novel.

The remaining industries continue to be commercial fishing and logging, on a restricted basis. There is no longer the wholesale stripping of resources and the environment. Tourism, however, has gained in prominence, and there has been a lot of entrepreneurial activity in the creation of new businesses, services, and tourist attractions. Activities include floatplane tours, whale watching, fishing, hunting, hiking, birding, surfing, and golfing. A large part of the attraction of tourists to Haida Gwaii is the work of Haida artists and artisans who have become world renown due to a renaissance of their art. Tourists may enjoy visiting their studios to observe and purchase products of their craft.

There are also many more businesses and accommodating facilities, including restaurants, hotels, bed-and-breakfasts, galleries, gift shops, a library, and the maritime museum. A new airport, built in 2008 with an asphalt runway that can accommodate 737 jets from Vancouver, assists in bringing tourists to the northern end of the islands.

An excellent source for information on Haida Gwaii and its communities is gohaidagwaii.ca. I have friends and acquaintances who have enjoyed a vacation on Haida Gwaii, and a trip to the Misty Isles is definitely on my bucket list. It has been recognized by many groups as a highly ranked tourist destination. *National Geographic*, for example, named it one of the top twenty "Must-See Places in the World" for 2015.

The Haida First Nation referred to the Queen Charlotte Islands as "Haida Gwaii," meaning "islands of the people." The second significant event since our departure occurred when "Haida Gwaii" was adopted as the official name of the QCI through the Haida Gwaii Reconciliation Act with the province of British Columbia in 2009. Many stalwart Haida have engaged in a long, hard struggle to reclaim their culture and their land, protesting the overuse of their resources by large logging and commercial fishing companies. This journey is traced in Ian Gill's *All That We Say Is Ours: Guujaaw and the Reawakening of the Haida Nation.*

A significant result of this struggle was the protection from exploitation of South Moresby Island through the establishment of Gwaii Haanas National Park Reserve, National Marine Conservation Area Reserve, and Haida Heritage Site. For expedience, this area is labeled simply as Gwaii Haanas National Park on the map in the front of this book. *Haida Gwaii: On the Edge of the World*, an award-winning documentary about the islands and the struggle for preservation of them, was released April 28, 2015.

"Running to Forever" is the longest part of the novel for two reasons. When I first began writing the story, it was to be a stand-alone novella; however, the lives of the characters were so intertwined, the secondary characters insisted that their stories be told. In addition to introducing the characters and their relationship to one another, Part I also establishes the setting for the novel. In essence, it is the foundation for the rest of the book.

An integral presence in the novel's setting is the Goose, described in Part I. At one point or another, each of the main characters had escaped to or from the islands on the Goose. The experience of riding in the Goose was definitely unique, and although TPA is humorously referred to as Toilet Paper Airlines, no disrespect is intended. The pilots were very skilled in potentially hazardous conditions. The Hecate Strait is known as one of the most treacherous water passages in the world. In 1993, Trans Provincial Airlines was purchased by Harbour Air, which, to my knowledge, also no longer services the islands. Although the Goose is no longer in use, one can still take a pontoon floatplane from Prince Rupert to Masset.

Many of the place names, such as Masset, Old Massett, the Tlell River, Tow Hill, Agate Beach, North Beach, Queen Charlotte City,

Skidegate, and Sandspit are real and are noted on the map, but they have been fictionalized for the purposes of the stories. Businesses such as Books 'n' Brew and Raven's Nook are fictional. Real businesses, such as the Seegay Inn and Trans Provincial Airlines, referenced in the stories are no longer in existence. Real institutions such as NWCC Masset Campus and the George M. Dawson Secondary School are used fictitiously.

"Play Under Review" digresses somewhat from the island setting in flashbacks to Sheryl and Deacon's youth at the University of North Dakota. For readers "in the know," there may be several points that perhaps need clarification of my fictionalized use of real events for the sake of the plot. Interested readers can find more detailed explanations about the following events and others on my author's website: the transition for the UND hockey team from playing in the "Old Barn" to the new Winter Sports Building in the early 1970s; the entrance of the Canucks into the NHL in 1970; the Canucks' early farm teams; and the team's actual visit to Haida Gwaii in 2013. None of the characters represent real people associated with the Canucks team or its operation. In addition, the history and controversy of the UND Fighting Sioux nickname issue and its transition to the Fighting Hawks are discussed in detail on my website.

Hockey fans will also note that the reference to the Fergusons and Parkers naming their sons after Zach Parise and Jonathan Toews is an anachronism, meshing their current NHL positions within the time frame of the story.

When I finished "Play Under Review," Willow started knocking on the inside of my head, insisting that I had to tell her story. I wanted to, but I was a little inhibited by the huge task of representing her realistically. Eventually, I began "Raven's Song."

I knew I could not write authentically from her perspective, but I delved into researching Haida history, culture, and art. I have included general information that was common from several sources to bring some authenticity to Willow's education of Corbin. An example occurs when Willow refers to Raven's creation story. Mythology of the past plays a large role in Haida culture and art. There are several sources for the creation story and others, but the one referenced for this novel is "The Raven and the First Men" in a volume of Haida mythology titled *The Raven Steals the Light* by Bill Reid and Robert Bringhurst. It was illustrated by Bill Reid, a renowned Haida artist. Please see the bibliography for details.

It was my good fortune to discover that my friend, Virginia Campbell, from our Sol Writers group in Florida, was able to connect me with her friend, the anthropologist Margaret Blackman, whose research on the Haida I had read. Dr. Blackman graciously allowed me to use her as a resource and to refer to her within the novel.

While searching for the date of the Masset Campus's establishment, I was put in touch with Marlene Liddle, Campus Officer of NWCC Masset Campus. I am greatly indebted to Marlene's input. She not only assisted me in my attempt to present Willow authentically, but also clarified many details about the islands that have either changed or have faded in my memory. She and Dr. Blackman gave me the background and impetus to write "Raven's Song."

It should be noted that Marlene is a talented artist and artisan in her own right in cedar bark weaving of traditional and contemporary creations. She also teaches others her art and craft. In 2013, she was awarded the BC Creative Achievement Award for First Nations Art. Please check out the website listed at the end of these notes to watch Marlene's video explaining and demonstrating her craft. Samples of her work can also be found on Facebook.

In spite of my research and good intentions, Willow's character and perspective may still be somewhat influenced by my own. This influence, however, may also be authentic to her character, because given her circumstances, her life was also influenced by white cultural factors.

Part III, like the others, is fiction, and my first responsibility is to the love story. Sometimes I had to remind myself that the fictional story was the purpose, and even though I was extremely interested in my research, I had to resist including too much detail as if it were a nonfiction research paper. I did, however, want to give enough general background information to lend authenticity to my character, and also to pique enough interest in my readers to explore Haida history, art, and culture further on their own. I hope I have achieved these goals and have not inadvertently misrepresented this fine First Nation. Please note the list of a few of my resources, suggested readings, and websites for your own exploration following this postscript.

Since the book is set in Canada, Canadian readers may question the use of US terms, such as miles, degrees in Fahrenheit, and US spellings of words such as "color." These were pragmatic choices since the book is being published in the United States. In addition, Crocus Plains is a fictional place, representing all small prairie towns in Manitoba. The private school in Wilcox, Saskatchewan, that Deacon attended is officially named the Athol Murray College of Notre Dame, but many western Canadians would refer to it colloquially as the "Father Murray School" or simply "Notre Dame."

This book, which began as one romantic novella, has grown to a three-part novel, and it has become much more than a trilogy of love stories for me. The novel and its characters have become very dear to my heart. It is my hope that the formation of this "family" of friends that crosses cultures, generations, and even borders has demonstrated for the reader that there can be unity in diversity.

I have experienced many serendipitous moments in the novel's writing, which have revealed to me that this project was meant to be. It is said that art often imitates life, and vice versa. In my research to get reacquainted with the islands, I was amazed to discover evidence of events or businesses that I had imagined in my early drafts had actually come to fruition in reality. I describe in detail both the serendipity and art's imitation of life in writing this book on my website.

As noted in the preface, "To the Reader," the time frame of the trilogy spans approximately ten years. The time frame, encompassing some historical and cultural events and references that have been incorporated into the trilogy, however, actually covers approximately twenty years. These events have been fictionalized, and the time periods have been meshed together for the purposes of the stories; therefore, some of the dates are purposely vague. For clarification and a description of my writing process in using these events within the novel, please check out my website. In addition, you will also find photographs in the site's gallery of places mentioned in the novel. These photos were taken in the mid-1970s, when we lived on the islands. Thank you for joining me on the Misty Isles.

www.rosemaryvaughn.com

# BIBLIOGRAPHY AND
# SUGGESTED READING

Blackman, Margaret B. *During My Time: Florence Edenshaw Davidson, A Haida Woman*. Seattle: University of Washington Press, 1992.

Duff, Wilson. *The Indian History of British Columbia: The Impact of the White Man*. Victoria, BC: The Royal British Columbia Museum, 1997.

Gill, Ian. *All That We Say Is Ours: Guujaaw and the Reawakening of the Haida Nation*. Vancouver: Douglas and McIntyre, 2009.

Harris, Christie. *Raven's Cry*. Toronto: McClelland and Stewart Limited, 1966.

Harris, Christie. *Raven's Cry*. 2nd ed. Vancouver: Douglas & McIntyre. Seattle: University of Washington Press, 1992.

Islands Protection Society. *Islands at the Edge: Preserving the Queen Charlotte Islands' Wilderness*. Vancouver: Douglas & McIntyre, 1984.

Reid, Bill, and Robert Bringhurst. *The Raven Steals the Light*. 2nd ed. Vancouver: Douglas & McIntyre. Seattle: University of Washington Press, 1996.

Smyly, John, and Carolyn Smyly. *Those Born at Koona: The Totem Poles of the Haida Village Skedans Queen Charlotte Islands*. Saanichton, BC: Hancock House Publishers, 1973.

# WEB SITES

**Tourism and general information:**

gohaidagwaii.ca (excellent source of information about Haida Gwaii with links to each village)

haidagwaiiobserver.com (island newspaper)

haidanation.ca (Council of the Haida Nation)

massetbc.com

oldmassettbc.com

**Haida Art:**

http://www.authenticindigenous.com/artists/marlene-liddle

Facebook search: Haida Cedar Bark Weaver – Traditional and Contemporary (Marlene Liddle)

dahliadrive.com (note particularly Reg Davidson and Van Riesen Designs)

facebook.com/PerchedRaven/?fref=ts (Cori Savard Haida Artist))

haidaweaver.com/MerleAnderson

robertdavidson.ca

regdavidson.com

http://www.bcachievement.com/firstnationsart/video.php?id=54
   (Marlene's weaving video)

# SEARCH ENGINE TERMS

Haida Gwaii (also Queen Charlotte Islands)

CFS Masset

Haida First Nation

Haida Art

Argillite

Bill Reid

Charles Edenshaw

Florence Edenshaw Davidson

Gary Edenshaw (Guujaaw)

Indian residential schools

Tlell River

Tow Hill and the Blow Hole

Hecate Strait

# ACKNOWLEDGEMENTS

*L*ike children, it takes a village to develop a book, and I am indebted to many people for assistance and support from the birth of the first novella to the book's full growth into a three-part novel.

I am grateful to my first reader, a Minnesota Lakes dear friend, Betty Cram, who encouraged me from the very first rough draft of "Running to Forever" through the ups and downs of developing a full manuscript.

My husband not only served as one of my early readers, but also as my medical and hockey consultant. Knowing how important it was to me to fulfill this dream, he, too, encouraged me through the highs and lows of the process.

I have mentioned in my author's postscript notes the willingness of Margaret Blackman and Marlene Liddle to answer my questions with regard to Haida Gwaii and the Haida culture. These women gave me the courage to tell Willow's story.

I have been inspired by Sol Writers, my women writers' group in Florida. Four of these women served as beta readers, volunteering considerable personal time to read and provide feedback to an early draft of my full manuscript. Thank you, Virginia Campbell, Jill Smith, Kathy Joyce Glascott, and Gail Blohowiak.

The publishing process is quite involved and challenging, and I am thankful for the team at Mill City Press, who guided me through the procedures. They were very patient in answering my many questions throughout the process.

*Rosemary Vaughn*

I am also grateful to Krista Rolfzen Soukup from Blue Cottage Agency who led a workshop for new authors in Brainerd, Minnesota, in September 2015. This experience provided useful information and prompted me to continue pursuing my dream of becoming a published author. This workshop also introduced me to Corey Kretsinger from MidState Design, who has designed my author's website and walked me through the process of its use.

I am naturally appreciative of members of my family, who are getting used to my periodically reinventing myself. My husband, as noted above, encouraged me to complete my dream of writing and publishing my novel. Until recently, my children were unaware that I had embarked on this new adventure. After telling her husband that her mother was writing smut, my daughter immediately wanted to read it. When I faced challenges along my journey, she would remind me of the resilience I have modeled for her. My son surprised me at Christmas with a gift of three different-sized journals. He said they were for me to start writing the Great American Romance. The tiny one was for me to carry with me for quick notes on the go, the medium one for more inspired writing ideas, and the large one for writing the novel's manuscript. I then surprised him by saying the first draft was already complete, though it was unlikely to be a candidate for the Great American Romance.

And last, I must acknowledge that the inspiration for my pen name came from my mother, whose name was Rosemary. Writing a book is very personal, and presenting one's creation for the world to see is a little scary and intimidating. Thank you to my village for supporting me in the creation and presentation of—in essence—*Rosemary's baby*.

Sincerely and respectfully,

Rosemary Vaughn

CPSIA information can be obtained
at www.ICGtesting.com
Printed in the USA
LVOW10s0345180317
527647LV00004BA/5/P